THE
Naturalist

BOOK ONE

THE HAPGOODS OF BRAMLEIGH

CHRISTINA DUDLEY

ISBN: 978-1-963408-00-3

To Cindy,
for all those stacks and stacks of Regencies we read

THE
Hapgoods of Bramleigh
RICHARD HAPGOOD = AUGUSTA ARBUTHNOT
ELFRIDA   ALICE   MARGARET   EDITH

CHAPTER ONE

Let the Naturalists explain these Things.
—Daniel Defoe, *Robinson Crusoe* (1719)

A soft but unmistakable *ploop* broke the early morning silence, followed by rustling. Joseph drew back from the water's edge, the jar he held nearly slipping from his grasp in his surprise. Could he be so fortunate? The frog specimen he sought was not rare, exactly, but one hardly expected to come upon it the very instant one set out in search.

Moving imperceptibly—creeping—placing one boot-shod foot before the other where no twig would crack nor mud cling, he edged along the pond's rim.

Just there, where the sweet flags crowded the bank, the outermost of them bending to meet the water, sat the frog. Not the rarer pool frog he sought, but a common brown one, its toes and fingers tucked beneath its moist body. It stared at Joseph, but once the naturalist spotted its lack of greenness and black dots, the interest was not returned. Joseph had dissected his first common brown frog when barely out of leading strings, after all. The man's attention was drawn, rather, to the unexpected sight of a fishing pole trailing in the water beside a bucket. In the bucket's depths, a glistening trout circled.

Joseph straightened, glancing around. "I say," he called. "Good morning—? Do come out. I'm sorry to have disturbed your peace."

He waited. There was no response. He could see, however, from the gaps in the rushes, that the shy fisherman had not gone far. He probably lay on his belly, keeping his head out of sight. A poacher, then, with a guilty conscience. Fishing Lord Marlton's pond without his lordship's leave.

"I mean you no harm," Joseph tried again. "I myself am a guest in these parts, and no relation to Lord Marlton or Pattergees." It wasn't the entire truth. While Joseph had yet to meet the viscount or his family, he was certainly a guest at Pattergees, having arrived late the previous night, letters of introduction from the Royal Society and Sir Edmund Chall in particular tucked in his waistcoat. But it was true enough—Joseph meant the possible poacher no harm and thought the viscount could well afford to share a trout or two.

The silence held, save one listless croak from the frog.

Curiosity began to get the better of him. Joseph leaned over the bucket. "I say, what a capital fish." Giving the handle a rattle, he picked the bucket up. "A plump fellow, as well. As it appears to be abandoned, perhaps I will take it with me and have it fried for breakfast."

"Catch your own, then!" came a shrill cry, and up popped the elusive angler. The movement startled the frog, which leaped back into the pond. Joseph found himself faced by a lad anywhere from twelve to fifteen in years, clad in rustic attire too large for his diminutive frame. His clownish appearance was capped by a floppy brown hat clamped down so hard that only a hint of nut-brown hair escaped over his forehead, the unruly lock exactly matching in shade his sparking, indignant eyes. "I'll have that back, if you please." And he extended an imperious hand for the bucket handle.

The temptation to tease the young upstart was too great. Joseph retreated a step, stirring the pail's contents with his fingers. "Common brown trout. *Salma trutta.*"

"Morpha *fario*," muttered the lad.

"I beg your pardon!" exclaimed Joseph, astounded. Common poachers in his experience were seldom versed in Linnaean classifications. "Did you say something?"

The boy froze, his eyes fixed on his interlocutor.

Most peculiar. Joseph cocked his head. "How *did* you manage to snare him here? Fellows of his age and size don't do much waiting around still spots, hiding under rocks—not before the heat of midday, at any rate."

The lad's pointed chin went up an inch. "That's as much as you know, sir. Now may I have my property?"

"Your 'property'? As we stand on Pattergees acres, would I be correct in assuming you are Lord Marlton's son, the Honorable Master Birdlow?"

The brown eyes dodged his. Joseph could almost hear the machinery whirring behind them as the boy mulled over some great whopper to tell.

When the lad spoke again, Joseph made two observations: firstly, his voice had dropped a register or two; and, secondly, he seemed to have lost both his refined accents and his grasp on standard grammar. "Oh, I begs yer pardon, yer lordship, if I be fergettin' my place. I be's no Master Birdlow. Only the—er—the gamekeeper's bastard. That's right. But I do asks yer leave if'n' I may have the fish there, as Cook be expectin' it for Master Birdlow's repast."

Joseph's mouth twitched. A better whopper even than he expected. As a reward for such creativity, he held out the bucket, which the boy snatched from him. "I wish Master Birdlow good eating, then, young—young—"

"Ali—ahem! Alec," said the boy. "No—no—William, I means. I be William the Bastard."

"Yes," said Joseph, a small laugh escaping him, which he masked with a cough of his own. "The gamekeeper's son. Yes, I caught that. Well, thank you, young—William. I bid you good morning."

He turned on his heel, pausing momentarily to retrieve his empty specimen jar from the rushes.

"Wait!" called William the Bastard. "What are—what be ye doing on his lordship's lands, sir? Be ye an unlawful angler?"

The boy's gaze ran over the man's well-tailored shirt, his buff waistcoat and nankeen breeches neatly tucked into Hessians that gleamed, despite the grasses and muck. Joseph no more looked the part of Unlawful Angler than William did Gamekeeper's Bastard.

"I am a naturalist," Joseph replied after a hesitation. It was an odd enough vocation for any man, much less a well-to-do younger son who should, by all rights, have become a clergyman. But what was he to say? That he disdained to pile the work of a parish on an underpaid curate, while he devoted himself to the world outside the study window?

"I study our native fauna," he added.

"I knows what a naturalist be's—is," said William stoutly, getting tangled in his adopted cant.

Joseph raised an eyebrow. "Indeed. I imagine you might, since you knew the specific variety of that trout in your bucket. No common piece of learning for a lad like yourself."

The boy got his stunned look again. Joseph watched his throat work. Another fabulous tale was clearly in the works, and Joseph was not disappointed. "My father—er—my old man, the—uh—the wicked blighter, 'e stole a book on natural 'istory I—I peeks into when 'e's fuddled—full-brimmer, 'e, that one."

"Astonishing. I suppose you learned your Latin when he was intoxicated, as well. Clever child. I would heartily love to make your father's acquaintance, as I hope to be observing and collecting hereabouts in the coming weeks. Perhaps later this morning..?"

"No, no—busy man my—my pot and pan. Not likely."

Joseph could not prevent the grin tugging at the corners of his mouth. "Alas. However, since you seem equally familiar with the lands here—to the point of knowing where the trout hide, all unsuspecting—perhaps *you* might be spared to assist me in my investigations?"

The lad's capacity for falsehood was here overmastered. He merely shook his head frantically as he backed away, pulling the brim of his hat ever lower, while the bucket banged his shins in what must have been a painful manner.

Joseph took pity on him. Touching the brim of his own beaver hat, he wished him good morning once more and headed in the direction of the Great House, leaving the young poacher to make his way home without further observation or questioning.

Lord Marlton kept country hours. Joseph returned to find the family gathering for breakfast, and he was conscious of wishing his boots better scraped on the mat. Lady Marlton spied him first. She was a faded beauty with sharpened features, decked in a morning gown of pale blue chintz, her graying curls tucked beneath a flowered cap. Joseph executed a quick bow, to which she raised her eyebrows slightly.

"Ah! You must be Joseph Tierney," cried a stately balding gentleman, approaching him with outstretched hand.

"Viscount Marlton." Joseph attempted the bow once more. "Your lordship—thank you for receiving me. Sir Edmund Chall has asked that I—"

"Yes, yes, I know all about it," Lord Marlton interrupted with a wave of his fingers. "Some great work—some massive compendium, eh?—detailing the flora and fauna of this blessed plot, this earth, this realm—or at least the miniscule portion of it represented by Pattergees and the larger county. Heh, heh! Chally was ever nose and ears in a book and running all manner of things through with sturdy pins in our Pembroke days. You a Pembroke man, Tierney?"

"No, my lord. Emmanuel."

"Emmanuel! Were you intended for the church?"

"Originally. Now I fear I would not do it justice."

"Never say you are one of those Nonconformists!" Behind the viscount, Lady Marlton was seen to give a *frisson* of distaste.

"No, my lady. I have no quibble with the Church. But my first love has ever been the study of the natural world. To contribute to Sir Edmund's work will be a very great honor."

"Hmmph. Well, so." The viscount thumped a hand on Joseph's shoulder. "On Chally's behalf you are welcome at Pattergees however long your endeavors require. Let me perform the introductions and then on we to breakfast, hey?"

There were not too many introductions to be got through, thankfully. Lady Marlton unbent fractionally on seeing her lord so affable. Master Birdlow was something of a shock, however, being no whipster still in the schoolroom, but rather a full-grown, portly Honorable *Mister* Birdlow. He bore little resemblance to either parent and was accompanied by his new-minted and equally round bride. The only other claimant to the title of Master Birdlow was disqualified by her sex, being the daunting Honorable Miss Birdlow, a young lady whose haughty good looks and silvery blonde hair hinted at her mother's former beauty, just as the mother's pointed nose and chin predicted the daughter's future. Young Mr. and Mrs. Birdlow were kindly enough, but Miss Birdlow's eyes flashed warning to Joseph: he was not to consider himself in any way her equal—she, with ten thousand pounds and an "Honorable" to her name!

Lord Marlton seemed the only one of his family inclined toward conversation, but it gave place in priority to concentration on food. Unused to silence at table but unwilling to accost his hosts, Joseph managed but little, and it was with relief he saw the viscount lay down his silver and wipe his mouth on the cloth. Apparently Joseph was not the only one awaiting such a signal, for at once the family began to bombard their patriarch.

"Papa, may I have the chaise today? Constance made me promise most earnestly to visit her and the ground may yet be too damp for walking."

"Hmmph. Suppose so."

"Father, I say, it is a shame that the hounds be kept another year at Bramleigh. The state of dilapidation of those kennels—!"

"Hapgood will never part with them, however broken down his kennels. Matter of Saxon honor, I daresay." Here Lord Marlton gave a puff and grunt as if stifling a belch, but Joseph realized it must have been a chuckle.

"My lord," began his lady, "I fear something must be done about the lad William. Ford complains to me that his attentions to the maids are ceaseless, and he causes many a row between them."

"William!" Joseph blurted. "Then there *is* a lad William?"

The viscountess blinked several times, not otherwise remarking his outburst. "'Tis a common name, to be sure," she said politely.

Joseph was too intrigued to refrain from asking, "Would this William be the gamekeeper's ba—the gamekeeper's son, rather?" He could scarce imagine the stripling he encountered earlier causing heartaches belowstairs, but one never knew.

Lady Marlton's acute gaze fixed on him, a line creasing her brow. "The very same. You are acquainted with our William, Mr. Tierney?"

"I came upon him this morning, my lady. The day was so fair I could not resist familiarizing myself at once with the Pattergees grounds. The lad was fishing."

"Fishing?" echoed Miss Birdlow, as if Joseph had suggested he found young William looting the Great House. Perhaps the Marltons *were* jealous of their brown trout.

"Amazed he would do something so industrious," grumbled Lord Marlton. "Pure trouble, that boy. But we must suffer him, Arabella. Think on his father and mother."

"I think on little else, my lord, else I would have sent him packing some months since."

"William's father is the gamekeeper," Joseph said again, "but I was given to understand his mother...that they were not...that his parents were not..." He trailed off, uncertain how to put the matter delicately.

"A most respectable woman, Mrs. Davies," said her ladyship in a tone that brooked no argument. "A goodly, respectable woman married to a goodly, respectable husband. The more shame to their son."

So no William the Bastard, son of a drunken father. Joseph drummed his fingers thoughtfully on the table. From the boy's countenance, Joseph would have thought the boy's explanations pure fantasy, from beginning to end. How odd that he would include details of truth, then—the name, the father's occupation.

"I will speak with William presently," pronounced the viscount, "but let us not forget our guest. Tell us, Mr. Tierney, your aims and objectives for the summer."

Joseph nodded. "They are both humble yet extensive. Sir Edmund Chall has proposed nothing short of an exhaustive natural inventory of the realm, for which the Royal Society underwrites a small army of budding naturalists."

"Such as you."

"Such as I."

"And you chose this portion of Somerset because...?"

Joseph's color rose. "Two reasons, your lordship. Firstly, the scale of such an endeavor requires the Royal Society to practice economies. As a personal friend of Sir Edmund Chall, he trusted to your understanding and hospitality—"

The viscount gave a bark of a laugh. "Yes, yes—I salute Chally! He must have 'naturalists' like you, Mr. Tierney, ensconced in the great houses of every Pembroke fellow he could impose upon. *Not* that you are an imposition, Mr. Tierney. Well, well. So much for the first reason Economy. Let us have the second."

"Secondly," continued Joseph, "I need not tell you, my lord, whose family have lived at Pattergees for generations, that your corner of Somerset is unequalled in natural beauty and variety. Variety of landscape yields variety of natural life. Birds, river creatures, plants. Consider but the insects, my lord, the dragon and damsel flies, the—" From the corner of his eye he saw Miss Birdlow's nostrils flare as she held fingertips to her lips, smothering a yawn. Joseph smiled ruefully. "But let me not bore the ladies with trifles."

"The ladies?" countered Lady Marlton. "You believe ladies have no interest in the natural world, Mr. Tierney."

Her daughter's face was all innocence and brightness again, and Joseph could only say, "Forgive me, your ladyship. I meant only that the natural world forms no part of a typical lady's education and interests. There is French to learn. Italian. Music. Painting. Needlework. History. Dancing."

"Are you being satirical, Mr. Tierney?" questioned Miss Birdlow.

"Oh, no!" cried Joseph, dismayed they would suspect him to be so ill-mannered. "Permit me as a man of science to speak as I find. I mean merely that, as natural history forms no part of a lady's education, one cannot expect the subject to scintillate in the drawing room."

"But surely," rejoined Lady Marlton, "despite your...enthusiasm...for the natural world, Mr. Tierney, you would agree that a 'typical' lady's education serves best in her sphere of life. You have received an excellent *gentleman's* education at Cambridge, and should you make a name for yourself as a naturalist—receive honor, perhaps recognition, from the Crown—you might one day marry a most excellent woman. One who would require just those accomplishments you enumerated."

"Yes," said Joseph.

"You would not expect any future wife of yours to trail after you, butterfly net in hand, or propose that she stick pins in your damsel flies," Miss Birdlow rallied him. Her sister-in-law gave a good-natured titter.

"No, indeed," said Joseph, though he had never given it a thought. Marriage formed no part of his present plans, and Miss Birdlow might rest easy that he would not besiege her fortress of eligibility, however rich, beautiful and accomplished she might be.

"We rejoice to hear it," said Lady Marlton, "for we do place one condition on your residence here—you may not spend all your time in the fields and streams. We are a sociable neighborhood and pride ourselves on keeping abreast of developments, whether they be fashionable, political or scientific. Please do not assume we will be bored by what you call trifles. We, even the ladies here, are people of the world, and list *curiosity* among our education and accomplishments."

"At least we at Pattergees and select families, Mama," corrected Miss Birdlow. "But Mr. Tierney had better steer clear of the squire's girls if he seeks to surround himself with education and accomplishment."

Lord Marlton interrupted another amiable titter from his daughter-in-law with a thump on the table. "Here, now, if we descend into county gossip, pray excuse me *and* our guest. I am sure Squire Hapgood is a very good man, and his daughters very good sort of girls, so let's no more of that." Sliding his chair backward, he signaled the end of the meal.

"After all, we cannot all of us be Fortune's favorites."

CHAPTER TWO

**The Misery of all Fathers who are
so unfortunate to have Daughters.
— Henry Fielding, *Tom Jones* (1749)**

Viscount Marlton never spoke truer words, for, indeed, Squire Hapgood considered himself a man under a curse.

What else could explain the series of misfortunes which had befallen him since he came of age, some decades earlier?

If anything, his twenty-first birthday had seemed to mark him as especially favored by heaven. As he sat at the head of the long board drawn up beneath the shade arbor, a board thronged with well-wishing local gentry and groaning under all the bounty summer at Bramleigh could offer, he imagined a prosperous life unfolding before him. He was the sole heir of all he surveyed: acres of parkland, artfully-landscaped, and the House itself, solid, if not elegant or modern, a house that had graced the county since the days of Good Queen Bess. By his side sat the lovely Miss Arbuthnot, his intended. She was perhaps not so spotlessly-pedigreed or richly-dowered as a Hapgood of Bramleigh deserved, but Richard Hapgood was a wealthy young man and need only demand respectability and a pretty face, two characteristics not even the most envious could deny Miss Arbuthnot.

No, as the neighbors and tenantry raised bumpers to toast him, as he rose graciously in acknowledgment, the sun glinting from his thickly waving golden crown, Richard Hapgood would be forgiven for imagining himself Fortune's Darling.

It did not take many years to disabuse him of this notion.

For one, Miss Arbuthnot, once she became Mistress Hapgood, proved a most high-strung, languishing, extravagant, whining woman, whose elevation to her august station went immediately and regrettably to her head. She must have Bramleigh new-furnished and papered. There must be jewels and carriages and gowns and seasons in London. As the oldest family in the district (far older than those upstart Marltons over at Pattergees), the Hapgoods must be seen to live in a manner befitting their descent from Saxon royalty. She was, moreover, susceptible to the blandishments and importunities of her spendthrift younger brothers Alec and Alwyn, and many the rents from Bramleigh quarter days found their way into the pockets of these would-be gentlemen and their creditors. Worst of all, a decade of admirable fertility on the part of Bramleigh's mistress yielded four bouncing, healthy, rosy...girls. Hapgood groaned inwardly to think of their dowries—outlays with no return, supposing he could even marry them off!

The squire found comfort where many men of his position did, who did not turn to politics or strong drink or womanizing—in sport. He shot pheasant and grouse in season; he stalked roe and red deer; he rode to hounds in loud pursuit of cunning *Vulpes vulpes.* The costs of the hunt and the keeping of the hounds hastened the Hapgoods further along the path to destruction. Small pieces of land were sold—none of the original patrimony, to be sure, only acres here and there added by the incumbent's grandfather. Portions of the House were closed off and a brace of servants let go. Longer and longer gaps separated the tenures of the girls' governesses. Yes, the neighbors began to agree, the Hapgoods of Bramleigh were in a bad way, and who knew what would become of them, especially those girls!

The only stroke of luck Squire Hapgood could lay claim to was his good lady's retirement from the field after ten years, when she took to her chamber as a permanent invalid. While Alec and Alwyn's visits and requests did not cease, and while doctors' fees were then added to the estate's financial burdens, the expenses of home improvement evaporated, as did the London visits and the London house. The situation stabilized.

"A tourniquet has been applied!" he crowed to his friend, the ancient doctor Mr. Lewis. "There is damage internally and various lesser open wounds—including your exorbitant fees, my man—but the limb may yet be saved."

"I congratulate you, Richard," replied the doctor, "and your medical metaphor could not be more appropriate. May time and prudence heal what remains. As for my fees, they might be kept to a minimum in future if you heed my advice. I must recommend your girls receive the benefits of exercise—"

"Did Mrs. Hapgood ask you to say this?" growled the squire, subjecting the drawing room chaise to several whacks with his riding crop. "If this is about that fool of a dancing master, we are well rid of him, and I will not have him back by any measure!"

"No, no, I do not speak of the dancing master," said Mr. Lewis soothingly, "but perhaps you might encourage your daughters to spend time out of doors, walking or riding their ponies. Your lady was never one to insist on it, and as you are again without the services of a governess to direct their time—"

"Blasted plaguey expensive things, governesses," interrupted the squire.

The doctor affected not to hear this and continued, "As you are again between governesses, I see the girls spend all their time within doors. They have all of them grown too pale and listless for my liking. Miss Alice in particular."

"Hmmph. I see you want to anticipate illnesses in my girls. Your receipts suffering? Wife clamoring for a new carriage, is she?"

The silent swelling of Mr. Lewis' chest was the sole indicator of his impatience, but he had known the squire too long to take offense.

"Hmmph," grunted the squire again. "Very well, very well. Alice's looks worry you, you say? I blame her wet-nurse Mrs. Davies. One need only compare Alice to her milk-brother William to know that woman gave the better nourishment to her ox of a son, despite the money we paid her."

"Softly," cautioned the doctor. "Mrs. Davies is a respectable woman who has nursed many a blooming child. But this is neither here nor there. I have given you my prescription, now do you carry it out."

"At once." The squire gave the bell-pull a mighty yank, and, after some minutes, when no servant responded to the summons, he struck the chaise once more and stalked to the door. Throwing it open, he bellowed, "Girls! Girls! Come!"

Mr. Lewis wagged his bearded head as he listened to the patter and thumps and shrieking of the girls' approach. Just before they entered the room, they stopped to arrange themselves.

The eldest, Elfrida, entered first, mincing her way with thirteen-year-old grace. She promised to be the requisite family beauty, having her father's thick golden hair, delicate features, and eyes the color of forget-me-nots. The eyes tended sadly toward the myopic, as her younger sisters pointed out, Elfrida denied, and her father ignored. Elfrida affected her measured, graceful movements as flowerings of maturity, but more to the point they helped her avoid collisions with the furniture. She also was the only Hapgood daughter in a clean frock that morning, the second eldest, Alice, bearing the unmistakable rusty splotches of the morning chocolate on her dimity and the two youngest bespattered with paint.

"Lewis here says you all need airing," began their father abruptly enough. "What—hey—Edith, Margaret—have you tumbled into the paint pots?"

"I was working on my miniature of great-grandfather in his youth," lisped little black-haired Edith.

"And I had need of the Terra de Siena, Papa. Edie was *lavishing* it on background," explained Margaret with a sniff, "and you know how costly it is."

"I could hardly be *lavishing* it when I am painting a miniature," protested Edith reasonably.

"You laid it on so thick it won't dry this fortnight!"

"There, there—decorum!" interjected their father. "What say you of this matter, Elfrida? Speak impartially."

"I cannot honestly judge, Papa," she returned. "I saw nothing."

"Indeed!" chorused Edith and Margaret, forgetting their quarrel to giggle together, Margaret adding, "Elfie couldn't see a thing unless we painted the tip of her nose!"

Squire Hapgood only scowled at this and rounded on his other daughter. "You, then, Alice! How came you and your sisters to be in this condition?"

A pair of nut-brown eyes were raised reluctantly from the volume she held and a finger inserted to hold her place. "I am sorry, Papa. What did you say? I was not attending."

Her father gave an exasperated cry usually reserved for when his pack had lost the scent of the fox or drawn a blank. "I say! Put down that book. Hasn't Lewis here just told me you must be more out-of-doors? You in particular, Alice!"

"Mama says I must not venture out of doors," she replied, "lest I catch cold and suffer her Fate."

These words unleashed the full force of Squire Hapgood's wrath, which, in truth, did not strike much fear in his daughters, they having long realized that his bark was far worse than his bite. Nevertheless, that day gave birth to a new regime. There must be pony rides and long walks. Books and painting and whatever it was that Elfrida spent her time doing were all very well, but they must be balanced with the promotion of healthfulness, the development of strong constitutions.

As the years passed and the girls' color and hardiness improved, they subsided into their familiar sedentary activities within-doors, with the sole exception of Alice, who had discovered not only soundness of body but also a passion for the natural world. It was not that she loved books the less, but she found that she might, as Lord Shaftesbury once put it, both eat her cake and have it. Linnaeus' *Systema naturae* replaced Richardson, and volumes of Buffon's *Histoire naturelle, générale et particulière* edged out Edgeworth.

While her father and Mr. Lewis had been Alice's first encouragers, their early prescriptions of sedate pony rides and ladylike walks were, sadly, the alpha and omega of approved exertions. Not for young ladies were hunting, fishing, dam-building, the rearing of hedgehogs, or the dissection of water snakes, all of which Alice was caught doing at one point or another. "No respectable young gentleman will saddle himself with you unless you hide these unmaidenly interests," grumbled her father. "You have not portion enough that anybody would overlook fossils in your pocket or frog guts on your hem." Alice was a biddable girl, in her way, but in this instance she chose to understand the squire rather too literally. She sewed herself boy's clothing and continued her pursuits in the early mornings, before her family was about. From the few remaining Bramleigh servants she purchased silence with gifts of fresh-caught fish and eels—even a pheasant or partridge occasionally.

This morning, when she delivered her bucket with its spotted trout, Button had no more than glanced in when Alice accosted her breathlessly. "Who has come to Pattergees, Button?"

"Mind your boots, child! You've got mud all over my floor, 'ee have. Best be headed abovestairs. I heard the squire tramping about unnatural early, even for him. If he should catch 'ee in your trousers—"

"But what do you know?" Alice insisted, clutching Button's meaty arm. "About the visitor?"

"Visitors? What would I know of other people's visitors?" Button demanded, shaking herself free to lean over the hearth. "In here slaving away all day, I am."

Smothering a sigh, Alice was about to give up when Dorcas whirled in, arms loaded with coal scuttle and polished chamber pot. "Took your sweet time, this morning," grumbled Button. "I suppose you think the family's breakfast makes itself."

"Dorcas!" cried Alice, "Who has come to Pattergees? What says your sister Tabby?"

"Oh, Miss Alice, don't you know?" breathed the girl, a skinny stripling not much older than Edith. "Tabby says 'tis a Mr. Joseph Tierney, a man of science who knows all manner of things and brought with him ever so many cases and instruments and books and nets and pins—"

"I'll net and pin you, if you don't mind this toast!" declared Button, giving Dorcas a push. The girl filled the gridiron with the thick slices of bread and carried them to the fire without pausing in her speech. "—and that he's come to study our country hereabouts as a guest of Lord Marlton and that he's ever so handsome—Tabby says a great strapping fellow and eyes the color of ambers at the bottom of a pond—only he's not a man of great means, otherwise Miss B would surely set her cap for him—"

"Miss Birdlow shan't have him!" Alice interrupted, her hands clutched to her chest.

"Miss Birdlow may have any man she likes." Button delivered this pronouncement as one recently descended from Mount Sinai. "A fair and a wealthy woman such as herself. She may marry where she pleases, if the man be respectable."

"Oh, certainly he's respectable," resumed Dorcas. "Tabby says he's a Cambridge man and that his uncle is a baronet in Buckinghamshire and Mr. Joseph's mother is somehow related to the Earl of Chiltern—cousin? great-niece?—but that Mr. Tierney would not please his family and be a clergyman—"

"Was there no living to be had?"

"There *was* a living, Miss, on his uncle's estate, and Mr. Tierney sent to Enamuel—Enemallow—"

"Emmanuel," Alice supplied, breathless.

"The very same, ma'am. But he refused it positively and has had a break with his family, but his man Chambers says they will forgive him presently because Mr. Tierney's brilliance has attracted the notice of a Distinguished Man of Science and perhaps Mr. Tierney himself will become one—a Distinguished Man of Science—besides which, Mr. Tierney's elder brother is fast becoming the saddest rakehell that ever broke his mother's heart. Those were Chambers' exact words to Tabitha: 'fast becoming the saddest rakehell that ever broke his mother's heart.'" Here Dorcas at last ran out of both breath and information.

"Mr. Tierney shan't marry Miss Birdlow," said Alice again, "be he ever so respectable."

"That's all you know, Miss," returned Dorcas, annoyed to have Alice pretend to inside knowledge of the exciting newcomer.

"Because he's going to marry me!" Alice declared. She gave her chest a thump with her fist.

The cook rolled her eyes and gave the ball of dough before her a good punch. She was well accustomed to Miss Alice's fits and fervors. There was no one like the girl for being taken with sudden, enduring passions: books, birds, blossoms, bees. True, Miss Alice's enthusiasms had never before taken a romantic turn, but, well, she was at that age now, Button supposed. Heaven help the squire. If Miss Alice should take it upon herself to fancy some gentleman, that was an improvement, at least, over the newts and spawn which usually captured her heart. Poor thing. She was not a bad-looking little creature, when she had a gown on and her hair dressed, but the squire would have a time of it marrying her off—make no mistake.

"What can Miss Birdlow know of the natural world," Alice went on, "unless it be to embroider it in her frame?" Pointing an emphatic finger at her fishing bucket, Alice proclaimed, "*Salma trutta* morpha *fario*!"

"Young men don't want to talk Latin nonsense with young ladies," said Button quellingly. "Worse yet, with young ladies who dress as common lads and truck with slimy fish. They want wives who will ornerment their lives with beauty and peace."

Dorcas nodded agreement. "Ay, that. If Miss Birdlow won't have 'im, Miss Hapgood surely will. So lovely and quiet. Never a book in her hand, not to mention boasting about what's in 'em."

"Elfie doesn't read because Elfie can hardly see a thing that's not three inches from her nose!" cried Alice, stung. "Not because she's more ladylike than I." Her companions merely raised skeptical eyebrows, and Alice felt the stirrings of guilt. Elfrida was her dearest sister, and, if Mr. Tierney would not marry her, Alice, she would far rather he chose Elfie than the haughty Miss Birdlow. And it was only too true that Elfie was the loveliest Hapgood, as well as the quietest.

"I can be quiet and ladylike, too," Alice amended, "if that is what the young men like."

"It is, in truth," said Button.

Alice's chin began to jut defiantly as she thought of Button's man Big Will. He seemed to like Button well enough, though she was neither lovely nor quiet and was a good ten years older than he. More than once Alice witnessed Button pound Big Will's shoulder with her heavy fist when he displeased her. Yet he continued to bring her posies and boughten sweets.

"And that right there, Miss"—Button slammed the tea urn on the worktable—"that face right there is exactly what I speak of. Willful and opinnernated. If you disagree with a gentleman—if you believe you know better than a gentleman, he doesn't want to hear of it. After you're wed is soon enough to reveal you've a mind and will of your own and intend to use 'em."

Dorcas gave another knowledgeable nod that made Alice want to stamp her foot, but such an action would only draw more unfavorable comparisons to Elfrida and Miss Birdlow. With difficulty, she swallowed her ire and managed a meek, "I will endeavor to profit by your advice."

"There's a good girl." Button gave Alice's cheek a painful pinch before suddenly releasing her to sniff the air. "The toast! You've nearly burnt it," she screeched, smacking Dorcas' hand. The girl withdrew the gridiron hastily, just as a bell was heard. "Miss Edie, I'll be bound. And that great commotion, coming down the front stairs, will be your father, Miss Alice. What did I say to 'ee? No more chatter and nonsense. Upstairs with you, quick like, and mind you come down a lady!"

Chapter Three

**It must prove...a work of much labour to inquire,
consider, research, and determine, what is needful
to be known concerning him.
– Izaak Walton, *Life of Hooker* (1675)**

Despite her frosty demeanor, the Honorable Miss Agnes Birdlow was by no means indifferent to the presence of the Pattergees guest. She waited only for her mama to remark upon it, which Lady Marlton did at last when they were alone the following day in the morning room.

"Quite a charming young man, do not you think, Aggie?" her mother asked from her desk, where she crossed out one of Cook's supper suggestions and scratched in another.

Miss Birdlow did not look up from her embroidery. "Of whom do you speak, pray?"

"None of that, now. You know very well I mean Mr. Tierney. He hails from good family, shows intellect and promise, and bears himself well. Not ill-looking, either."

"Mama, I do wish you were more ambitious for me."

"My love, if dukes grew like dandelions I would fetch you a bouquet. As it is, a baronet's nephew under our very roof is nothing to sneer at. If your father will not consent to a second Season for you, you had better have Mr. Tierney or your cousin Geoffrey. There! A baronet's nephew or a viscount's nephew."

"Geoffrey," echoed Miss Birdlow, with what, in a less well-bred young lady would have been called a groan. "I suppose it will have to be him, as well you know. Admit that you only propose this Mr. Tierney to make me like Geoffrey the more."

"Do not accuse me of such subterfuge, pray! I mean my praise of Mr. Tierney sincerely. Your father speaks of reviving the Midsummer Ball in honor of his visit, and you and Mr. Tierney will open it."

"Will Geoffrey come?"

"I hardly think we could keep him away."

Miss Birdlow considered this as she chose another shade of embroidery floss. The cherub's curls should be silvery fair, like her own locks.

She and Geoffrey had known each other and been loosely betrothed from the cradle, a fact they used to tease and torture each other with, when they were children. Now that they were nearly of age, they had ceased to discuss the matter altogether, but they knew it ever lurked in the minds of their family. Miss Birdlow imagined more than once how she would reply to Geoffrey, should he refer to it—sometimes she answered in the affirmative, sometimes in the negative—but he never did refer to it.

She thrust her needle through the scalp of the cherub. "Had not you better ask Mr. Tierney if he would like a ball given in his honor, Mama?"

"What objection could he possibly have? It would be a signal honor and bring him to the attention of the best folk in the County. Who knows but that one of the gentlemen he meets might become a future patron? I am certain, my love, that for all his talk of 'Chally' and Economy, Mr. Tierney descends on Somerset with no other object."

Unknown to the female inhabitants of Pattergees, Joseph had no such object in mind. His ambitions were rather humbler: he wished to find a suitable assistant. More specifically, he wished to find the so-called 'William the Bastard' because he believed that, apart from a propensity to spin far-fetched tales, the lad would make an able helper. But where to begin?

With the bewildered guidance of an upper housemaid, Joseph located the entrance to the servants' staircase and descended its cramped steps with one hand along the bricked wall. From the smoothness of the surface, he imagined this was the common *modus operandi*, though how the chambermaids ever made their way up the narrow passageway with the coal scuttle or down with the slops amazed him. The lower door could only be opened with a shove, and Joseph burst into the kitchen more dramatically than he intended. Heads turned; activity halted.

"Have you lost your way, Mr. Tierney? How may we assist you?" Girdles the butler recovered first, hastily slipping his shoe back on to hide the stocking hole he had been showing Mrs. Trapp and springing to his feet.

"Indeed. Forgive me for disturbing you," Joseph said to the company as a whole. "I am not lost, but I did hope you might direct me to the young Master William Davies, son of the gamekeeper."

All eyes darted toward a strapping fellow in livery with straw-colored unruly hair, who rose reluctantly to his feet from a settle against the far wall. "I be he." At a sharp jerk of the chin from Mrs. Trapp he added, "Sir."

Joseph nodded. One glance sufficed to show this was not the William he encountered earlier. "It is as I suspected. Do you by chance, my good man, understand much of the flora and fauna hereabouts?"

"The only fauna that Will knows about is what you find in petticoats," came a grumble from another corner, followed by a squeal of protest. Joseph imagined the tale-teller had suffered a retributive pinch.

William Davies straightened to an even more impressive height. "I serve at the house, *sir*."

Unlike his gamekeeper father, this particular Davies would not be found mucking about out of doors, Joseph interpreted this. He bowed his comprehension. "Perhaps, then, someone might direct me to a likely young lad. One who knows his way around the county and shows a curiosity for the natural world. I—uh—thought I saw a possible candidate yesterday morning: about this high"—he indicated with his hand—"brown eyes and hair. Pointed chin. Quick thinker. Surprisingly well-spoken for his station. "

"What was he—what was he about, sir, when you came upon him?" Joseph recognized his questioner as the girl who made the saucy remark about William a moment before. She stepped forward, all angles and bones and hair coming loose from her cap.

"Fishing. He was fishing. Do you know him, Miss—?"

"Tabitha," she supplied. "Not Miss. Just Tabitha. Or Tabby." Her eyes studied him briefly before flicking away. "No. 'Fraid not. Many a lad hereabouts answers to that description."

"Any lad in particular at Pattergees?"

"Brown hair, yellow hair, brown eyes, blue eyes, hazel eyes," Mrs. Trapp put in. "We have 'em all, to be sure."

"I'm less particular about the hair and eye color," Joseph said with a laugh. "It's rather the mental facility and willingness to work in all weathers outside that I prize." When no one volunteered further information, he slapped his thighs with finality. "Very well. I will explore on my own. But if anyone does come to mind, please send him my way. Thank you."

He was no sooner gone than a buzz of conversation rose.

"What an odd gentleman, to be sure," said Girdles.

"I'll warrant you know who he saw, Tabby," accused the more observant Mrs. Trapp. "Some lad with brown hair and brown eyes and more than two wits to rub together. And what was that about him being 'well-spoken for his station'?"

"Certainly rules out most fellows around here, those last bits," Tabby shrugged, causing William Davies to ball his fists.

"Just because I'm not leaping to drag buckets and net butterflies for his royal highness—" he sputtered, before Tabby waved the conclusion of his speech off.

"Who spoke of you, William Davies? Not every girl at Pattergees has you on her mind 'round the clock," she sniffed. Tying her apron more snugly about her, Tabby eyed the bell marked *Morning Room* just as it began to ring. "That'll be Lady M, Mrs. Trapp. Ten to one she's put a line through 'Stuffed capon.'"

"The more for us, then. Go fetch the menu for me, lass."

Joseph set out to retrace his steps, notebook in hand and knapsack slung over one shoulder, half his mind noting birdcalls while the other mulled over the mystery of William the Bastard. Whoever the lad had been, he knew the players well, naming real people and occupations. And that girl Tabby knew the lad's identity, Joseph was certain. But was the lad then not affiliated with Pattergees, if no other servant had shown similar awareness? Perhaps he was a younger sibling of Tabitha's, whose illicit activities she protected, lest they both be turned out. He wondered whom he could ply for further information about Tabitha's background, without arousing the suspicions of the Marlton household, upstairs and down. Suppose he were to—

Here his thoughts were interrupted by a loud hallooing and the faint sound of horse hooves approaching. He must have wandered closer to the road, such as it was, a compacted dirt track winding through the fields, here a muddy wallow, and there bordered by a stone half-wall. Shortly, a spotted hound vaulted over just such a wall a hundred yards ahead, a fine, lithe creature with tongue hanging out and paws filthy to the knee. Upon catching sight of Joseph, it drew up short, pivoting in a large circle to gallop back to him. The hallooing broke off and the next sight to burst into Joseph's field of vision was a mighty black charger with a square-built, ruddy-faced man on its back, hat held on with one hand and cravat askew.

"Caractacus! Crack! Damn your hide!" bellowed the squire, pulling up as suddenly as he was able. In response, the dog (to whom the lofty name referred) trotted over, plopped his backside down and began nonchalantly scratching behind his ear with a muddy leg.

After an instant's hesitation Joseph advanced, hat in hand. "Good morning, sir. How do you do?"

"Eh?" The squire wheeled around, eyeing his witness head to foot as his horse sidestepped beneath him. "Oh. I see. How do you do." After aiming another brutal glance at the misbehaving dog, which Caractacus ignored, he slid down and marched over, hand extended. "Squire Richard Hapgood, of Bramleigh."

"Joseph Tierney, sir. I am a guest of—"

"Marlton, yes. You see, news travels quickly in this corner of Somerset. We have been alive to your arrival for some weeks. I was headed to Pattergees to make your acquaintance. That and to recapture Crack, here. But I see you are not at home."

Joseph grinned. "Begging your pardon, sir, without casting aspersions on my generous host, I am much more at home where you find me than in the drawing room of a viscount."

"That so? Bit stuffy, they? I say, then, if your morning's travels take you by Bramleigh"—he pointed westward— "and you would like some refreshment, do you call on us at your convenience. Share our collation. Or come for some tea, if that be too soon, though we take our tea earlier than at Pattergees, I suspect." (The squire gave a doubtful frown here, as he recalled what an unpredictable, haphazard affair tea at Bramleigh was. The collation, though, could be counted on, the Hapgoods preferring a solid repast mid-day.) "We would be glad to know you. Have some interesting features on our land. Animals. Plants. That sort of thing."

"I should be delighted," Joseph agreed with alacrity. "And we had better say tea, if you don't mind. I have a few items to attend to."

"Certainly, certainly." The squire wrenched his cravat back into position, tugging on it as if his valet had tied it a trifle too snugly. "Tea, yes. Four o'clock. Capital. You will excuse me, then." Mounting his horse again, he tipped his hat and bellowed at Caractacus, "Home, bedamned to you! On the instant!"

The beast trotted off obediently enough, having no mind to torture his master further if the master's heart wouldn't be in it, and it was plain enough to Crack that he could run to Cornwall, if he pleased, without being followed. The master's mind was now elsewhere.

"Elfie?" roared the squire, hurling the drawing room door open and stomping in. He interrupted what would have been a scene to warm his heart, had he been less excited: Elfrida working most intricate embroidery, which required her to sit closest the window and hold her frame not five inches from her nose; Alice striking a jangling discord on the spinet as she whisked a book from the music desk and sat upon it before launching into a tune; and Edith and Margaret's heads bent over a tablet, where their father assumed they wrote answers to questions Elfrida posed, but where in actuality they considered Edith's drawing of the music master who lately instructed them.

"Yes, papa?" answered his eldest calmly, laying aside her embroidery and regarding him with hands folded.

"What have we for tea today?"

She blinked. "Why, I suppose we could ring Button for tea and toast, but had you rather not eat some cold meat and sandwiches first?"

"Blast cold meat and sandwiches!" proclaimed her father. "And a plague on tea and toast! Tea and toast will not do, for we expect a visitor."

Alice blanched and then just as rapidly went scarlet, but thankfully no one was looking at her. "Who, papa?"

"Mr. Lewis may have tea and toast," put in Margaret. "I'm sure it has been well enough for him many a time. Perhaps we might toast cheese."

"Confound Lewis!" Hapgood did away with him as well. "It's the gentleman Mr. Joseph Tierney who has come to stay with Marlton at Pattergees. A very learned young man."

"A young man!" gasped Margaret.

"Do you want him to marry Elfie, Father?" asked Edith, her eyes enormous.

"Of course I want him to marry Elfie," he cried impatiently. "He could hardly marry you, Miss, now, could he? A girl still in the schoolroom."

"He might marry Alice," Margaret recovered enough to point out, at which Alice's playing, which had grown more and more quiet and disjointed, here ceased altogether.

"Alice? Nonsense. Oldest must marry first. Has your mother been out of bed today? This should be her job, by rights, to foist you on eligible gentlemen. I'm sure I haven't her subtlety and skill at getting her way. I will rouse her. She must rise to the occasion. We haven't every day young men thrown our direction. Elfrida must snatch him up, or by heaven, she must marry the next man who begs my blessing, if he has two eyes and two legs to 'im!"

"But Alice eats the most," said Margaret reasonably. "So it stands to reason you should send *her* packing first."

"Hush, you!" her maligned sister hissed, trilling two bass notes threateningly.

"Eats? Eats! That's just it!" boomed their father. "Tierney must have something to eat and see that this household runs the more beautifully for having Elfrida at the head of it. My child, you must go see Button immediately. Tell her to pay no mind to any luncheon, but we must have some cakes for tea. Cakes and strawberries. No—tell her we will take our luncheon alongside the tea. And do you, Alice, run up to see your mother and see if you can't convince her to get dressed."

"Yes, Papa."

"Of course, Papa."

He clapped his hands together with satisfaction. Those matters attended to, and the midday eating all but cancelled, there was still plenty of fine weather for riding before four o'clock came around. Squire Hapgood beamed at his four daughters. "Very well. Very well. Those are my girls. I'll be off, then."

Margaret waited until the door shut behind him to spring from her seat. "Oh! Won't Button be fit to be tied! She hates changes in routine."

Elfrida's brow furrowed. "She does indeed. Alice—" her gaze sought her sister's, and Alice obligingly came closer so that Elfrida wouldn't have to squint. "Do you think you might tell Button about the tea? You know your way around her so much better than I."

"Certainly! I will face down Button, especially if *you* tell Mama she must get dressed and come down," Alice answered. "You know how Mama will do whatever you like."

"Not without her share of fuss, however," admitted Elfrida.

"Exactly. And Button will do whatever *I* ask," said Alice, "and with a very great deal of fuss."

"Never mind Mama's and Button's fussing!" cried Margaret. "What will you wear, Elfie, to charm Mr. Tierney?"

Elfrida stared. "Why, I will wear what I am wearing at this moment." Spreading her arms, she indicated her long-sleeved, dotted white muslin.

"Because she's already always beautiful," piped up Edith, crawling into the window seat beside her oldest sister.

Elfrida put an arm around her and gave her a playful hug. "That's right. Because how could I possibly be even more beautiful? But, in truth—if Mr. Tierney is to please Papa and fall in love with me at first sight, he had better see me exactly as I am." Margaret and Edith laughed at this, but Alice turned away.

"Exactly as she was"! Easy enough for Elfrida to say. Elfrida, who was more than presentable from the moment she opened her eyes in the morning to when she shut them at night. Alice knew—the two girls shared a bedroom. Nor did Elfrida's gowns ever seem to be plagued by tiny rents or blossoming mystery stains, like Alice's. She frowned down at her own striped dress, which had once been white but had since been tea-dyed after Alice dribbled some of that beverage down her front. (She was not usually clumsy, but in that instance she had glimpsed a lizard on the window frame and had bounded up without thinking.) Yes, the wondrous Mr. Joseph Tierney would shortly see the enchanting Miss Elfrida Hapgood exactly as she was, but, more to the point, he would also see Miss *Alice* Hapgood exactly as she was. Alarming thought! Never mind whether her gown be clean or no—would he recognize her? Be shocked and horrified to discover that the boy he met earlier was no boy at all? Would he expose her?

He would not expose me, she told herself. *He is too much the gentleman.*

And who was to say he would fathom her disguise? People saw what they expected to see, Alice had learned. If you presented them with a young boy, they saw a young boy. That was all there was to it. She herself had chosen to share her secret with Button and Dorcas, more for her own convenience than anything else, but, as to the rest of the neighborhood, Alice had evaded discovery easily over the years.

Nevertheless, she would tread cautiously. Men of science were gifted observers, after all.

After Alice informed Button of the change in plans (and quenched the flames of the good cook's predicted towering rage), she escaped for a long walk out of doors. In her dress she dared not seek the woodlands, and she kept unwillingly to the overgrown walks of Bramleigh's surrounding gardens while thinking of Mr. Tierney.

She saw again his smiling mouth as he questioned her and the gleam of humor in his eyes. How the sun shone on his crisp brown hair and how he had loosened his neckcloth for ease. He had a quick, graceful way of moving. All about him was quick and graceful, for that matter, his movement and his manners. See how easily he spoke with her, whether the subject was trout classification, poaching, or offers of employment! Alice had never met any man like him before.

A naturalist. She whispered the word as she trailed leaves in the algae-ridden reflecting pool that no longer reflected. Then she spoke it aloud, trying it out. Mr. Joseph Tierney, Naturalist.

She had never imagined, in her eighteen years, that she would find something more compelling than the world around her, but here it was. More fascinating than any creature that swam or flew or burrowed, more winsome than any plant that blossomed or leaved or fruited.

Mr. Joseph Tierney, Naturalist.

Chapter Four

Doe not demaund why I am mute:
Loves silence doth all speech confute.
—Philip Rosseter, *Book of Ayres* (1601)

From the squire's bluff manner and Miss Birdlow's remark on the Hapgood girls' lack of refinement, Joseph had no great expectations of the afternoon's tea. He was half sorry for making the engagement, when he finally arrived and was announced by the goggle-eyed, breathless maid-of-all-work. But once ushered into the small but elegant drawing room, he forgot his regrets.

The squire stood with his back to the modest fire, his boots clean and breeches unwrinkled, cravat perfectly crisp and knotted. The mistress of Bramleigh, trussed in gray muslin and pink with the effort of sucking in her breath, favored Joseph with a bobbing curtsy as introductions were made before dropping into the nearest armchair, her skirts billowing about her as if they, too, exhaled with relief that the courtesies were dispensed with. "My eldest, Miss Elfrida Hapgood," Joseph's host continued, raising an arm in the direction of the golden-haired beauty on his left.

"Miss Hapgood," Joseph murmured, bowing to her curtsy, and understanding all at once the reason for Miss Birdlow's ill-will. Miss Hapgood might not be the daughter of a viscount, but she bore herself with the beauty and grace of a duchess. He studied her some moments longer than propriety allowed, but it was with the interest of a naturalist. What *did* cause certain members of a species to be deemed more pleasing than others? Symmetry and regularity of feature, a clear complexion, generous proportions—it must be that these qualities were indicators of health. Health and—yes—fertility.

Elfie colored faintly under his gaze, but her own remained clear and blue and steady. Her sisters knew that Elfie couldn't make much of Mr. Tierney, the distance he stood from her, but she saw enough to recognize his face was still turned toward her.

"And my next—Alice," the squire went on, not bothering with the grand arm gesture this time. He merely pointed. "Alice, Margaret, Edith."

More bows and curtsies. The younger girls retreated to the window seat, Margaret with a book she held upside down the entire visit (she had been forbidden on pain of banishment to speak, lest her sharp tongue give offense), and little Edie with a sheet of drawing paper, upon which she pretended to sketch Margaret while actually capturing their guest.

It was some minutes before Joseph was free to look at the young ladies again. The squire questioned him on his views of the West Country and whether his morning's wanderings had proven satisfactory. Joseph outlined some differences he observed between the landscape of Somerset and his home county Buckinghamshire, and verbally retraced the route he had taken earlier, a speech to which only Alice paid close and covert attention. Apart from one visit to London when she was younger, she had spent her life entirely within a five-mile radius of Bramleigh, and she yearned to see more of the world. For her part, Elfrida glanced up from time to time as she bent over her embroidery so her father would not later accuse her of coldness to their guest. She was careful to work only on the boundary because she could not hold it near enough to see the shepherd's features in the center, and she had no wish to spoil months of stitchery. Alice imitated her, having stolen Margaret's embroidery frame not ten minutes earlier, with a solemn promise that she would only put in big stitches around the very edge that she could pick out later. The truth was, Alice could stitch well enough if her task were to sew up a frog or snake whose organs she had removed and inspected, but embroidering flowers and scrolls and cherubs and simpering couples made her want to poke her own eyes out with the needle. Worse yet, in this moment, all she cared to do was stare at Mr. Tierney and see if he really were as handsome as she remembered, this brilliant man of science who fell from the sky to fascinate her. As a result, it was fortunate for Alice that Margaret could not see the long, thoughtless stitches she put in, one after the other, as she listened.

"Begging your pardon, sir, there could never be a better time for such an undertaking," Joseph was saying. "With the war on, both practicality and patriotism require that we British look inward as we seek to advance knowledge. There is neither leisure nor funds at present for voyages such as Captain Cook made, but there is much yet to be discovered within our very borders!"

"Boney's the only frog I'd like to capture and slice to ribbons," growled the squire. "And when we get him, we'll beat him! Exile him to the Antipodes, by G—"

"My love," his wife interposed mildly.

"By gum," finished the squire. He marched up and down the room twice before spreading the tails of his coat and plopping on the chair opposite Joseph. "If I were twenty years younger, why, I'd—say, Tierney—young fellow like you had no desire to take a commission and have at the Frenchies?"

There was a brief silence. Alice stole a glance at their guest and saw color rise under his sun-tanned cheeks. He cleared his throat. "I did, at one time, sir, have thoughts of enlisting with His Majesty's navy. A fit of patriotic zeal, you know. But I held that wish in opposition to my family, who chose me for the clergy."

"Churchman, hey? And yet here you sit, neither sailor nor vicar, captain nor curate."

"I believe I have found my true calling, nonetheless."

The squire appeared to waver between wanting to quiz Joseph further and fear of driving off Elfrida's potential suitor, and all were relieved to see Dorcas come in with the tea tray, Button close behind her, bearing a second platter heaped with fruits and tiny custard tarts. Only Alice knew what those tarts had cost: the roast scorched on one side because Dorcas was sent to collect eggs and Button up to her elbows in flour and butter. After Alice returned from her walk, Button let her turn the spit until she saw how red in the face and blowzy the task made her. "Let it be, child. If it burns, it burns, and your father would well deserve it for laying this task upon me. But we canna be sending 'ee to tea looking like the fishwife's beggar maid. And you so much in love with the gentleman! Best spend your efforts making yourself presentable." Alice didn't need to be told twice. She raced upstairs to find a gown with no stains or rips and to scrape her stick-straight hair atop her head in what she hoped were becoming scallops.

Elfrida performed the perils of the tea service with nary a spilled drop, but Alice was glad Button left the room before Mr. Tierney politely abstained from the custard tarts. All that fuss for naught!

The squire, at least, appeared to enjoy them. Having been robbed of his cold collation, he devoured a half-dozen of the pastries in rapid succession, pausing only to say around a mouthful, "All right, then, Mr. Tierney. You have found your true calling as a naturalist, and this Sir Edmund fellow has provided the employment. What will you do first?"

Joseph set his teacup lightly in his saucer. "I begin with an inventory, sir, of the common flora and fauna, with ever the hope of discovering new varieties and species."

"Will you—ahem!"—his host choked on a stray pastry crumb and got it down with some struggle—"catch 'em and pin 'em, or merely sketch 'em?"

"Neither, if they be long familiar. But if I chance on plants or creatures unrecorded, I will have to capture them for study. I'm afraid I'm a shabby hand with the pen, unlike the artists hired by the President of the Royal Society, Sir Joseph Banks. The beauty and wonder of the drawings commissioned from Cook's voyage!"

Alice poked herself with her needle and stifled a cry, having brought her hands together in awe. "You have seen the drawings?" she squeaked.

Gladly Joseph availed himself of the opportunity to look her direction, and he caught one flash of her glowing brown eyes before she dropped them to her work. "Do you know of them, Miss Alice?" In answer she only shook her head, regretting her impulsiveness. "I consider it a great shame," he pursued, "that they have not been published. But, yes, I have been fortunate enough to see some of the proofs at Somerset House and then—not a fortnight since—at Sir Joseph Banks' home in Soho Square, when he hosted our company of men to mark the beginning of this new endeavor." This elicited no response whatsoever from the young lady—she had, in fact, turned completely away and appeared to be watching something out the window—and Joseph sat back in his chair, abashed, remembering Miss Birdlow's smothered yawn. He *would* go on and bore people with his passions! But, no—she had asked *him*, after all. Could it be—worse—that she thought him boastful of his acquaintance with the illustrious Sir Joseph Banks?

He took a custard tart.

"So, I say," the squire valiantly tried to resuscitate the conversation, "My Elfrida is a pat hand at drawing. She could assist you, if you needed some bug's likeness taken."

This utter falsehood drew stares from his other three daughters and surprised Margaret into breaking her vow of silence. "Why that's nonsense, papa! Elfie was the despair of the drawing master. It was only Edith's ability that checked him from hurling himself off the parapets, or so he said. If anyone should take a bug's likeness, it should be she."

"Oh—heh heh—was it so?" Her father tugged on his cravat and shot Margaret a withering look. "Elfie, Edie. Mix 'em up, sometimes."

His host's discomfort made Joseph forget his own. "What a capital suggestion, though, Miss Margaret, if Miss Edith were willing."

"Edie cannot abide dead things," blurted Alice, to rescue her little sister, who had paled at the thought of painting impaled insects and stiffened squirrels. "Though I don't know what there is about them to be in a ruffle over. Whatever injury they might have done one—"

"Can't say I approve of the subject matter for vulnerable female minds." The squire broke in, with an ominous raising of the eyebrows. Alice pressed her lips together. Oh, dear. This was terrible. The bold question on Sir Joseph Banks' drawings was bad enough, and now this! Would she never learn? Gentlemen did not like young ladies who were fearless of dead things. As Button said, they wanted wives who would ornament their lives with beauty and peace. The ability to be beautiful was beyond her control, but Alice could at least be peaceful, could not she?

Joseph, too, was struck dumb for the second time that afternoon, interpreting the squire's comment as a rebuke to his own suggestion. He took a second tart.

To general family amazement, it was Mistress Hapgood who dislodged them this time from the conversational mire. "How I miss London," she breathed in her papery, fluttery way. "I have not been this age—my health has not permitted." Smiling over the guest's murmured regrets, she sighed. "If you have been much in Town, you must tell us the latest. What have you seen? *Whom* have you seen? Had you leisure for the theatres?"

Joseph had the good fortune of seeing Miss Sarah Siddons at Covent Garden, and a thorough discussion of the production and how favorably and unfavorably Miss Siddons' talents compared with newer and younger actresses occupied some minutes. Elfrida roused herself to ask a gentle question or two, and the visit might have wound up on this pleasant footing, had not nature intervened.

One of the sad consequences of the Hapgoods' earlier financial difficulties had been the release of many servants. They employed but three at the time of our story: Button, Dorcas, and a shiftless but strong lad Hal, who handled the out-of-door work and occasional repairs. As a result, Bramleigh was neat, if not precisely clean, and functional, rather than immaculate, in its workings.

Thus it was, that while Mr. Tierney answered Elfrida's questions about the cavernous Theatre Royal and attended to Mrs. Hapgood's sighs for the more intimate Old Drury, Alice made a terrible discovery. Dangling by its thread and slowly but surely descending ever closer, a spider hung not ten inches above their visitor's head. It twirled on its string, drawn perhaps by Mr. Tierney's curling brown hair.

Please, Alice whispered in her head. *Please do go back up. Leave him alone and find some comfortable corner to spin your web in!* She shot her younger sisters an agonized look, jerking her head as imperceptibly as she could toward the spider. But Margaret and Edith were too far away to perceive it and thought Alice meant to communicate something about Mr. Tierney. Margaret gave a tiny shrug and Edith shook her head.

Alice bit her lower lip. *Please let it be gone.*

It was not. Horror-struck, she saw the spider lower itself another few inches. When Mr. Tierney laughed, his head tilting back, the movement set the arachnid swaying, swaying in the air. If he were to swing into their guest's mouth—!

"I could not agree more, madam," Mr. Tierney said, "and the days of Mr. Kean—"

Rattle and *slap!* Alice's teacup hit her saucer as she sprang across the room to clap her hands around the eight-legged intruder. Elfrida and Mrs. Hapgood shrieked; Joseph started in alarm; the squire cursed; and Margaret and Edith cried, "*Aaa*-lice!"

"I beg your pardon!" Her horrified gaze met his startled one. "It was a—I—I—beg your pardon." Backing away, she turned toward the window as if she thought of putting the spider out, but Edith gave another minute shake of the head, and Alice fled the room, spider and all.

The remaining Hapgoods returned their attention to their guest, their expressions ranging from mortification (Elfrida) to puzzlement (Mrs. Hapgood) to resigned exasperation (the rest of them). To their surprise, Mr. Tierney's shock had given way to thoughtfulness. Setting aside his own teacup and the remains of the second tart, he frowned at the squire. "Excuse me, sir, but—do you have any other children that I have not met today?"

"Other children?" echoed his host, dumbfounded. He struck the arms of his chair. "Do you refer to baseborn children?"

"Richard!" gasped his lady, falling back against her seat in a faint. Elfrida rushed to her side and fanned a handkerchief in her face.

"Good gracious! No, sir! By your leave, I meant nothing of the kind. I referred to...legitimate children. There was no implication of—"

"Oh, well then," returned the squire, ignoring his wife's attack and his eldest's ministrations. "No, to answer your question. That's all of them." He swept the room with a gesture. "These three. And, of course, the one that disgraced herself not a moment ago. Heaven's blessing, such as it is. Four daughters."

"I see," said Joseph, not seeing at all. A bell of recognition had rung, when Miss Alice lunged at him, and he saw the stricken look in her wide brown eyes. Eyes the very shape and color of those belonging to the mysterious William the Bastard. His acquaintance with the Bramleigh folk being of such recent vintage, he could not discern if Mrs. Hapgood's extravagant reaction to his question demonstrated grief over her husband's past betrayals or simply hypochondria. Nor had Squire Hapgood refuted the idea of fathering bastard children, after himself raising the topic, Joseph realized. Perhaps this William the Bastard lied about the "William" portion but spoke truth about "the Bastard." Could the squire have a natural son? And if he did, who knew of him?

Joseph certainly could not pursue the matter further here, and he was sorry to have distressed the mistress of Bramleigh and her beautiful oldest daughter. He rose soon after to take his leave, contenting himself with repeating his request for an apt assistant.

"Perhaps Hal might serve, father," suggested Edith, bobbing her curtsy.

"Not Hal," declared Margaret, "unless Mr. Tierney wants all his traps sprung and his birds' eggs trod upon."

"Not Hal, indeed, then," said Joseph with a smile and a final bow. "But if a more suitable lad comes to mind, please send me word at Pattergees."

Scrambling away from the other side of the door before her father could open it for Mr. Tierney, Alice darted around the corner into the library. Her breath came short, but not from the fear of being caught eavesdropping. No—it was that Mr. Tierney had indeed recognized her—or nearly. It had been a close thing. His suspicions had been raised, but then diverted down the wrong track. Ah, well—let him think what he might, so long as he did not hit upon the truth. As her heart slowed, she dismissed Mr. Tierney's notions to focus on what interested her far more: he still sought a suitable assistant. Thankfully he made no mention of William the Bastard, and she berated herself for spinning a tale that could be so easily unwound.

No. William the Bastard could not and would not reappear.

But if Mr. Joseph Tierney persisted in wanting a helpmate with his work, it so happened that Miss Alice Hapgood knew where he might find one.

CHAPTER FIVE

Use of Spectacles weakneth the sight,
unlesse you wear them for need.
—James Smith, *A Complete Practice of Physick* (1656)

Girdles leaned over him as the gentlemen were enjoying their sherry after dinner. "Note for you, sir. Awaiting your reply."

Unfolding the sheet, Joseph read: "If ye be still needing holp in yer endevers, there be a likely lad Arthur a perish ward availerble early mornings by the Bramleigh Downs Church. Please answer, care of Button. Bramleigh."

Alice had been at some pains to affect a round, untutored scrawl, but her anxiety over it paled in comparison to what she felt as she watched from her chamber window for the reply. Two custard tarts and a story that Mr. Tierney had forgotten his list of West Country toad varieties sufficed to send Hal on his way to Pattergees with the note, but Alice hoped he wouldn't ask too many questions about why Mr. Tierney should send a reply to Button.

Hal didn't, having been welcomed in the Pattergees kitchen with a mug of small beer and some toasted cheese. When Alice intercepted the thirteen-year-old boy on the side path at Bramleigh, he held out the envelope unasked. "'E didn't reply to you, Miss, but to Button."

"Thank you, Hal. How peculiar of him."

"The Quality," answered Hal, as if this accounted for all manner of odd behavior.

Tucking the missive in her sleeve, Alice plunged into the next step of her plan. "By the by, Hal, I heard my father and Miss Elfrida remark on the state of your clothing."

"State o' me *what*?" demanded Hal, his blush hidden in the twilight. The thought of the beautiful Miss Hapgood noticing anything about him flooded him with a mixture of longing and horror.

"Clothing," repeated Alice firmly. She reached for the bundle at her feet. "So I have taken it upon myself to stitch you this shirt—nicer linen than that you currently wear—and trousers. Please to give me the ones you have on, and I will see they are laundered and darned."

Hal clutched his arms to his body as if he were that instant naked before her. "That—that's not ladylike, Miss, begging your pardon."

"Oh, go behind the bushes, Hal. I won't look," promised Alice impatiently. "But you can't go another minute in such as you have on, and these ones I have for you are clean and nearly new." That is, she had only worn them perhaps three times since last they were laundered, and they were free, for the most part, of mud, blood, or other ordure.

Having little choice in the matter, the boy complied, snatching the bundle from her and disappearing into the shrubbery with a rustle. Shortly, hurtling upwards like birds taking flight, his own rough and stained attire sailed into her eager hands.

By the time Hal emerged, newly dressed in her castoffs, Miss Alice was gone.

The ancient church at Bramleigh Downs stood since the 12th century, with major work undertaken in the 17th, when Alfred Hapgood of Bramleigh saw fit to improve and repair all that belonged to him. Since that time, despite regular attendance and an ordinary level of devotion from surrounding residents, the small chapel building grew somewhat dank within and overgrown by moss and ivy without. The living attached no longer supported even a modest vicar's family, and, indeed, the vicar who held Bramleigh Downs added to his income with three other parish churches and was rarely seen at the poorest of these. Rather, the duties of Bramleigh Downs, including those usually given to a sexton, fell upon a humble curate, nearly as ancient in age as the Jacobean pulpit from which he delivered his sermons. This Mr. Thomas, or Father Thomas, as his flock began to call him some decades past, received a fright when he shuffled in the following morning and discovered a young lad asleep on the forward-most pew. He wore rough, loose-fitting, none-too-clean clothing, muddy boots, a snug cap from which no hair escaped, and round spectacles.

"Good morning, my boy," said Father Thomas, when he had recovered from his surprise. He gave him a gentle prod in the calf with his cane.

Instantly the boy sat up, going to rub his eyes until he realized he wore spectacles, and then crying, "Oh, dear! Have I missed him?" He looked around in a panic before finally lowering the spectacles and recognizing the curate. "Father Thomas. Forgive me. I stole in early to wait and must have been more tired than I thought."

"You are forgiven, lad, freely. Only help me—I do not know you."

The boy dropped his voice and spoke more quietly, but at the same time the pitch of it rose. "Do you not? It is I, Father Thomas. Alice Hapgood. Only you mustn't say anything, if you please."

"But, Miss Alice!" breathed the astonished curate. "Why are you dressed thus? You are not running away, are you?"

"No—by no means. I only hope to serve as an assistant to the naturalist who has come to Pattergees. But you understand, he can't have a female assistant. It wouldn't be proper. That is why you must not expose me."

"And I perceive you think disguising yourself as a boy is proper, Miss Alice?"

"Not exactly, no," she admitted. "But Father Thomas, have you never loved something so much that you thought it worth a sacrifice or two? In this case I sacrifice only propriety—and only in my own eyes and…and a few others'. Because I would so love to help him and learn from him. It is not fair! I love God's creation every bit as much, but I cannot go to university or be elected to the Royal Society, that I might study it and teach others."

He patted the hand that had grasped his arm. "I see your dilemma. And, yes, there are things so beloved they come at a cost, but I must point out to you, Miss Alice, that you sacrifice not only propriety, but also the trust of others."

Brown eyes pleading above the spectacles, she fell to her knees. "I mean no harm! I mean only to help him, and by keeping it secret, I hope to hurt no one by it. Please, Father Thomas. I confess to you now that I've been disguising myself many a morning to go fishing or exploring because Papa said such pursuits were not suitable for young ladies. But no harm has come of it. I pray you, say nothing to anyone."

"Shhh...get up, my dear. I will say nothing for now, but we will speak again of this another day. I must think this over. Wherever did you find the spectacles?"

Alice bit her lip. "I suppose I ought to confess that, too. Mr. Lewis left them weeks ago by Mama's bedside. He has so many pairs that he did not even remember or notice the lack. I took them to give them back, but then I kept forgetting. Or—I forgot them until I had a use for them. But I must wear them, Father Thomas, because Mr. Tierney might recognize me, else. He already asked Papa if we girls have a brother—"

Out came tumbling the story, beginning to end, from the encounter by the pond to the previous day's visit, and barely had Alice finished telling it than a step was heard at the south door. Giving her accomplice's hand a final squeeze, Alice pushed her glasses back up and advanced, taking care to remain in the shadows. "Good morning, sir. Be ye Mr. Tierney?" she asked in a gravelly voice, bowing because she dared not remove her cap. Behind her she caught the shuffling of Father Thomas, most likely retreating to his office to avoid implication in the deceit.

"Good morning," returned Joseph, peering into the dimness without success, his own hat in hand. He was dressed much as Alice had seen him the first time, though his waistcoat was brown today, and over his shoulder he carried a satchel from which a net poked. "I am he. You must be Arthur, friend of Mrs. Button of Bramleigh."

"That I be. She said ye be needing an under-fellow, like. What knows the country hereabouts. I be yer—I be the one for the job."

"Splendid. We will begin at once, if you are ready. Say four mornings per week, about this time, at the rate of...a shilling a fortnight?"

Alice gave a soft gasp, her plans not having included remuneration. She rarely had any coin to call her own, the insufficient pin money doled out by Squire Hapgood first passing through Elfrida's thrifty hands.

"Not enough?" asked Joseph, frowning. He honestly had little idea how to go about this, or if the boy would prove able, and hesitated to commit more.

"Bob a fortnight," agreed Alice. "What shall I show ye first? Bugs? Birds? Fish? Game? Flowers?"

"If you don't mind, shall we step out of the church? The first thing you may show me is yourself. If we are to work together, the good Mrs. Button's recommendation notwithstanding, I would prefer to put a face with the voice."

Alice gave a wordless grunt and raced past him, stubbing her toe painfully on the low-relief effigy which marked her great-great-great-uncle Hapgood's remains in the aisle. Mr. Lewis' spectacles effectively blinded her, so blurred did they make the world, but she pushed them up her nose again before turning to face her employer, whose countenance was an indistinct oval crowned with cloudy brown hair. Was this what everyone looked like to Elfie?

For his part, Joseph saw a young lad in ill-fitting clothes, anywhere from twelve to fifteen, with delicate, flushed features and eyes magnified like the specimens he was wont to examine under a microscope. Brown eyes—enormous orbs filling the lenses—and a certain challenging set to the chin—"Ah," said Joseph lightly. "Just so. You wouldn't happen to be acquainted with a lad who calls himself William the Bastard, would you, Arthur?"

Her mouth dropping open, Alice took a step back. "N—no, sir. Mrs. Button—my—my—cousin twice removed—why, she would tan my hide if I kept company like that."

"You know to whom I refer, then," persisted Joseph. "I cannot speak for his character, whatever his birth, but he bears a remarkable likeness to you, Arthur, in build and coloring. Though certainly he has the advantage in eye-sight."

Alice fairly squirmed, but she hid it with artful scratching. Or possibly not so artful. Without time to wash it, Hal's shirt was not only fragrant, but also abrasive. "You are new to these parts, sir," she said, "so ye aren't so very familiar with the peoples. Many of us be distant cousins to each other, born either side of the blanket, if ye ken. Best not to be mentioning it overmuch."

Joseph's mouth twitched, but he only nodded. "Sound advice, I am sure. Only yesterday I called upon the Hapgoods at Bramleigh, to whom William the Bastard (and thus you) also bear a resemblance. More 'distant cousins,' I suppose. Alas, the good squire has only daughters, and my inquiries as to sons set everyone at sixes and sevens. I certainly do not want to be thought casting aspersions on anyone's reputation."

"That's right. No tittle-tattle like the village gossips. Hadn't we best be getting on, sir?" strangled Alice. She threw out an arm to point behind her companion. "A shrew! Out late, this one! I can show you where he keeps his home."

"If it be *Sorex araneus*, you needn't trouble yourself, Arthur," Joseph called after his assistant, who was bolting for the cover of the trees, the better to hide her features from further examination.

"No, no—*Sorex minutus*—I mean to say—" Alice clapped a hand to her mouth. No Latin! What would Mr. Tierney think? That this corner of Somerset was awash with boys of questionable bloodlines, all educated beyond their station! "Off it goes!" she amended, crashing into the undergrowth. No sooner was she shaded by the woodland canopy of spruce and hemlock than her foot caught a fallen branch and she tumbled to the ground, Mr. Lewis' spectacles bouncing from her nose into the foxgloves. In a flash, Alice was on her hands and knees, groping for them and smashing them back on.

A firm hand caught her beneath the arm and hoisted her upright. "I say," spoke the blurry face of Mr. Tierney, "how fortunate you saw where those shot off to. I would have judged, by the thickness of those lenses, that we would spend the better part of the morning searching for them." Not only the thickness of the lenses, he added inwardly, but also the lad's propensity for stumbling over objects in his path.

"W—what?" The warmth of his hand penetrated the coarse material of her sleeve as if it were an iron fresh from the fire, and Alice jerked her arm away. "That pair of spectacles be precious necessary to me, sir. Gift of a—er—benefactor. I would sooner lose the nose on my face than them."

"Hmm." Bending quickly, he plucked a budding foxglove stalk and held it up. "I also value keen eyesight in any assistant of mine. Tell me, Arthur, how many bells do you count on this stalk?"

Alice swallowed hard, her hands clutching at her baggy woolen trousers. She saw only streaks of pink against the green—that and her head was starting to hurt. *Think, Alice Hapgood—think!* How many bells were typically found on *Digitalis purpurea*? Her chin lifted. "Mean you already blown or still in the bud?"

"Say blow*ing*—no longer green," returned Joseph.

It was but late May. The foxgloves had more weeks yet until they were in full bloom. "It's hard to count, sir, without holding it meself, but I'd guess twelve or so, and more to follow."

"Mm." He tossed it away, and Alice guessed that her assumption was correct.

Grinning, she put her hands on her hips. "Shall we be getting on, sir? Did you be wanting to see about that shrew?"

Ignoring her suggestion, he pointed back across the field to Bramleigh Downs Church. "And how many headstones do you count, in the first row, Arthur?"

Headstones? Were there headstones? She could not even make out the church building amidst the surrounding elms.

Had Alice not gone to that tiny chapel every Sunday in living memory, she could have vouched for no more than a vague, gray-white heap of *something* in the distance. Feeling Mr. Tierney's eyes on her, she dared not lower the spectacles to peer over them. *First row…first row…there was Obadiah Hapgood and his three wives. How many children had they?* She couldn't recall. A half-dozen? Oh, it was impossible to know. "Six?" she ventured dully.

"I count ten," said Joseph. "If you would permit me—" Reaching over, he plucked the eyeglasses from her face.

"Oh." Alice blinked several times. Affecting a squint, she counted the now distinct headstones. "Holla! God save the King!" She rubbed her eyes and blinked some more. "My condition! The haze over my vision be gone now! It be a miracle, no less."

"That 'haze' over your vision some might attribute to wearing spectacles when you have no need of them," Joseph replied wryly.

"Begging your pardon, sir, I had great need of them." *As a disguise,* Alice added in her head.

"Arthur. Look at me, please."

Unwillingly, Alice obeyed. She was glad to see his handsome face clearly again, but discomfited by the stern expression it wore.

"If we are to work comfortably together, let there be no mysteries or falsehoods between us." The boy's eyes widened even further, if it were possible, and Joseph found his irritation receding. What ailed the lad? Sir Edmund Chall had prepared his team of young naturalists for difficulties with patronage, weather, supplies, and so forth, but of the management of dishonest natives of the humbler class he had said not a word.

"Come," prodded Joseph, giving an encouraging smile. "Tell me once again: who are you, and do you bear any relation to the lad William I met two days since?"

Over her racing heart Alice croaked, "I be he, sir."

"Thank you. And is your name William or Arthur or neither?"

She licked her lips. "A-Arthur."

"Why then the story, the first day?"

Heaving a genuine sigh, Alice braced herself for yet another fable. Mr. Tierney was so very good-natured that she hated to impose upon him, yet what choice did she have? If she confessed all—that she was the legitimate *daughter* of the local squire—she would be dismissed instantly, having lost his esteem and all further possibility of his company, not to mention any opportunity to learn from him.

But being by nature an untalented liar, all her previous fabrications had yet to take him in.

She had best keep to her most practiced lie: the Arthur story. At least that one was rehearsed before her looking glass a good half-hour the previous night.

Taking a deep breath, Alice grumbled, "Sir, please forgive me. My name be Arthur. Baddely. Arthur Baddely. Related somewhat to both Mrs. Button and the squire's family, although it be best not to mention that part to parties concerned, if you catch my meaning.

I told you a tale when first we met because, like you said, it were unlawful for me to be fishing at Pattergees. I didn't want you to peach me to his lordship. But I did be wanting to assist you in your tasks, what they be. Only I figured as you wouldn't want the other one, what you caught doing something wrong. So I counterfeits myself. And there be nothing wrong with my eyes. I only—er—wore the spectacles what I found fair and square at Bramleigh, so's that I wouldn't be so easily recognized by you, like."

"I see." His face was unreadable, even without Mr. Lewis' spectacles. "And if you would permit me to ask—the first time we met, when you were fishing at Pattergees, both your accent and vocabulary were somewhat different than they have been since. I heard nothing of the Somerset 'Zs' from you. 'Zomerzet' and so forth. Nay, even the pitch of your voice—"

"Ay?" squeaked Alice, fighting down another swell of panic. "The pitch? That—uh—you see, my voice only recently underwent the change of life. Don't always have it under my control." As if to prove her point, her uncooperative instrument cracked twice during the delivery of this speech.

"That makes perfect sense," returned Joseph. "Do you find your accent and vocabulary similarly unpredictable?"

At this, Alice buried her face in her hands for some moments while her interlocutor waited in silence. Let him think her ashamed. She *was* ashamed, but not for the reasons he thought. "I have, sir, what Mrs. Button does call an unfordinate gift for mimicry. Sometimes I'll talk likes what I expects people expects to hear. Please don't be angry 'bout it. I meant no trickery or insult. If I put on the gentleman-talk when first I saw you, 'twas only because you looked the gentleman."

By the end of this explanation, her companion was smiling. Drawing the net from his satchel, he handed it to Alice. "Why don't you hold this? Thank you for speaking the truth, Arthur Baddely. I pardon you, and assure you with my whole heart of my discretion. Not only that, but I hope I will prove actually to be a gentleman, and not merely to bear the appearance of one. Now that that is taken care of, I expect we will get on famously."

He took a few steps in a slow circle around her, considering the woodland and the fields, his expression thoughtful as he caught the birdcalls and the angle of the morning sun. When he looked at her again, his gaze warmed her as much as the sunlight.

"What say you, Arthur? Shall we begin?"

CHAPTER SIX

**He now began to fear he had made a choice
the most injudicious, and that coquetry and caprice
had only waited opportunity, to take place of
candour and frankness.
—Fanny Burney, *Camilla* (1796)**

If Lady Marlton and her daughter hoped to be bothered by Joseph hanging about, angling for occasions to ingratiate himself with them, they were soon disappointed. Most days they saw no sign of him until dinner at five o'clock. He was cheerful and dressed for evening and polite then, if somewhat distracted. Joseph had learned that, however much he might like to retreat in the evenings to sort and document and compile the day's findings, manners required that he lay these aside and participate in the social doings of the family. These doings usually consisted of music and cards, but one evening, some ten days after his arrival, they were joined by the Porterworths and the DeWitts, two prominent families whose estates lay to the west of Patterton village.

As all of them were long familiar to each other, Joseph's presence added much piquancy to the gathering, and he found himself placed between the elegant Miss Birdlow and her dearest friend Miss Porterworth. Across from him sat the long-nosed Miss DeWitt. That lady was the wrong side of thirty and plain as plain could be, but she had resigned herself to it with good nature and did not discomfit him with the coquetry of Miss Porterworth or the disdain of Miss Birdlow.

"You must tell everyone where you go, Mr. Tierney, these long mornings," commanded Miss Birdlow, when they had finished with the bouillon and moved on to fish. Leaning around him to address Miss Porterworth she added, "I vow, Constance, our guest leaves the house before dawn, and we never lay eyes on him until it is time to dress for dinner!"

"You don't say!" cried Miss Porterworth. With her upturned nose, unfashionably wide mouth, and a scattering of what could only called freckles, she had not the elegance of Miss Birdlow, but she could be relied upon to follow her bosom friend's lead. "How shocking, Mr. Tierney! How rag-mannered of you." Her voice caressed the words, and she lowered her lashes over her green eyes to regard him.

"Indeed," said Miss Birdlow. "Every day when we sit down to dinner and he makes his appearance, I am reminded anew of his existence." She wore a new blue mull gown which she knew well became her, and she imagined someone beside her mother should tell her she was the picture of a summer's day.

Mr. Tierney did not appear in danger of flattering her. "Forgive me, if I have not been the most social of houseguests. There is more to do and see than can be seen and done. My days have never seemed shorter."

"But where do you *go?*" insisted Miss Porterworth. "Pray, do not be secretive. I cannot think what there is to see and do around here."

"He is a naturalist, after all," put in Miss DeWitt. "I suppose he wanders out of doors." Such a commonplace observation pleased neither of the young ladies and was duly ignored.

Seeing their talk had the attention of the whole party now, Joseph laid down his fork. "Why—Miss DeWitt has hit upon it. I go everywhere and nowhere. Ground familiar to you all from birth, I imagine. This morning, for example, my assistant and I were making observations where the stream bordering the north of Pattergees joins with the Holliton."

Miss Porterworth leaned toward him, her generous bosom threatening to come atop the table like twin walruses heaving themselves ashore. "What...manner of observations?"

"Otters," said Joseph. "We were numbering the otters."

"Oh!"

"This assistant of yours," interjected Lady Marlton, "who is he again?"

"A ward of Bramleigh Downs parish, my lady. I am certain you are not acquainted with him."

"Of that, I too am certain," said Miss Birdlow, archly. "Please accept the apologies of the neighborhood, Mr. Tierney, that you could find no one here more fitting for your labors than this uneducated, unfamilied urchin."

A flash of irritation crossed his face, which no one outside of his family would have been quick enough to catch. "Please do not worry yourself, Miss Birdlow. Arthur Baddely is everything I require. He may not have formal education, but he has missed no opportunity to teach himself from books and from experience. He lacks family—it is true—but whoever his forbears were, they have gifted him with cleverness and an easy disposition."

"Such praise!" remarked Miss Birdlow with mock awe. "How you do heap it on! I see you do know how to compliment when you choose. Well. 'Cleverness and an easy disposition'—you have just nicked our Somerset character. Hit right upon it. Therefore that will be no assistance in determining the lad's parentage."

"Are we Somersetians so clever and easygoing?" asked Miss De-Witt.

Feeling a surprising surge of protectiveness toward his humble assistant, Joseph could only spare a smile for Miss DeWitt's demurral before answering, "His parentage matters not a straw in the work he does for me, and I have not inquired into it. The most august family would not render Arthur a hair more helpful. And I have not met his equal for sharp eyes and fast fingers, two advantages in my line of work that cannot be overpraised."

"You've caught many things, you have, with your sharp eyes and fast fingers," Mr. Frank Birdlow called down the table. "Or you and your assistant have. My father's library begins to resemble a curiosity shop."

"Say, rather, a museum," said Lord Marlton.

"Whatever you may choose to call it, I am grateful for its existence," Joseph said. He was grateful as well to have the subject turned from Arthur Baddely's antecedents. "My chamber was growing rather cluttered with specimens and equipment."

"I should like to see this wondrous display," interposed Sir Cosmo DeWitt, a cadaverous man as plain and long-nosed as his daughter. "And so should my sons"—indicating the gentlemen placed on the other sides of Miss Porterworth and Miss Birdlow—"Perhaps after dinner, Mr. Tierney?"

Mr. Roscoe DeWitt threw Joseph a hostile look. He was used to monopolizing Miss Porterworth's attention when he was home from university, and she had not glanced at him all dinner. The other DeWitt appeared willing enough, only because he never took his eyes or his attention from his food and wine.

"Yes, let's," agreed Mr. Porterworth. "Have you any grouse, Mr. Tierney? I have a fondness for stuffed birds. My father made a collection of them. Grouse, partridge, some other."

"I do not claim any stuffed grouse as yet, but I should very much like to show you what I have gathered," said Joseph. "I daresay there are a handful of species which have never before been documented."

Lady Marlton caught her daughter's gaze narrowing in annoyance as the conversation drifted to these dull and exclusive subjects. Nodding at the footman to signal the serving of the partridges, she said smoothly, "A visit to the library for the gentlemen will be in order, then, I suppose. But I insist the tour be brief. I had in mind that we might push back the furniture and have the young people dance."

Sir Cosmo shrugged. "Dancing enough for them, Saturday next at the assembly."

"Sir Cosmo!" his wife chided, a jolly woman from whom the daughter inherited her amiability, "do not gainsay Lady Marlton. I am sure you may make a quick inspection and then join us in the drawing room. How the girls love to dance, and probably young Mr. Tierney would rather stand up with them on a summer's eve, than spend the time fiddling about with fossils and faded flowers."

Here Lady DeWitt was mistaken, but of course Joseph could not say so. The chance to explain his ambitions and progress to two of the leading county gentlemen—what could standing up with Miss Birdlow and Miss Porterworth and Miss DeWitt be, but a nuisance? Could they not dance with Miss DeWitt's two brothers and Mr. Birdlow?

"Needless to say," Joseph answered, "it would be an honor to partner the young ladies."

"It is settled then, Papa," Miss Porterworth told her father. "The tour must be whirlwind in nature. No monologues from you about Grandfather's stuffed birds!"

When the ladies withdrew after the meal, the men lingered over their port until Joseph was hard-pressed not to fidget with impatience. Time was a-wasting! At this rate, they should barely have the library door open before Lady Marlton swooped in to recall them. To make matters worse, the older gentlemen seemed to have forgotten their earlier interest. They plied him with questions to be sure—and not very subtle ones—but these were all related to his background and financial prospects. How precisely was he related to the Earl of Chiltern? And was there not also a baronet in the family? Did either man have heirs? Was Joseph's older brother likely to marry?

Joseph could have kissed Roscoe DeWitt's feet when the young man finally snapped, "Are we satisfied with our observation of Mr. Tierney, father? Shall we on to his animal-and-plant odds and ends? Mr. Tierney, you could not have observed those otters by the Holliton more closely than we seem to be scrutinizing you here."

The library tour proved as abbreviated as Joseph feared. While Lady Marlton was too well-bred to interrupt them, Mr. Porterworth was disappointed by the scarcity of stuffed specimens, and Sir Cosmo made inattentive by his desire to whip his sons into a frenzy of interest. Joseph suspected Roscoe and Norman were no men of science. Norman was polite but said little, and Roscoe plopped himself upon a sofa and determinedly hid behind a newspaper, answering his father's comments and questions in monosyllables, if at all. Only Lord Marlton evinced his usual pride and fascination in his guest's progress, but he was too good a host to insist upon a longer visit when the others proved so disinclined.

Before fifteen minutes had passed, Joseph's hopes of luring future patrons had been frustrated for the night, and he entered the drawing room with a false brightness pasted to his face, hating himself as he said and did all the polite things expected of him. He listened with seeming appreciation to the young ladies' musical offerings. He stood up multiple times with Miss Birdlow, Miss Porterworth, Miss DeWitt, and even Mrs. Mary Birdlow.

"How admiringly Mr. Tierney looks upon your Agnes," he heard Mrs. Porterworth say to Lady Marlton, as he and Miss Birdlow circled by.

"Nay—I am sure his eyes are all for your Constance," replied Lady Marlton.

Joseph's mouth clamped shut, and all Miss Birdlow's witticisms and asides thereafter could not succeed in drawing more from him than the minimum required by courtesy.

Then he must tread another measure with Miss Porterworth, who flirted and coquetted relentlessly until Joseph thought Roscoe DeWitt would take up the fireplace poker and murder him with it.

Miss DeWitt noticed his reticence and danced with him in easy silence, but by then, Joseph could not help feeling Sir Cosmo's eyes upon them, perhaps calculating whether his daughter's thirty-one was too vast an age to marry with twenty-three.

To his relief, Mrs. Mary Birdlow did not talk much because she never did. The one remark she did venture, however, was enough to steal what remained of his peace of mind. "How well you do this, Mr. Tierney. Frank and I are forever stepping on each other's feet. It will be a treat to see you and Agnes open the Midsummer Ball. You know they are reviving the tradition, do you not? Just for you. And it has ever been, that whoever opened the Midsummer Ball was married by Michaelmas."

Joseph suppressed a grimace and wished the present company at the devil. Married by Michaelmas! Not he! The next morning could not come soon enough. Then he would trade the smothering confines of Pattergees' drawing room for the open air of the cool streambed and exchange these maritally machinating companions for the honest Arthur.

Whatever the burdens of bastardy, thought Joseph savagely, *Arthur is spared at least the ambitions and intrigues of well-meaning parents and their tiresome daughters!*

One mile, as the crow flew, from the exasperated Joseph, his "bastard" assistant sat curled in an armchair beside her youngest sister Edith, two candelabras perched nearby to shed light upon an issue of *Curtis's Botanical Magazine*. The squire had gone to see to his hounds, and the girls abandoned the drawing room for the cozier quarters of their mother's chamber. Margaret read aloud from Fanny Burney's *Camilla* while Mrs. Hapgood dozed in her chair and Elfrida lay on the bed, staring up at the ceiling. Evenings were the only times Elfie let herself be idle, her eyes being usually so tired by then from straining all day.

Alice found her own head drooping. As such an early-riser, she was not much good past nine o'clock, but Edie's comments and the rustling of the magazine pages as they turned them helped to rouse her.

"How lovely this one is," breathed Edie, admiring Sydenham's illustration of the flax-leaved broom. "See those delicate yellow petals! Perhaps I will give over painting people and try plants."

"You will find they sit still a good deal better than people," murmured Alice. She smothered a yawn. "I will gather you some field turnip tomorrow morning."

"Field turnip! That does not sound pretty at all."

"It is, though." Alice yawned again, openly this time. "*Brassica rapa*. Little yellow flowers almost like these. Smaller petals. Mr. Tierney says he has eaten some."

"Mr. Tierney?" cried the keen-eared Margaret, looking up from the orations of Dr. Orkbourne, which, in truth she read without attending to. (She much preferred love scenes.) "When did you speak with Mr. Tierney?"

"What? Oh—oh—I am certain it must have been when he came to call," said Alice, coming full-awake at once over her blunder.

"Did we discuss field turnips then?" questioned Elfrida mildly.

"I'm sure we didn't," said Margaret. "And Alice said hardly a word, so it would have had to be Papa and Mr. Tierney, and I don't think Papa knows a field turnip from a city turnip."

"What is a city turnip?" put in Edith.

"Margaret is being clever," said Alice. "Very well, then. It must not have been Mr. Tierney. Perhaps—Hal ate some and told me of it."

"Hal never eats anything green," Edith pointed out.

Alice threw up her hands. "Then I do not know where I got it! I must have dreamed it."

"Are you, then, dreaming of Mr. Tierney, Alice?" said Margaret, provokingly.

"No. I am not. Don't be tiresome, Margaret. I regret even opening my mouth."

"Elfie is the one who should be dreaming of Mr. Tierney," said Edith. "Isn't that right? Papa said she must try and love him."

Slapping *Curtis's Botanical Magazine* shut, Alice bounded up, nearly tumbling Edith to the floor. "Papa said she must try and marry him. He said nothing about love."

Elfrida rolled up on one elbow, squinting slightly to regard her sister. "Well, I will try to do both, the very next time I see him. I am afraid not much progress has been made, as yet. He did not look at all on the point of proposing during his one call, and I did not look at all on the point of accepting."

"How can you jest so, Elfie?" Alice accused. "Of course you must come to love Mr. Tierney, if you would marry him. You could not marry him, could you, if you did not? Even to please Papa?"

"Marriage would be much more comfortable if I could love him," was Elfrida's musing but unhelpful reply. "In the meantime, may we have more *Camilla*, Margaret?"

It was Margaret's turn to huff and toss aside her reading material. "I would rather talk about love and marriage. I care not for Dr. Orkbourne's educational philosophies or Eugenia's *hic haec hoc*. Can we skip to the next bit about Camilla?"

"Better to be Eugenia than Camilla," Alice retorted, still stirred up. "I should rather have Eugenia's fine education than the heart of that prig, Edgar. How often Edgar believes the worst of Camilla!

How easily he is persuaded she is nothing but a coquette! I would never marry a man who did not know me and believe the best of me."

"Picky, picky," spoke up Mrs. Hapgood, the argument having wakened her. "If ever a man comes along for you, duck, you will have to take the flaws with the fineness."

"Such a flaw as that would outweigh any fineness," muttered Alice.

Their mother reached to pet Elfrida's head. "And a little coquetry serves its purpose. Else how would a man know to be interested in the first place? Remember that, Elfrida, if you would captivate Mr. Tierney. I should never have won your father, if I did not trouble myself to make him feel he was heaven's gift."

"What do you mean, Mama?" asked Margaret, all fascination. "How did you go about it?"

"Why—" Mrs. Hapgood smirked and ducked her head, as if she were once again inhabiting those long-ago assembly rooms— "I made much of him. Fixed him with my eyes. Hung on his words—"

"Asked questions about his hounds," suggested Edith.

"Many, *many* questions," said her mother.

Alice loved her father dutifully, but the thought of her parents' courtship inspired no flutterings of the heart in her. She picked up the volume of Burney and ran her finger over the cover. "I should still prefer Eugenia's education to Camilla's lover," she declared.

Her mother favored her with a critical look. "Eugenia's education is well enough for *her*, poor pock-marked creature, but for the rest of us females, Greek and Latin make poor bedfellows."

"Since I have 'small Latin and less Greek,' I suppose I must settle for ensnaring my own Edgar Mandlebert," answered Elfrida lightly.

"Mr. Tierney is no Edgar Mandlebert!" Alice could not help crying. "He is in every way superior to that stuffy, mistrustful—"

Fortunately for that young lady's secret, Margaret interrupted her. "At Saturday's assembly, you must cast your eyelashes down, Elfie, and agree with everything the gentleman says. And if he tries to be witty, you titter behind your fan."

"And you dart melting glances at him when he is not looking, which he just turns and catches you at," added Edith.

"Girls!" laughed their mother along with them. "What would you know of the matter?"

"I shall do nothing of the kind," said Elfrida, crossing her arms over her stomach.

"Well," said Mrs. Hapgood, "you are so beautiful that perhaps you need not make the effort. What say you, Alice? Should Elfie exert herself?"

But, after catching herself and sending a grateful prayer heavenward that she had not revealed her relationship with Mr. Tierney, Alice had returned to ruminating over her mother's earlier speech. Was Eugenia's fine education, with its Greek and Latin, only useful as a consolation because she might never know love? Miss Burney implied at the end of *Camilla* that Eugenia, too, found love, but it was an afterthought. Camilla's triumphant match with the tiresome Mr. Mandlebert took precedence.

It was what Button had said, in so many words—that gentlemen did not want educated young ladies with minds of their own. Alice felt the weight of this universal opinion heavy on her shoulders. Sighing, she took the candelabra nearest her. "I do not know, Mama. Elfie must shift for herself. But I am tired. I must to bed."

"I will come presently," said Elfrida.

"Remember, Alice—no dreaming of Mr. Tierney and his wild turnips tonight!" Margaret called after her.

Thrusting her head back in the room to favor this sister with a scowl, Alice shut the door with a bang.

CHAPTER SEVEN

And twenty of these punie lies ile tell.
—Shakespeare, *The Merchant of Venice* (1600)

For Alice, the two weeks that followed her employment by Mr. Tierney were among the happiest, yet most tortured of her young life. Happiest, in that she did what she most loved to do, in the company of the young man whom she admired above any other. And tortured, in that she knew her friendship with Mr. Tierney was founded on deceit, a deceit added to day by day and minute by minute.

May passed into June. The pair of them wandered the Pattergees and Bramleigh acres. They collected grasses and flowers and seeds; they followed tracks and located burrows; they surprised mothers with their young; they caught insects by the score.

"Have you the jar?" Joseph asked, the morning following the Pattergees dinner party. He reached a hand back for it as they waded in the stream for water bugs.

She had been somewhat absent-minded that day, turning over and over in her head the discussion with her sisters and mother, and the jar had been forgotten as she followed him. Alice glanced toward the bank where the satchel lay, but before she could reply, Joseph said, "No matter—hand me your hat, and we will transfer it to the jar by and by."

Eyes widening, she clutched her floppy cap more tightly to her head and stumbled backward. Joseph looked around upon hearing her splashing. "Softly—you'll chase them away—Arthur, what ails you?"

"I—err—Mr. Lewis told me straight-like I must be keeping my hat on out of doors. Prevents—ah—nermonia, like."

"Pneumonia!" echoed Joseph, forgetting the escaping water bugs altogether to stare at her.

"I were a sickly babe," added Alice. That, at least, was the truth. But in her eagerness to be truthful where she could, she overreached herself. "And my pap insists I watch out for my health. So I keeps my cap on. Doctor's orders."

There was an odd light in her companion's eyes, and he sloshed a few steps nearer her. "Then you do know your father, Arthur. You are not entirely a parish ward, with origins shrouded in impenetrable mystery?"

Alice felt her insides constrict, both at being caught out and at having him so near, his hazel eyes fixed on her and his mouth curving at one corner in bemusement. Gasping, she drew an unsuccessful breath. "I—I—"

"There now. You've gone pale. You had better climb up on the bank and sit down for a spell." Before she knew what he was about, he had one hand under her armpit to hoist her upward while the other gave her an unceremonious push on the backside. All the color which had fled her face returned with a vengeance, and Alice busied herself with the satchel after tumbling down beside it, to hide her response. She had never, never, never been touched by anyone so intimately! Waltzing with the long-ago dancing master, his gloved hand at her waist, was as nothing compared to Mr. Tierney's splayed, bare fingers on her seat!

"I am sorry if I have pained you," said Joseph, trying without success to catch his assistant's eye. She shoved the requested jar at him, and he carelessly turned it round and round in his grasp. "We have not discussed your...antecedents...since you first entered my employ."

"Don't know what you mean by 'antecedents,'" grumbled Alice, "but if you means my parentage, you didn't make bones about it then."

"Nor do I now. You misunderstand me, Arthur. But as we spend increasing time together, I find myself curious and concerned for you. You said once you were in some wise related to both Mrs. Button and to the squire's family. I had no idea you knew exactly how. Does your...father...recognize you?"

The boa constrictor wrapped about her midsection tightened a notch, and Alice wondered if she would faint. Not even the corsets she so detested wearing were as uncomfortable as deceit. She shook her head. "Not what you would call recognize, sir. 'E would be ashamed of me, if you gather my meaning." With difficulty she resisted burying her face in her arms. What would her father say, if he knew the implied aspersions his second-born cast on his character?

"Ah." A long breath escaped Mr. Tierney. "Sadly, I imagine I do gather your meaning, Arthur." Before her puzzlement at his reply could blossom into alarm—had he guessed her secret?—he went on. "But your father has not entirely forgotten his duty, I hope. You are a ward of the parish, but perhaps he provides some additional support? A stipend? A place to live? Guardianship?"

"I—I—he" —her hands twisted the straps of the satchel— "I'm not in the village workhouse. I be placed with a modest family in Bramleigh."

"I am pleased to hear it. A farmer, then? The baker? Or the candlestick-maker?"

"A farmer," she choked.

"And, in addition to helping me in my work, do you also work for your guardian? Does he intend you to farm?"

"Yes." That lie nearly finished her. Supposing he should ask the name of this farmer guardian? Would she next have to invent names out of whole cloth? As for what Alice's actual father intended for her, that was no puzzle. Why, he intended for every one of his daughters to marry respectably and do her part to replenish the family coffers.

"How generous of him, then," mused Joseph, "to allow you these early mornings. I know how hardworking most smallhold farmers are, in this busy season."

"You do pay me, sir."

"So I do. A bob a fortnight." She could hear the smile in his voice. "Which I perhaps ought to increase, if you share it with your guardian's family." His brow knit. Far more likely, he thought, Arthur was compelled to turn over the *entirety* of his earnings. But as his assistant made no response, Joseph let the subject of payment drop. "Have you never wished for more from life, Arthur? Some schooling, perhaps."

Another shake of the head. And, gruffer even than before, "No, sir. Nothing. I be—perfectly content." That, at least, was only a partial fable. Were it not for wearing Hal's scratchy clothing, pretending to be someone she was not, spinning lies about all and sundry, and knowing she could never attach him, Alice would, in fact, find herself perfectly content in Mr. Tierney's company. Her early infatuation had suffered no dampening effects from greater familiarity. If anything, she found him more clever and kind, graceful and at ease, than ever. And she had been able, these sunlit mornings, to study him to her heart's content, so much so that he occupied her dreams, both sleeping and waking, despite her avowal to Margaret. The previous night had not been the only time Margaret teased her, and the squire on many occasions had to shout Alice's name to get her attention, but as she had always been thoughtful and absorbed, no one suspected much. She fell in love in perfect peace.

Silence fell between them for some minutes. The stream bank was a trifle damp from a recent shower, but Alice was not going to move if he wasn't. Birds called, water chuckled and glinted below them, breezes stirred the grasses and rushes. Alice watched as Mr. Tierney continued to turn the jar round and round, his gaze fixed on it, but unseeing. She loved the look of his hands—strong, with long, clever fingers. The very fingers that pressed her—her cheeks flamed again, and she looked away.

"You say you are perfectly contented," he began again. "I have much to learn from you, Arthur."

"Oh, no."

"Indeed. One would be inclined to pity a lad in your—humble—situation, but perhaps that pity would be wasted. It may be that ambition, and an unwillingness to accept one's allotted role in life lead to greater grief."

It was not Arthur Baddely's place, as a supposed bastard and parish ward living on the generosity of an unwilling father, to advise a gentleman such as Mr. Tierney, but the Miss Alice Hapgood in Arthur could not help uttering, "Are you—ahem—be you not content with your lot, Mr. Tierney?"

Laying the jar gently on the bank, he leaned back to clasp one of his knees. "Shall I make you a confidant, young Arthur? I rather envy you your father's indifference." He heard her suck in her breath and dropped his knee, the heel of his muddied boot digging into the earth. "Forgive me—that sounded callous. I meant only that, from your father's indifference or unwillingness to claim you, you are, in your way, free from his expectations."

"Yes," said Alice, her pulse seeming to rise to her throat. "Be you not, sir? Free from expectations?"

"I tell myself I am, after much heartache I have both endured and caused in my family." He paused, and she held her breath, hoping he would continue. She would far rather he talk about himself than pelt her with questions to which she must invent plausible stories. However, it would not, she reminded herself, be Arthur Baddely's place to press him.

After another moment, Joseph did go on.

"Apart from our work, Arthur, we occupy wholly different spheres. In my world, I am the younger son of a gentleman—a wealthy one, by your standards, but by society's only a modest country squire. Rather like Squire Hapgood at Bramleigh. But unlike that good man, with his bevy of lovely daughters, my father has two sons: my elder brother Frederick and me." Another pause, in which he retrieved the jar and rubbed at the wet grass sticking to it, while Alice stared dazedly at the stitching on her cuffs, wondering if that 'bevy of lovely daughters' Mr. Tierney referred to included herself. Or did he only call them lovely because Elfrida's beauty spilled over her sisters like sunshine over a meadow?

Her attention snapped back when he spoke again. "Frederick will, naturally, follow in my father's footsteps and inherit the estate, while I—I have always been intended for the church."

She nodded, saying nothing. She knew this much from Dorcas.

Joseph glanced at the bowed head beside him, with its cap pulled low against possible pneumonia. He could only see the curve of cheek, as yet untouched by any beard, and he speculated again how old Arthur was. He wondered if Arthur even knew. For all the boy's awkwardness—nay, it might even be because of his awkwardness—he put Joseph at his ease. How could he not? Unlike the drawing- and dining-room encounters with the viscount's family and friends, and even the uncomfortable call upon the Hapgoods, the time spent with Arthur was free from the burdens of propriety and polite conversation. With Arthur, out in the cool, fragrant mornings, there were no undercurrents of the unspoken, no traps laid by the fair sex or the older generation to snare the unwitting. There was only the excitement of discovery, the easy conversation or the silence. That Arthur admired him and wanted to please him was clear, and Joseph certainly had no complaints on that score. The lad was punctual, fearless of weather or terrain, eager to share his knowledge and to add to it. The only blot on his character was his initial dishonesty, but given his background, Joseph could forgive such diversions from the truth.

If only all of life were so straightforward.

"I have no objections to the church," Joseph continued at last. "No crises of unbelief. But I felt my diffidence, my tendency to distraction, would not serve any congregation entrusted to me."

"Not to be contradicting," said Alice in a low voice that he needed to bend toward her to catch, "but you be a kind man. Kind like Father Thomas. And you speak fair."

To his own surprise, Joseph felt himself color with gratification. How his brother Frederick would mock him, to see how he appreciated some bastard-born nobody's praise! "You see the world topsy-turvy and inside-outwards," Joseph could hear him jeer, "which is why, however much I disappoint our father, we understand each other. He cannot make heads nor tails of you. Throwing away a career to scramble in the mud for polliwogs."

To clear his head and banish Frederick's words, Joseph clapped his hands together and sprung to his feet. "This will never do, Arthur," he cried. "We must be insect-gathering, not wool-gathering. You have been kind to indulge my muddled thoughts. It matters not now whether I should have made a fine clergyman or no—my father intends to sell the living put aside for me, and I must make my own way."

Alice scrambled up with the net and another jar, pretending not to see the hand he extended to her. "Be you—disinherited, sir?"

"Cast off on the merciless world? Not a bit of it," he declared, making his careful way down into the streambed once more. "Like you, Arthur, with your kindly guardian, I have been blessed with my patron Sir Edmund Chall. I have work, my curiosity and hopes, the generosity of the Marltons, a modest competence, and your able assistance. I must strive to be 'perfectly content,' as you are."

"You must truly love your work, sir."

"Above all things." His hazel eyes met her brown ones, and Alice felt her heart flop like a fish on dry land. But it was Joseph who looked away first. Something in the lad's searching gaze made him feel like Arthur saw the dissatisfaction beneath his easy words. What this dissatisfaction consisted of, Joseph had not cared to probe too deeply. There was his father's disapproval, yes, and his brother's derision, but those he had been used to bear. He suspected the new source of restlessness lay in the county's reception of him, as the last night proved. Where Joseph hoped to find patrons who would interest themselves in Sir Edmund's project, he found that he himself was their object of interest. And not Mr. Joseph Tierney the Naturalist, but rather Mr. Joseph Tierney the Somewhat Eligible Young Man and Nephew of a Baronet.

"Sir!" Alice interrupted his train of thought, pointing past him. "Pied flycatcher, male. Patch on its wing and forehead."

The handsome little black-and-white bird hopped through the crowding grass, flicking its tail, and Alice almost hopped in response. "See him? 'E's caught something. Has to fatten up for breeding season. Find a lovely little brown mate. Suppose she's yonder, in the ash trees? Shall I go for the net?"

"Leave him, Arthur," said Joseph, holding up a hand to stay her. "I have no plans for dissection this morning, and it would be a shame to rob him of his mating and breeding chances. Some creature among us should be fortunate in love." He bent down, closing in on an overhanging shrub, where a flat black water scorpion clung to a leaf.

The last of this speech halted her in her tracks, and for once Alice felt no stir of interest in the insect world. "Be you—crossed in love, sir?" The moment the words escaped her she could have bitten her tongue off, and she quickly muttered, "Begs yer pardon. I—it be not my concern."

But Mr. Tierney only gave a rueful chuckle. "Have no fear, my good Arthur. I have not taken offense. We are on a fast way to becoming friends, are we not?" With a swift movement, he scooped his quarry into the jar, tossing in the leaf after it.

She reached for the specimen like an automaton, thinking he did not mean to answer her, but he surprised her. "I have the good fortune not to be crossed in love because I am not in love," Joseph said.

Alice could not help her face brightening. Then he did not care for the wealthy Miss Birdlow? Nor for the beautiful Elfrida? Of course—if he did care for either of those young ladies—he would hardly confide in his humble assistant, she realized, his kind words notwithstanding.

Indeed, a cloud passed over his brow, as if the same thoughts occurred to him. "And I am doubly fortunate not to be in love," he went on, "because I have not, as yet, the income to marry on."

Clutching the captured water scorpion to her breast, Alice hid a smile. She cared not a whit for his poverty, if it meant the two of them could spend morning after morning thus, indefinitely.

Joseph's hand came down on her shoulder, and he gave her a playful shake. "I say, all this talk of love. Ought you to stand in the muck so long? Suppose you should fall victim to pneumonia?" Releasing her, he gave her cap a mischievous bump.

With an unmanly squeal she clamped it to her head, nearly dropping the glass jar in her panic. Her employer doubled over with laughter. "I could not resist. You looked so serious. Now you must forgive *me*, Arthur."

"My health be no laughing matter," groused Alice as she struggled to move away from him.

"Certainly not. Come now, if I pardoned you, you must pardon me," he insisted, still laughing. But seeing the mulish set to his assistant's jaw, he added, "What would you say, if we preserved your delicate health this morning? Shall we cut our travails short? You should accompany me to Pattergees and see how our findings are taking over the viscount's library." It would be a pleasure to show them to someone who would truly appreciate them.

This time Alice did drop the jar, and she scrambled to recover it, swooping the water scorpion back in before it could float off. "No!" she cried. "I means—sir, that wouldn't be recommended." Knowing very well that water scorpions despise swimming, and wanting to avoid his gaze, she kept her head down and tried to pour out some of the cloudy liquid. "Them at Pattergees be all upon the hoity-toities and not wanting the likes of me about."

"True enough," agreed Joseph. "But if you keep mum and forbear to stumble over your own feet, as you are wont, you might be in and out before you were discovered." He aimed a teasing blow at her shoulder blade, and Alice crashed to her knees in the stream, bug and jar floating off once more. "Great heavens!" he exclaimed, taking off in pursuit. "I had no idea your footing was so precarious, Baddely."

And Alice had no idea young men engaged in such horse-play, when apart from the fair sex. She rose, dripping, from the stream, alarmed to see the rough weave of her trousers clinging to her. Why, she could see the shape of her limbs! Forgetting all pretense at boy-ishness, she began to scramble up the muddy bank, thinking she would flee for the cover of the trees.

"Arthur! Wait—Arthur!"

But Alice was too panicked to heed him, and she had nearly gained the top when she heard him splashing noisily behind her.

"Do calm down, boy! I assure you, you will not catch pneumonia, despite my best efforts." His hand closed around her booted ankle, and the frantic Alice kicked out at him. Her other foot lost purchase on the slope; she toppled down, feeling a sharp twinge in her left ankle as she trod awkwardly on him.

"Blast!" he hollered, sitting down hard in the water.

Both the pain and his shouted oath roused Alice from her instinctive flight, and her eyes were round to see him on his backside in the water, grimacing and massaging his own ankle.

"Oh, blimey," she whispered.

Without a word, she helped him struggle up, though the wet weight of him almost overset her once more. He would be furious, she was certain.

He would dismiss her.

She might never see him alone again.

They stood facing each other, each favoring his uninjured foot as the water rippled past them, ankle-deep. He was wet to the waist and she not much better. Water dribbled from them; clothing clung; grass stuck. Alice's precious cap still rode low over her hidden hair; Joseph's hat perched at a rakish angle. The specimen jar lay in the streambed, half-filled with mud, while the water scorpion had made its escape.

When she finally dared raise her eyes to his, her mouth fell open in relief. There was no anger in their hazel depths. Rather, a glimmer of something.

"Sir—"

"Arthur—"

Bending simultaneously to retrieve the jar, they cracked heads. Off went Joseph's beaver altogether, but Alice managed to lay hands on the jar through the stars she was seeing. A great roar of laughter assaulted her before her vision cleared. Joseph was clutching his knees, positively *howling*, even as his hat floated away.

"Sir—your hat!"

"No—don't touch me!" he cried, batting at her outstretched hand, his eyes streaming with mirth. "We are fatal to each other."

"But your hat!" Thrusting the jar at him (and thus besmirching his waistcoat with mud, which led to another whoop), Alice floundered downstream to pluck it from the rushes. Any weight she applied to her own twisted ankle made her grimace in discomfort, but when she limped back to Mr. Tierney to present him with the waterlogged item, she was smiling herself. "Glad you see the humor in it, sir."

"In these situations, Arthur, one must laugh or weep." He clapped the beaver back on his head, sending rivulets coursing down his hair and neck, and then Alice did laugh. A pealing, girlish laugh that she choked down instantly to a manlier ho-ho-ho.

"Have you something in your throat?" demanded Joseph.

Alice shook her head and struck a solemn face. "Must be the nermonia coming on."

"I do believe you're right. Pneumonia. And I was so cruel as to tease you."

They grinned foolishly at each other.

"Well—considering we are the both of us dirty, wet through, specimen-less, and suffering sprained ankles, I think we had better retire from the field today. Can you make it home all right?"

"Yes, sir. Thank you, sir. Same time tomorrow?"

"I think not. We had better give ourselves a few days to recover and launder our clothing. I will occupy myself with what we have already collected. Say Monday."

"Monday," Alice agreed, her heart sinking a little. Monday lay three days off. Even if she were to glimpse him in town or at Saturday's assembly ball, they would have no opportunity for conversation. And if they did, she did not imagine he would have much to say to Miss Alice Hapgood.

But there she was mistaken.

Chapter Eight

No, no, look off, don't smile at me.
—Jonathan Swift, *The Journal to Stella* (1711)

The assembly rooms at Patterton, always a popular resort of the young people, were this evening positively packed and stifling. Through the doors and windows propped open for air came the lively strains of Sir Roger de Coverley and the shuffle and stamp of dancing feet.

"What's this, then?" asked a burly young man who had just alighted from his gig and handed the reins to one of the Marlton grooms. "Bit more crowded than the usual, hey, Cox?"

"On account of his lordship's guest, Mr. Geoffrey," explained Cox. "Man of science come to survey the likes of us, while all the parents and young ladies in the county be surveying the likes of him."

"*Are* there so many eligible young ladies in the county? I was not aware." To Geoffrey Wynstanley, this corner of Somerset signified only his Marlton relations and the awkward informal betrothal to his cousin Agnes. He took care never to visit more than absolutely necessary, lest his aunt Arabella decide the time had come to apply the screws.

"All of 'em seem to have erupted at once," was Cox's phlegmatic reply.

So close were the quarters inside, that the chain of dancers extended nearly to the door. Geoffrey Wynstanley no sooner handed his cape and stick to the attendant than up whirled a vision in white, golden hair piled on her crown, cheeks pink with exercise, and gloved hands clapped together. Blue eyes met his and then dropped modestly, but not before the gentleman made an unconscious grasp at his chest—*even so quickly may one catch the plague?* a more literate man than Geoffrey might have wondered. As it was, he merely thought, "Gadzooks! Cox calls this fair creature an eruption?"

His uncle the viscount spotted him first and clapped a heavy hand on his velvet-clad shoulder. "Geoffrey. We welcome you. How long mean you to stay with us at Pattergees? Your visits are ever too brief, in your aunt's opinion."

"I can't say, sir," said his nephew, his dazed eyes continuing to follow Miss Elfrida Hapgood through the figures. Only when she crossed before another young lady did he come to himself, finding his mooncalf look intercepted by the narrowed gaze of his cousin Agnes. She was paired with a man he didn't recognize, her mouth pursed in a thoughtful fashion that brought his aunt Arabella forcefully to mind. His dear aunt, whose too-capable airs and exalted marriage cast the rest of her Wynstanley siblings in the shade, including Geoffrey's father.

Miss Hapgood and her partner had been the last pair to perform the cross, leaving Miss Birdlow and Mr. Tierney to begin the promenade. Having exchanged but a few niceties during the preceding minutes, Joseph was surprised to have his partner suddenly turn upon him a glowing countenance. "I adore the promenade, Mr. Tierney. How well you manage it."

"Indeed? I mean—I thank you. I believe a graceful partner lends skill." He delivered the compliment calmly enough but hoped Miss Birdlow had no expectations of a flirtation. An indifferent dancer to begin with, Joseph was this evening troubled by his bad ankle.

"La!" cried Miss Birdlow, fluttering at him sidelong under her lashes. "Do you stoop to flattery today? You are not wont to speak much to ladies, I have noticed, unless it be to answer a question put to you directly. I fear we cannot hope to compete with the valve snails and lark's eggs and meadowsweet you have collected. Always examining and categorizing and studying, you are."

"Forgive me that, Miss Birdlow." Releasing her hand, he retreated to his position in the line, swallowing his grimace in what he hoped was a pleasant expression.

From his position by the entrance, Geoffrey scowled at the pair of them. "Who would that be, uncle? Partnering Aggie?"

The viscount puffed up visibly. "That, my good lad, is Mr. Joseph Tierney, naturalist and protégé of Sir Edmund Chall, F.R.S.—Fellow of the Royal Society. Tierney lodges with us. His findings have quite taken over my library, and I account myself delighted. What a fund of knowledge that young man has! We will read about him in later years, I imagine. In the meantime I plan to aid his cause by introducing him to possible patrons. A wonderful thing, to witness the advance of knowledge."

Geoffrey's scowl deepened, having always been no more than passable as a scholar. "Well, he's a wretched dancer," he observed. "Favors one foot. Amazed he doesn't lose his balance. I will have to rescue Aggie at some point."

His uncle made no response but turned away with a smile.

Geoffrey's priorities were somewhat muddled by his urgent desire to be introduced to Miss Hapgood, but to his delight he saw Mr. Tierney returning Agnes to Aunt Arabella, who sat not two yards from where Miss Hapgood's partner returned her. Hastening over, Geoffrey made his bows and greetings, following them with, "I say, Aggie, anyone nabbed you for the supper dance?"

Almost succeeding in not looking at Mr. Tierney, Agnes shook her head.

"Done then, hey?" Geoffrey let out a sigh of relief to see Lady Marlton beam approval. He turned to Joseph. "Privilege to meet you, sir. My uncle speaks warmly of you and your work."

Joseph bowed.

"Maybe do some shooting, one morning?" Geoffrey suggested. "Unless you only pin 'em and object to shooting 'em."

Joseph thought of his prized mornings, tramping through wood, water, and hedgerow with the eager Arthur, and suppressed a sigh.

But perhaps he would be fortunate, and Mr. Wynstanley should prove a late riser. "With a day's notice, sir, I am at your disposal."

"Say Thursday, then."

"Thursday!" echoed Lady Marlton. "Will you favor us so long?"

"Even longer, ma'am, if you'll have me."

Amidst her effusions of delight, both Geoffrey and Joseph were aware of the Miss Hapgoods passing nearby, and Geoffrey contrived to step backward, bumping into Miss Hapgood and treading squarely on Alice's slippered foot.

"I beg your pardon!" he cried, turning round as Alice—tears in her eyes—swallowed the exclamation that rose to her lips. "Please forgive my clumsiness, Miss—"

"Geoffrey—for pity's sake," chided his aunt. "Miss Hapgood and Miss Alice, do pardon my abominably clumsy nephew. Allow me to present Mr. Geoffrey Wynstanley, son of my brother Geoffrey Wynstanley. Geoffrey, these young ladies are our near neighbors. Miss Elfrida and Miss Alice Hapgood of Bramleigh."

Another round of bows and curtsies followed, after which Geoffrey tried to say as nonchalantly as he was capable, "Miss Hapgood—please show me you bear no grudge by accepting the next dance."

Color rising to her cheeks, Elfrida nodded assent.

"I rather think you owe the greater debt to the younger Miss Hapgood," Joseph said dryly, "whose foot you have mangled in such a way that dancing the two next with her would hardly begin to remedy."

To his surprise, the girl went all over scarlet, putting her elder sister's faint blush to shame as the corn poppy's hue does the apple blossom. What ailed the girl? Since the time she had captured a spider above his head and fled the room, she had never once met his eyes, and her reaction to his teasing made him feel like a brute.

"It would be an honor, Miss Alice," said Geoffrey dutifully, "to dance the next but one with you."

Alice only gave a shake of her head, setting the handsome chestnut curls trembling, and muttered in a subdued voice, "I thank you, sir. But I do not dance tonight."

"Sadly, my sister turned her ankle on her morning walk yesterday," interposed Elfrida. "Indeed, we passed this way because I was assisting her to that settee by the palms."

"Allow me," Joseph said, extending his arm to Alice. "I sustained an ankle injury of my own that same morning—it must be something in the air! I would welcome a chance to sit down."

At this close range, Elfrida would not have missed the stricken look that came over Alice, even if it were not accompanied by her grip tightening on Elfrida's forearm, but before Elfrida could demur, the notes struck up for the country dance and she was obliged to pass Alice off, that Mr. Wynstanley might lead her to the floor. Elfrida did miss the flash of Miss Birdlow's eyes, however, when that young lady saw the admiration so plain on her cousin Geoffrey's face.

Torn between trepidation and joy, Alice placed her gloved hand lightly on Mr. Tierney's arm. Though they not infrequently came in contact with each other in their morning work, hands brushing together as they captured specimens, or jostling each other when climbing a stile or such—not to mention the streamside calamities of the previous day—to touch him deliberately as herself, as *Alice*, filled her with alarm. As if her every feeling would spill out and communicate itself to him through the antennae of nerves in his skin. Ridiculous, really. How could anything be imparted, muffled by the layers of her glove, his jacket and shirtsleeves? Still, she hardly dared to breathe.

"Miss Hapgood," he began, when they were settled and half obscured by palm fronds. "I hope you did not mind my little jest a moment ago. I had no intention, when I rallied Mr. Wynstanley, to cause you discomfort."

"No," she answered, hardly above a whisper, her eyes fixed on the couples hopping forwards and back.

"And I regret to hear of your mishap," he went on. "Did you chance to step in a rabbit hole?"

A vivid memory of treading on the ankle of the man next to her as she collapsed on him rendered Alice unable to speak for some moments, but as her companion merely waited it out, she was forced to reply, "I was not heeding where I went. Uneven ground. What—what happened to you?"

"Alas. A combination of mud, sloping bank and strong emotion. We had in our possession briefly a prize water scorpion before a series of mishaps."

Alice could not help herself. "'We'?"

"My assistant and I." It was Joseph's turn to shift with uneasiness. While he made no effort to keep Arthur Baddely a secret, he hesitated to mention him, tied up as young Arthur was with the genealogical irregularities of the neighborhood—Bramleigh in particular. The conversation about Arthur at Pattergees had been uncomfortable enough, and they cared nothing for him, other than as an object of passing curiosity.

"What does your assistant do, Mr. Tierney?" Alice persisted, her gaze now fixed on that gentleman's knee, which meant she failed to catch the smile that pulled at the corners of his mouth. He was thinking of Arthur darting through the woodlands in quest of the finest ferns and bluebells; Arthur leaping about with the net to capture a Large Blue or an especially magnificent Duke of Burgundy butterfly; Arthur dripping wet and muddy and fearful of catching 'nermonia.'

When Mr. Tierney did speak, however, Alice could hear the smile in his voice. "A more apt question might be, Miss Hapgood, what does my assistant *not* do? He leads me, he follows me. He knows a prodigious amount about everything that interests me: plants, animals, *habitats*—by which I mean the natural places in which natural things would be found. He has proven remarkably adept at catching specimens. He answers nearly as many questions as he asks. When I have completed my study of this part of Somersetshire, I wish I might take Arthur wherever I go next, not merely for my own convenience but because his innate desire for knowledge would be so pleasant to gratify!"

To this his companion made no answer, finding herself incapable of one. She was a-tremble with delight to receive such praise and turned her countenance as far from his gaze as she could manage, to hide her expression. If he should see her now—if anyone should see her—would they not be compelled to ask what filled Miss Alice Hapgood with such elation? But to think he found her helpful! Nay—not merely helpful—that he claimed to learn things from her as well! That he should wish to keep her on as an assistant, even after he had left Somerset!

This pulled Alice up short. *Leave* Somerset? "Complete his studies" here, and then depart?

Of course. Of course he would. Would and must. She had been blind not to realize. And then—and then, even if he found funds enough to offer Arthur Baddely a future position, Arthur Baddely could never accept because Alice Hapgood could never accept! Their partnership would be at an end. Mr. Tierney would be disappointed and Alice crushed.

Clutching her gloved hands together, she willed the tears not to form. What was the use of thinking of such things now? Should she not simply revel in the praise? There were a few weeks yet, surely. Possibly months. She would be sure to tell him, as Arthur, of the changes of autumn he would miss if he cut short his project. Perhaps she could, like Scheherazade, spin out the tales of wonders to be revealed as the seasons changed, that he might never be free to leave! Yes, yes—

For his part, Joseph found himself presented with the back of Miss Alice Hapgood's head and her apparent complete indifference. He understood her not a whit! She would ask him questions with every indication of interest, only to meet his answers with utter silence. First regarding Sir Joseph Banks' illustrations, and now this.

If she did not care to hear his answers, why did she ask the questions? At least in the drawing room of Bramleigh she had torn her eyes from her needlework once to look at him. Here she most rudely kept them trained on the damned potted palms.

Not that the back of her head was unappealing. While Joseph the naturalist might observe every variation in a bird's feathers or a butterfly's scales, he rarely noticed the same in a woman's coiffure. Perhaps because he never looked so long at women as he did at God's other creatures. Miss Hapgood's unconventional behavior, though frustrating, gave him the opportunity to mark how her rich, shining hair well became her when it was curled and gathered to the top of her head, a rose ribbon winding through it and trailing down her neck. She was almost lovely, he supposed. Not as admirably constructed as her elder sister—being rather too thin—nor as flawless in her complexion—being unfashionably tanned from exposure to the sun—and without Miss Elfrida Hapgood's graceful, pleasing manner, but Joseph imagined Miss Alice Hapgood would have her share of admirers, when not eclipsed by her sister.

Yet how she might *sustain* any admiration she aroused was another matter altogether, he thought. He had never met a girl so deficient in the arts of conversation, and he wondered again if he had said something to bore or offend.

"This...Arthur...you speak of," came Miss Hapgood's soft voice then, just audible over the music and movement of the dancers, "you find him...so promising?"

Joseph gave a guilty start and was glad she still kept her face averted. It felt uncharitable to praise Arthur when he had been denigrating Miss Hapgood in his mind. But honesty must be given its due. "He's a humble lad, not suited by birth or education or deportment to be thrust upon society, but he's quick enough. Amiable. Under other circumstances, he would have made a promising naturalist."

"Other circumstances." She ventured a glance at him here, but finding him looking at her, Alice withdrew it instantly.

Joseph cleared his throat of an obstruction. "Naturally. I suppose I mean, were he so fortunate as to secure the approbation of a more moneyed person than myself, he might be sent to school." He frowned. It would be nigh impossible for the boy to overcome the misfortunes of his bastard birth, however. Perhaps, gifted with a truly generous patron, a position on an expedition to the Americas or the Indies might be secured, where birth was a muddled matter in any case.

"It can never be," murmured Alice, as if she overheard his thoughts.

The mournful note in her voice brought him to himself. Good heavens! In his eagerness to praise Arthur, it had not occurred to him that the mysteries surrounding the boy's birth might have been penetrated by more than himself and the housekeeper Button. Could Miss Alice Hapgood suspect her father's past indiscretions? Did she, too, recognize the striking resemblance between Arthur Baddely and legitimate members of the Hapgoods?

Decorum forbade him pursuing the subject, and he liked Miss Hapgood well enough to have no wish of disturbing her tranquility. And she *was* disturbed, he decided, considering the tremble of her chin. He went on to admire the fine curve of her cheek when she took him aback by turning to face him once more.

"Do you recall, Mr. Tierney, how you suggested my youngest sister Edith might like to draw some of your specimens?"

"Indeed. Of course," he returned, collecting himself. "As well as I recall you saying she 'could not abide dead things.'"

Alice colored at the memory of her indecorous remark. "Nor can she. But—but I can."

"Can—?" he prompted.

"Abide dead things." Alice clutched her gloved hands together that she might not wring them. Why must everything tumble, unguarded, from her mouth, when in the privacy of the bedchamber she shared with Elfrida, she was perfectly able to compose flowery speeches which would charm an educated gentleman like Mr. Tierney?

She pressed on, nevertheless. "Abide them *and* draw them, though not so well as Edie by half."

Joseph tried and failed to imagine presenting Miss Hapgood with the half-rotten starling corpse Arthur discovered the day before. Her assurances aside, he feared she would scream and faint, at best. "Ah...I see..."

"Have you none—specimens, I mean—that you could send along with Arthur, who could give them to our boy Hal? I would be happy to make the attempt, if it would be of use to you."

"How kind of you," said Joseph. With an effort, he forebore fidgeting under her urgent gaze. "Perhaps...I might send along some hawthorn flowers and branches...?"

"Hawthorn!" Alice could not keep the note of disdain from her voice. "Surely the Royal Society has illustrations enough of a shrub found in every hedgerow in England? Not only could I draw it, but I could give you a jar of Button's haw jelly, which might do the greater good."

Her companion laughed. "Forgive me if I have offended you, Miss Hapgood, but I assure you, even Sir Thomas Lawrence must have ventured a sketch or two, before being asked to paint Queen Charlotte."

His teasing reprimand could not have embarrassed her more effectively than if he had been in earnest. Why, she was catching Margaret's ailment of too-pointed remarks! *Peaceful and ornamental*, she reminded herself. She must be peaceful and ornamental. Even the suggestion that she might be of use to him had been too forward. Alas!

To her mingled relief and regret, she saw Mr. Wynstanley approaching with Elfrida. Mr. Tierney, probably glad to escape their tête-à-tête, sprung to his feet, suppressing a wince. "Would you like to be seated, Miss Hapgood?"

Elfrida smiled her thanks and murmured, "But your ankle, sir?"

"Think nothing of it. These fifteen minutes resting beside your sister have done the trick, not to mention the compresses and herbal remedies Lady Marlton and Miss Birdlow have insisted on since the fearful injury."

"Have they?" grunted Geoffrey Wynstanley, looking annoyed. "Deuced mother-hen of them, kicking up a fuss."

Mr. Tierney blinked in surprise at the young man's hostility. "They meant well, to be sure, even if their concern was not warranted." To pass over the awkward pause that followed, he heard himself say to Miss Hapgood, "Perhaps you would like some refreshment, Miss Hapgood? And—if I am not too late, might I engage you for the supper dance?"

Elfrida dropped her eyes and shook her head, a becoming flush stealing over her cheeks. "You are not too late, Mr. Tierney. I would be honored." She laid light fingers upon his extended arm and they strolled away, his limp barely perceptible, leaving two not very pleased people behind.

Mr. Wynstanley slumped into Joseph's vacated space on the settee, chewing his lip and watching them go. "And what am I to do, until it's time to fetch Aggie, I'd like to know," he muttered.

Alice didn't even hear him. She was too busy lamenting inwardly how Mr. Tierney's eyes shone at Elfie, and how eager he was to flee her own presence. Her one opportunity to charm him as a girl—as Alice! All wasted. All failure.

"Upstart. Nobody. Failed clergyman. Nearly penniless," her companion continued to growl. "What does anyone truly know of him?"

Alice didn't reply, for the simple reason that she was not attending. Neither she nor Mr. Wynstanley made any further attempts at conversation, and at length he rose to go in search of his cousin. He gave Alice a nod that in its curtness acknowledged his own bad manners and his ruefulness that it should be so, and, moved by her first impulse of sympathy toward him, she replied in much the same fashion.

And then she was alone.

Chapter Nine

Therwith the fyr of jalousie up-sterte
Withinne his brest, and hente him by the herte.
—Chaucer, *The Knight's Tale* (1385)

"Where can Geoffrey be?" asked Lady Marlton, settling her shawl about her shoulders in the barouche as her lord climbed in. "Means he to ride to church?"

"Yes," the viscount answered shortly. The carriage bounced as he took his seat beside her, facing his daughter and Mr. Tierney. "But not to Patterton." He signaled the coachman, who saluted with his whip and set them in motion.

"What other church can you mean, my lord?"

"He tells me he intends to ride to Bramleigh, to hear this Father Thomas preach."

"Bramleigh!" exclaimed Miss Birdlow, her eyes snapping. "I am sure this Father Thomas can be no especial sermonizer. He must be all of hundred years old."

"No matter," replied her father. "Any man can read from Blair's, if he be not blind."

Lady Marlton raised delicate eyebrows and said dryly, "Perhaps Bramleigh holds other charms for my nephew."

Tossing her head, Miss Birdlow said, "Well, we are spared a fearful crush in the pew, Geoffrey being as outsize as Frank and Mary." With a smile that could only be described as simpering, she shifted to face Mr. Tierney. "How fortunate for us, Mr. Tierney, that you are on the slender side. There would be room in the Marlton pew for three of your kind."

"And four of yours," he replied, fighting the urge to draw away from her. He did not mind the Honorable Miss Birdlow in general—only in particular, when her attention fastened on him. He rightly suspected that she wanted him to admire her, not from any mutual liking, but because she was there. Looking about, he turned the subject. "And will Mr. and Mrs. Birdlow be joining us at church?"

The viscount tugged on his gloves, his gaze fixed on the curving drive. "Not so devout, that son of mine. He and Mary spoke of checking on the progress of renovations at the lodge, and then attending the afternoon service."

Not far into the service at Patterton did Joseph wish he had a lodge that needed renovating or the freedom to order a horse and ride where he would on a Sunday. The Marlton party was first in consequence, and many eyes drifted their direction during the rector's dry musings. Making a match of him and Miss Birdlow, Joseph supposed.

That young lady held herself perfectly still, head high. She could not be accused by even the most malicious of her neighbors of "setting her cap" for Mr. Tierney. But he was ever aware that she was aware of him. Not a movement—not a glance betrayed it—and yet he knew. Miss Birdlow held him in reserve, for whatever schemes she had in mind. Or, perhaps, for schemes she might come to have in mind.

When they were safely back to Pattergees, Joseph retreated to the library, to his classifications and specimens. His ankle was much improved. He hoped the same for Arthur's and looked forward to the resumption of their morning work. Moreover, the butterflies they captured some days past were drying beautifully: a dull-brown Grizzled Skipper, the more vibrant orange Marsh Fritillary, the camouflaged Green Hairstreak that Arthur spotted, where Joseph saw only leaves.

A thought stopped him, and he set down his monocle. Why—butterflies were harmless enough. Dead, yes, yet nearly as innocuous for a young lady to draw as the suggested hawthorn plants which so offended Miss Alice Hapgood. Perhaps if he were to bring this tray to Bramleigh, they could continue their frustrating attempts at conversation?

Shaking his head, he gave a silent chuckle. Now *why precisely* would he want to make another attempt? She was such a puzzling mix of curiosity and reticence, and then there was her touchy pride, and whatever she might suspect about Arthur Baddely's background. If he were in his right mind, he should rather call on the elder Miss Hapgood, with whom he had passed the supper dance and supper itself with nary a painful silence or flash of perplexing emotion. Miss Elfrida Hapgood was lovely, amiable, calm, and...uninteresting. Their conversation ranged from dancing to card-playing, to whether orgeat or negus were to be preferred at assemblies. They canvassed Somersetshire weather, his opinions on the progress of his work, her taste in music and reading. She read surprisingly little herself and confessed that she was more likely to occupy herself with needlework while a sister read aloud. All the while she favored Joseph with her mild blue gaze, the vagueness of which he found himself contrasting to her younger sister's. Miss Alice, whenever she would deign to look at him, had something in her eyes that always caught him off guard. He could never predict whether she would show him alarm or wonder or sadness. In fact, he could predict nothing about her, and that in itself interested him.

He thought of the graceful line of Miss Alice's neck. How her shining brown hair lay against it, trailing the rose ribbon...

"Knock, knock."

Starting, Joseph looked up to see Miss Birdlow in the doorway, her mouth pressed in a thin line.

"Miss Birdlow. Am I needed?"

With an effort she attempted a smile. "I require amusement, Mr. Tierney. My father and mother have gone over to the lodge to advise my brother and his wife in their renovations."

"And you had no wish to assist them?"

"None. I have participated too many times already. No sooner does Mary choose one paper or carpet than she changes her mind. I have done with her."

"And your cousin Mr. Wynstanley?"

Her mouth pressed flat again. "Not yet returned from Bramleigh. Why, Mr. Tierney, how ungallant of you. One would almost suspect you of wishing me gone."

"Not at all," he replied. "Only, how might I amuse you?"

"Oh, I know you have your precious work to do." She wandered into the room, her eyes moving from the tray of butterflies before him to the stack of volumes in which flowers were being pressed. Pausing beside his brass microscope, Miss Birdlow trailed her fingers along its body tube. "How do you use this instrument? Would it be too much trouble to ask for a demonstration?"

Joseph swallowed a sigh of impatience. But better to show Miss Birdlow himself, than to have her fiddling with the delicate parts and perhaps wreaking havoc. He pushed aside the butterflies and thoughts of Miss Alice for the time being. "Of course. Would you prefer to examine an insect under the lens, or, say, the minute living creatures present in Pattergees pond water?"

"Oh!" Plainly the thought of either gave her shudders, and he hastened to correct course. "Better yet—shall we inspect something far more familiar?" He reached for her, and Miss Birdlow drew back in surprise, but Joseph only plucked a stray hair from her shawl. She tittered in relief, although her brow remained furrowed as she watched him press the silvery strand between strips of glass. "I hope there will not be found any minute living creatures *there*, sir!"

He carried his microscope to the table by the window, squinting through the eyepiece and adjusting the mirror below the stage repeatedly until he was satisfied. Then he placed the slide containing Miss Birdlow's hair below the lens. "Put your eye here." He tapped the eyepiece.

Gathering her courage, she obeyed.

"What do you see, Miss Birdlow?"

"I say—my hair looks thick as yarn through this."

"Is it clear? Sharp? If not, you can adjust here—"

"Where?" She raised her head and stepped back, bumping into him.

"Here." He took her hand and placed it on the round focusing mechanism. "This way to raise the stage; this way to lower it."

"I see." Miss Birdlow blushed rosily and put her eye to the scope again.

"What's this?" bellowed a new voice behind them. "Doing some out-of-the-way research, Tierney?"

The two investigators leaped, as if they had been caught in a reprehensible act. Miss Birdlow even snatched at Mr. Tierney's waistcoat, releasing it an instant later and flushing an even deeper hue.

"Mr. Wynstanley," said Joseph, bowing. "We were just looking at a strand of Miss Birdlow's hair. Perhaps you would like to take a gander?"

"I don't go in for all that," growled Geoffrey. "Aggie's hair looks fine as it is."

His cousin's face softened at this compliment, but she stiffened again when Joseph asked, "And how did you find Father Thomas, over at Bramleigh Church?"

Geoffrey cleared a bird's nest and a basket of feathers from an armchair so that he might sit down, a smug smile spreading across his face. "Can't say that I recall much of what the man said. My attention was drawn elsewhere. Lovely, lovely family, those Hapgoods."

Joseph heard Miss Birdlow's huff of irritation beside him, but when she spoke, her voice was light. "La! Geoffrey, what an idea of yourself you will give our guest. You must pardon my cousin, Mr. Tierney. He has never the mind nor the inclination for serious matters. When we were children he was called Geoffrey Jump-about."

"And you were called Agonies," her cousin retorted, "for the suffering your sharp tongue inflicted."

"Charming family stories," said Joseph with a smile, attempting to dispel the tension. Neither acknowledged him.

"How *were* the lovely Miss Hapgoods?" Miss Birdlow asked. "I hope the two younger had clean frocks on."

"They were—"

"I know Miss Alice Hapgood would as soon read a book as have her hair dressed properly," she trilled, interrupting him, "but I can't say as I blame her—with such a brown complexion, one would be hard put to make the effort."

"One thing I might say with all certainty," declared Mr. Wynstanley, rising from his seat and talking over the top of her, "is that the eldest Miss Hapgood was a perfect vision. A perfect vision! And as gentle and biddable a spirit as one could wish for in a girl."

"A paragon, indeed. I wonder you could tear yourself away, Geoffrey." With that, she turned her back on him and set her eye to the microscope once more. "What an amazing world we live in, Mr. Tierney! That there should be such detail, such minutiae, invisible to us. How clever of you to devote yourself to its study. I should dearly like to be a naturalist."

"You—a naturalist!" scoffed her cousin, all but shaking his fist at her. "Unless you have grown to be an entirely different creature from the Agonies I knew, you wouldn't know a robin from a rain puddle. Nor would you care to."

Joseph saw Miss Birdlow's hand clench around the base of his microscope, and he was grateful she held only the wooden piece and not any of the delicate brass instrumentation.

"I admire any man with ambition," she flashed. "What woman would not? How may humanity hope to rise above mere eating and drinking and pursuit of wealth, if no one will lead us?"

"Easy to criticize pursuit of wealth, when one has always had more than enough!" cried Geoffrey, positively bouncing on his toes and going red in the face.

"One would hardly describe you as impoverished," she retorted, "and you certainly have done your share of eating and drinking. No, no—Geoffrey Wynstanley is not a man for the new age—"

"If you would permit me—another engagement," Joseph muttered. Sliding the glass cover onto the butterfly tray, he lifted it gingerly. He regretted leaving the sparring cousins in possession of the library, but he trusted Miss Birdlow's temper would not extend to throwing things at Mr. Wynstanley.

"Mr. Tierney, pray do not let Geoffrey disturb your work," protested Miss Birdlow when he gained the door.

"Or Aggie here," threw in her cousin.

"No disturbance at all," he replied. Waving them both off, he made his escape. Before he was two steps from the room, the voices rejoined in argument.

Nay. He doubted he would be missed.

"See here, Elfie," announced Margaret, bursting into the sitting room with Edith tumbling after her. "It's that Mr. Tierney, come to see you! Papa must have passed him in the gig because they come together."

"And Mr. Tierney holds a wooden case of something," added Edith breathlessly.

"I cannot imagine Mr. Tierney would bring me a case of anything," answered Elfrida with maddening calm. She returned her gaze to her needlework, but Alice saw her color rise.

"Does he mean to propose?" asked Edith.

"Featherbrain!" Margaret pinched her. "They've only danced the one time together."

"And sat at supper," her little sister pointed out with a scowl.

"You know nothing. But he has certainly come to call, Elfie," said Margaret awfully. "Should you like us in or out of the room? May not Edie and I hide in the window seat, if we draw the curtains?"

"You may do anything but hide," Elfrida replied. "And where are you going, Alice?"

"He does not come to call on me, I am sure," murmured her sister, gathering the torn breeches she was patching.

"You may hide with us in the window seat, Alice," suggested Margaret generously.

"We cannot all fit," said practical Edith.

"I said no hiding!" cried Elfrida. But there was no time for further arrangement because Dorcas flung open the door with a shout of "Mr. Joseph Tierney!" The younger two sisters leapt for the window seat and smoothed their skirts, while Alice found herself stranded in the center of the room, breeches spilling from her arms.

"Miss Hapgood." Joseph entered and made his bow first to Elfrida. "Miss Alice. Miss Margaret. Miss Edith."

"But where has Papa gone?" asked Edith artlessly, after they had made their curtsies. Margaret elbowed her because now Mr. Tierney would know they had been spying out windows.

"I am afraid I interrupted his jaunt. He goes now to finish his errand." Laying his case upon a side table, Joseph advanced into the room, waiting politely for Alice to be seated before he chose the squire's usual chair. When Edie opened her mouth to point this out, she received another elbow to the ribs and her mouth snapped shut.

"Your ankle appears greatly improved, sir," said Elfrida.

"I'm certain by my performance last night you thought me crippled for life," he teased. Elfie squinted at him to tell if he was joking, and Joseph mistook it for annoyance. He turned abruptly to Alice. "And you, Miss Alice? How is your injury today?"

"Better. Ahem! Better, thank you." Whatever needlework she had been working on was now wadded into a ball, and she did not appear disposed to take it up again. Instead she fiddled with the tasseled cushion beside her. Her hair was uncurled today, simply twisted in a knot with a bandeau around her crown, and she wore a simple ivory gown with violets embroidered at the hem. He had been right in deeming her lovely. One had only to tear one's eyes from the golden aura of Miss Elfrida Hapgood to notice it. Studying the shadows cast by Miss Alice's thick dark lashes upon her cheeks, Joseph felt a surge of determination to make her look at him.

"Miss Alice." He cleared this throat. "You were so kind yesterday evening to offer your assistance in drawing my specimens." She said nothing and raised her eyes only so far as the tops of his boots, listening. "Therefore," he continued, a mischievous quirk to his lips, "I took the liberty of bringing the hawthorn you suggested—"

"But I said—" breathed Alice, flashing him an indignant glance from those wide brown eyes.

"—which your sister Miss Edith might attempt," he went on smoothly, "while you took on these butterflies."

"Oh."

He presented her with the case, laying it on the marble-topped tea table, and Margaret and Edith sprung from their window seat to crowd around. Even Elfrida lay down her needlework to draw closer.

"Are they real?" gasped Edith, paling.

"Of course they are, goose!" said Margaret. "What else should they be? Paper?" But she, too, grimaced upon seeing the pins stuck so emphatically through the middles of the tiny bodies.

"They are marvelous," Alice said softly. "However did you spread their wings thus? Every butterfly I ever caught became brittle—" She broke off, realizing she had said too much.

But Joseph only said, "Have you caught butterflies, Miss Alice? Yes—it's a trick to relax them. I dip the body briefly in boiling water and press down the wings, after I've mounted it, using paper and pins."

She didn't answer, but he saw the little smile she gave as she examined the Green Hairstreak. "You need keen eyes to spot that one in its native habitat," he said. "I wish I could say the eyes were mine, but alas." To the others he added, "My assistant spied the green one there. See how it looks like a leaf?"

"Have you found an assistant, then?" asked Edith. "Someone at Pattergees?"

"A neighborhood boy," replied Joseph, after a hesitation. What an inordinate amount of his time he spent discussing Arthur Baddely! The boy was like a sore tooth that the tongue could not cease to probe. "His name is Arthur Baddely." If he feared this admission would agitate the entire family, he was soon relieved. The name meant nothing to them, and a lively discussion on whom such a person might be ensued. Only Miss Alice did not participate, though her color came and went. Then the secret of Arthur's parentage was suspected only by her..?

"What do you say, Miss Alice?" he prompted. "Would you be willing to try a few sketches?"

"I could color them for you, after you had drawn them," Edith offered, bouncing up and down on the sofa beside Alice until she received another pinch from Margaret.

"Thank you," Alice answered. "I would like that, Mr. Tierney." Her gaze flitted to his and back to her hands in her lap, and with that he must be satisfied.

Conversation turned to the assembly, and Joseph did his duty by Miss Hapgood and Miss Hapgood her duty by him, so that when the squire returned some time later, he was besieged by Margaret and Edith.

"Papa, Papa! Mr. Tierney was here, and he must be head over ears in love with Elfie because he stayed *twenty-five* minutes!" cried Edith.

"Hush, Edie," snapped Margaret, pushing her away. "You are too young to speak of love. But Papa, he told Elfie that she was so light on her toes and 'as un—undemanding a supper partner as she was a quadrille partner'!"

"That so?" said their father, beaming upon his eldest as if "undemanding" were the highest honor accorded a young woman. "If that's what he likes, he'll be well satisfied with our Elfie. And what of that Geoffrey Wynstanley? Has he called, as well, after goggling at you in church all morning?"

"No, Papa."

"Harrumph. Can't say I'm astonished. Suppose his high-and-mighty family would have something to say about any attachment to you." The squire dismissed the Pattergees clan with a flourish of his arm. "Mr. Tierney, then, it is. What have you to say for yourself, Elfie?"

"He is a very nice gentleman, to be sure," she replied.

He bestowed a rare kiss to the top of her golden head. "And you'll have him, when he offers?"

"Yes, Papa, if it pleases you," Elfie said placidly. "I am sure everyone thinks well of him. But I must say, I am not certain he meant anything beyond mere politeness in his call. If anything, he showed far more enthusiasm talking about butterflies. Would not you say, Alice?"

But Alice was not listening. She had taken the case of butterflies to the window and sat hunched beside them, sketching furiously, the Green Hairstreak taking shape beneath her eager pencil.

CHAPTER TEN

**...He will steal himself into a man's favour and
for a week escape a great deal of discoveries;
but when you find him out, you have him ever after.
—Shakespeare, *All's Well That Ends Well* (1616)**

Geoffrey Wynstanley thrashed in his bed. He dreamed he was
on the point of wedding Miss Elfrida Hapgood when the
chapel darkened and the doors flew open. In swooped enormous
black birds, two of them, blood-chilling creatures with the wings of
ravens and the heads of his aunt Marlton and cousin Agnes.

"No-o-o-o-o-ooooo!" he cried aloud, sitting bolt upright. Sweat
bathed his hair and back. His nightshirt and the bed coverings twisted around his legs, and Geoffrey kicked them off frantically.

It was early yet, the late spring morning still the gray that preceded
dawn, but Geoffrey rose and bathed his brow at the washstand,

swabbing himself with the towel. He hoped no one had heard his shouts. Now that he regained his faculties, he felt foolish for being so upset. What fear need he have of his Marlton relatives? He would reach his majority in the autumn; his name and his fortune would be his own, to bestow where he pleased. And it would serve his aunt and cousin right if he chose to bestow them on such a fine, glorious girl as Miss Hapgood! These were not the dark ages of the world, when children could be betrothed in their cradles with any seriousness. Why—if he pleased, he would sleep another few hours and then ride straight to Bramleigh to pay court to the fair Saxon. He would have yesterday, he told himself, had he not got in such a row with Agnes that he required a long ride to settle his nerves, only to have them aggravated again by watching her flirt wantonly the rest of the day with the thrice-blasted Mr. Tierney. Although Mr. Tierney did not prove particularly responsive, that aggravated Geoffrey as well: how dare the upstart be so indifferent to the attentions of the Honorable Miss Birdlow?

Scowling, Geoffrey pushed these thoughts away. Yes, he should like to see Agonies' face when he told her he intended to call at Bramleigh. A shiver ran through him as he stood barefoot in his nightshirt, and he was on the point of bounding back into bed when a movement out the window caught his eye. The sun was rising, pushing back the gray with long fingers of apricot and rose. And there below on the east lawn strode that Mr. Tierney, boots on and satchel over one shoulder. A muted whistling rose to the glass—"Betsy Belle and Mary Grey," it sounded like. What right had Mr. Tierney to be so cheerful, when he created such havoc in Geoffrey's life?

He abandoned all thoughts of sleeping. He needed no more sleep than this so-called naturalist, whom his cousin praised to the skies. What was so ambitious about rising with the sun to collect bugs? Whatever all this Joseph Tierney did, Geoffrey Wynstanley could do as well, thank you very much!

Although he had not dressed without assistance in years, Geoffrey abandoned all thoughts of cravats and boot polish, and not five minutes passed before he, too, was downstairs and out of doors. Mr. Tierney was well out of sight, but once more Geoffrey caught the faint notes. Blessing the plague-stricken girls of the whistled ballad, he hurried after.

"Halloa there, Arthur!" called Joseph when he caught sight of the boy by the boundary stream. "How does your ankle?"

"All better, sir," came the gravelly reply. "And yer own?"

"Much, much improved. I don't doubt that this fresh air and morning light has cured me completely. What say you to some bird-watching today?"

Bird-watching! From his cover behind the trees, Geoffrey smothered a groan. What was there to watch, after all? Little brown hoppy things, one much like another, chirping. The assistant clapped his hands and grinned like a great fool, however, as if the man had suggested they crown him a prince and install him in a palace. Idiot. Perhaps the great naturalist was not worth spying on, after all. If

Geoffrey were to cut his losses, he could steal back to Pattergees and find someone to make him some tea and rashers.

Before he could decide to abandon his post, however, he heard Joseph add, "And keep a good look-out for stray feathers, Arthur. I must have something to show inquiring ladies beside insects and pond alga. Miss Birdlow turned up her nose at such things, and I was reduced to putting her own hair under the microscope."

"Nice hair, to be sure," said the boy grudgingly. "Did she let you pluck it from 'er noddle, or did you beg it from 'er to make a ring of?"

Their auditor found himself assailed by a new series of emotions. That—that this—this ill-spoken, ill-dressed *nobody* should bandy about a viscount's daughter as a topic of conversation—! That he should suggest a flirtation between a lady so far his superior and this failed clergyman of a Joseph Tierney! Geoffrey fought an urge to spring from the trees and knock their heads together.

"Do I detect jealousy, my good lad?" teased Mr. Tierney, pelting the boy with a twig. Like lightning, the boy snatched the twig where it fell and aimed it back at his assailant. "Nothing like!" he declared in indignation. "What I would have to be jealous of—a high and mighty Miss Hon'rable—she can keep her fine airs!"

Both Mr. Tierney and the unseen Geoffrey stared at this display, Geoffrey from speechless outrage and Mr. Tierney from astonishment. Joseph was the first to recover. "My dear Arthur, beware. Such language better becomes a jilted lover, or someone who has suffered at Miss Birdlow's hands. Has there been unpleasantness between you?"

Arthur's hands flew to his cheeks as he struggled to regain his composure. "No. No. Naught like that. I hardly know the good lady but to look at her. I be...out of sorts today. I begs yer pardon."

He 'begged his pardon'! Geoffrey ground his teeth. If Tierney were any man at all, he would beat the boy soundly and have him put in the stocks for such a speech about his superiors!

"Pardon granted," said Joseph, to his auditor's disbelief. "I am sorry to hear you are unhappy. You, who are usually so 'perfectly contented.' Is there anything it would relieve your spirits to discuss with me?"

Arthur's lips parted as if he were about to speak. The wide brown eyes searched Joseph's. Then, slowly, he shook his head. "No. No, sir. Nothing. Let's—we better be getting on with it. Sun's full up now."

His employer hesitated, debating whether or not he would press the lad, but he decided against it. Let him be. He would force no confidences. Gesturing for Arthur to go before him, he only said, "Lead on, my brave boy. You boasted of knowing where every bird makes its nest and when."

"Not *boasted*, sir!"

"There can be no other word for it, Arthur," Joseph rallied him. "I still blush for your sake, to think of it."

When they were some yards ahead, Geoffrey reluctantly made to follow. He had rather crawl back to bed and hatch plans to avenge his cousin Agnes' honor, but perhaps she would be inclined to forgive this urchin one heedless remark, especially if Mr. Tierney took his part. He must go on.

Geoffrey could not help himself. Despite the overheard insults to his cousin, to whom some considered him betrothed, and despite his desire to gather unfavorable information about Mr. Tierney, the early hour and loss of sleep played against him. Not to mention the deep dullness of his eavesdropping task after Mr. Tierney and the lad abandoned their banter and personal topics of conversation for those ornithological. Some business about "redstarts" and "wood warblers," talk of nest composition, counting of eggs, incubation periods...Mr. Tierney boosted Arthur into trees; the two of them explored shrubbery at the base...More discussion of colored supercilia, tertial edges, tail length...

When Geoffrey awoke and crept to his knees again, it was just in time to see Mr. Tierney finish buckling his satchel and stride off, calling over his shoulder, "Tomorrow, then, Arthur!" The boy watched him go and then sunk down against a beech tree trunk with a sigh. Geoffrey hoped he didn't plan on sitting and ruminating there for long—his own limbs were cramped from hunching beside the oaks which hid him. *Go home, boy*, Geoffrey mouthed.

Instead, the lad gave another sigh, stretched his arms and pulled off his cap to scratch at his hair.

His hair!

Geoffrey's eyes bulged. Where he expected to see a rough thatch of yellow or brown, he saw instead a coronet of braids. Braids! Plaits of a deep chestnut brown.

What manner of boy was this? No boy at all! The boy...was a girl!

Mesmerized, Geoffrey's gaze fell to the boy-girl's chest, under its coarse linen shirt. There was nothing to give secrets away there, but perhaps the creature bound herself. If further doubts assailed him, they gave way entirely when the girl began to hum and then to sing, the very tune Mr. Tierney whistled earlier:

> *O, Betsy Belle and Mary Gray,*
> *they were two bonnie lasses.*
> *They biggit a bower on yon Burnside*
> *and theeked it o'er with rashes.*
> *Fair Betsy Belle I loved so well*
> *and thought I ne'er could alter,*
> *But Mary Gray's two cheeky eyes*
> *caused all my fancy falter...*

The singer—the creature—he had heard that lilting soprano only recently...but where?

The girl bounded up, holding her loose trousers out like a skirt and dancing a little hornpipe. Then she laughed and whirled around, stumbling to a halt facing Geoffrey's direction, hands clasped together and glowing face lifted.

And thus he recognized her.

It was Miss Alice Hapgood, sister of the glorious Miss Elfrida Hapgood, and just yestermorning in Bramleigh Church had Miss Alice clasped her hands together, so, and lifted just such a glowing face during the Methodistical hymn-singing part of the service which left Geoffrey Wynstanley uncomfortable. He had wrestled, thinking he could feel no great admiration for a girl whose family showed such Nonconformist, Low Church tendencies, but unable to prevent himself admiring the incomparable Miss Elfrida all the same. He had returned to Pattergees, undecided whether he would call on Miss Hapgood or seek her no more, but upon finding his cousin Agnes cloistered with Mr. Tierney, all his wavering fell to the ground, and he found himself throwing the Bramleigh clan in Miss Birdlow's teeth.

That wavering now returned full force. Such a family! Impoverished, undignified—and now to have one among them, engaging in such activities! Could the graceful Miss Elfrida Hapgood have any notion what her younger sister did, Geoffrey wondered, in full view of all who might happen upon her?

Eventually the disguised Miss Alice Hapgood took herself off, but it was some time before Geoffrey followed. He had first to analyze what he had witnessed, and he was not in the habit of much analysis.

Did Tierney have any idea this "Arthur" was not what he seemed? Geoffrey ran over all the conversation he had heard before he fell asleep; he considered the naturalist's behavior toward his assistant and decided, no, Tierney was innocent of the scheme. Did that make Tierney any less guilty, however, of breach of propriety, if not outright scandal? No, again. The more fool he, that he was taken in! (Here Mr. Wynstanley conveniently forgot that he, too, had been taken in, until "Arthur" removed her hat.) Tierney's innocence would not spare him the consequences.

What earthly motive could Miss Alice Hapgood have, for behavior so ungentlewomanlike and reprehensible? She must mean to entrap the man. To compromise herself thoroughly before she revealed her true nature. Well, it was a disgusting trick. Undeserving of the name of woman. But, as Geoffrey was not her victim, he felt small pity for Mr. Tierney. Rather, he felt incredulity. What was it about that penniless pupil of pipkins and polliwogs, that women should chase him? Go to such lengths to ensnare him? Should not designing women prefer to practice upon men like himself, in possession of comfortable fortune and nephew to a viscount?

No matter.

The fair sex would always be something of a mystery. If this Miss Alice Hapgood wanted this Tierney enough to practice such arts, she was welcome to him. And perhaps—here Geoffrey looked up suddenly and held very still as he worked it out—perhaps this horrid contrivance of Miss Hapgood's might play out to the advantage of all. In particular, to the advantage of Mr. Geoffrey Wynstanley. A married Mr. Tierney could pose no threat to Geoffrey, not where Agnes Birdlow was concerned.

A smile spread across Geoffrey's square face. Why—could he not devise his own stratagem? If he hurried Miss Alice Hapgood's plans along, would she not be grateful, rather than resentful?

Yes. Yes, indeed.

That would do. *That* would do very, very well.

CHAPTER ELEVEN

**There is no society in the world without
scandal-mongers and tale-bearers.
—Nicholas Amhurst, *Terrae-filius* (1721)**

Lady Marlton prided herself on the lateness of the dinner hour at Pattergees, and it was not until fully eight in the evening that the gentlemen rejoined the womenfolk in the drawing room. The viscountess then called for her daughter-in-law to play for them on the pianoforte. Mrs. Mary Birdlow was no very superior musician, but she was obedient and hopeful of pleasing. When she had performed two movements of a concerto, she turned to the viscountess and asked, "Now may we please hear Agnes sing?"

"We've heard Agnes' repertoire three times over," complained Frank, with brotherly tactlessness. His wife's offerings must have been long familiar as well, for he had been staring into the fire and twiddling his cuffs throughout. "Let us rather have cards."

His mother gave him a freezing look that silenced further protest.

"Would you give us "Robin Adair" again?" Joseph prompted Miss Birdlow, as she rose to go to the instrument.

"If you will turn the pages for me," she replied with a smile.

"*I* will see to that," announced Geoffrey Wynstanley. He stalked past a surprised Joseph and took a proprietary stance beside his cousin, leaving the guest to resume his seat.

"I never knew you to take an interest in music, cousin," said Miss Birdlow dryly. "I thought you unresponsive to the arts of Aiode."

"The what—? Never mind that. I like your singing well enough." He perched an elbow on the pianoforte and urged her, in a carrying whisper, "Better to let me manage this. You can never be too careful of the company you keep."

Joseph's head jerked up, and his was not the only startled expression.

"The company I keep? I beg your pardon, Geoffrey," said Miss Birdlow. "What on earth can you be referring to?"

"I refer, cousin, to—"

Here the door to the drawing room swung open, and the maid Tabitha entered bearing the tea tray. Instantly the faces of all were wiped blank, but after a pause, Geoffrey went on more loudly than before: "—I refer to the conduct of Mr. Joseph Tierney. In particular, his carryings-on with one of the Hapgood daughters of Bramleigh."

"Geoffrey!" snapped Lady Marlton, more indignant that her nephew made such pronouncements before the servants, than by the pronouncement itself. Indeed, it was too bizarre and unexpected an accusation to be absorbed at once.

Miss Birdlow was too well-bred to continue the conversation under such circumstances (though her eyebrows seemed in danger of rising off her forehead altogether), and Mr. Wynstanley availed himself of the continued silence.

"Under the guise of his studies, I fear Mr. Tierney has been *consorting* with—"

"*Geoff*-rey!" shrieked his aunt.

"—Miss Alice Hapgood, compromising both her reputation and the Marlton name because we appear to sponsor him."

Etiquette forgotten, a clamor of voices burst out, so loud and instantaneous that not a person in the room noticed Tabitha dropping the sugar bowl and having to chase it under the settee.

"I demand to know what you mean," cried Joseph, springing to his feet and red with fury.

"Miss *Alice* Hapgood?" demanded Miss Birdlow. "Surely you mean Miss Elfrida."

"Geoffrey, I cannot have you insulting any guest under my roof—"

"Will no one have a care for the servants?"

"I say, which one was Miss Alice again?"

"You have damaged that young lady's good name and my own, and I demand a retraction." Joseph loomed over Mr. Wynstanley, who held his ground, only the whiteness of his knuckles as he gripped the instrument betraying his emotion.

"I say Geoffrey, this scandal-mongering ill becomes you," interposed Miss Birdlow, recovering her equilibrium. She despised the eldest Miss Hapgood as a potential rival but had never had two thoughts together about Miss Alice. She doubted anyone had.

"I have never met Miss Alice Hapgood, except in the presence of her family when I called there, or when I sat beside her at Saturday's assembly, in full view of all," Joseph declared.

"But you will admit, Mr. Tierney, that you have been assisted in your endeavors by a so-called lad named Arthur?"

"Yes—what of it? I have made no secret of it. And what do you mean 'so-called lad'?"

"A lad of small frame, medium height, tanned skin, brown hair and eyes? He wears rough, loose clothing and hails from the parish of Bramleigh?"

"Oh, Lor'!" gasped Tabitha, the sugar bowl dropping from her fingers once more.

"For pity's sake, girl," snapped Lady Marlton, recalling the maid's presence. "Leave that. Don't you know when you're not wanted?" If the viscountess could not put the genie back in the bottle, she could at least drive off some of the witnesses. The girl Tabitha was no gad-abroad, but the story would be all over the county by morning, nevertheless—how could it not?

"I do not follow you," said Joseph in an icy voice, when the door shut behind Tabitha. "And my patience grows thin. What has Arthur Baddely to do with your accusations?" Even as he spoke it, he felt a chill hand take his insides. He cared too much now for Arthur and—yes—for Miss Alice Hapgood, to have their names connected and Arthur's irregular parentage revealed. But how could Arthur's bastardy compromise Miss Alice in particular? Would it not rather disgrace the squire?

"Shall we ride over with my uncle to Bramleigh tomorrow morning, and put the question to Miss Hapgood herself?"

"We certainly shall not," retorted Joseph, "involve that young woman. Have the courage to make your meaning clear or make your thorough apologies."

"Very well." Geoffrey tugged on his waistcoat and shook out his cuffs. "Very well. In so many words, what I *mean*, sir, is that, when you have been out and about early mornings—"

"—Pursuing my work with the help of Arthur Baddely—"

"—Pursuing your work with the help of someone you assumed to be one Arthur Baddely," rejoined Geoffrey, "you were, in actuality, spending all manner of unchaperoned time with Miss Alice Hapgood. Extraordinary conduct, sir!"

Joseph threw up his hands. "If I were with Arthur, how could I be spending unchaperoned time with Miss Hapgood?" he demanded. "If Miss Hapgood were even present, which she was not?" He gave a humorless laugh as he swept his gaze over the assembled company, with their various expressions of puzzlement and disdain. "Arthur would be an unusual chaperone, to be sure, but I assure you—all of you—that I have been accompanied by young Arthur and only young Arthur."

Geoffrey slapped a triumphant hand on the pianoforte case. "Just so. But did you realize, Mr. Tierney, that young Arthur, as you call him, is in fact none other than Miss Hapgood in disguise?"

The others broke their stunned silence, following this revelation.

"Miss Hapgood in disguise? My good Mr. Wynstanley, how much of your uncle's port did you imbibe?" cried Joseph before the din drowned him.

"Mercy's sake, Geoffrey! Have done, or we will be forced to ship you home to my brother in disgrace."

"Honestly, Geoffrey—may I begin my song, or have you more preposterous bomb-shells to hurl?"

Mr. Wynstanley crossed stubborn arms over his chest and waited for the hubbub to die away. "There *is* no Arthur Baddely. He does not exist," he insisted. He scowled at Lady Marlton. "Banish me if you please, madam, but do me the courtesy of investigating my claims."

"Your claims are ridiculous and insulting to my guest!" declared Lord Marlton.

"And you have made them in the most indelicate manner possible, I am sorry to say," added Marlton's lady. Rising with a rustle of skirts, she extended a placating hand to Joseph. "Mr. Tierney. Do forgive my nephew. He has ever been an impulsive sort. If he will desist now and apologize, we will have some tables of cards."

Geoffrey faced down the ire of the Marlton clan. "I retract nothing."

His aunt and uncle glared; Miss Birdlow played a series of impatient trills; Mrs. Mary Birdlow whispered to her husband, who nodded, muttering, "Demmed nuisance."

Joseph waited for his breathing to calm before he replied, as evenly as he could muster, "Then we must investigate. Not only to vindicate Miss Hapgood's reputation, but also my own." He turned to the viscountess. "My lady, would you be so kind to call back the maid? Please," he added, when he saw protests bubbling to her lips.

Shortly, Tabitha reappeared, bobbing a curtsy and glancing at the still-untouched tea things.

"Tabitha, is it not?" asked Joseph, approaching her with his hands clasped behind his back.

"Yes, sir." Her own long arms hung by her sides while her eyes darted from one person to the next, before returning to Mr. Tierney.

"Tabitha, does your family belong to the parish of Patterton or of Bramleigh?"

A hesitation. "Bramleigh, sir."

"Then perhaps you are familiar with one Arthur Baddely, a ward of Bramleigh Parish?"

Her throat worked. "I—don't know everyone in the parish, sir."

"But you've never heard of any Arthur Baddely, have you, girl?" interjected Mr. Wynstanley.

"I 'aven't," she admitted. But no sooner had Mr. Tierney's shoulders drooped and Mr. Wynstanley's countenance lit up than she added, "Could 'e though, beggin' yer pardon, be about this high"—she indicated with her hand—"brown eyes and hair. Pointed chin. Quick thinker?"

Joseph gave her a sharp look, to hear her parrot back to him what he had once said in the Pattergees kitchen, though she left out the bit about Arthur speaking above his station. Tabitha's face was blank.

"That could describe half the lads in Somerset," said Geoffrey, annoyed by her waffling. "Simply say you know of no such person, and have never heard tell of such a person, and have done with it."

"Yes, sir," agreed the maid.

"Thank you, Tabitha. You are dismissed," Lady Marlton said.

Keeping her head down, the girl bobbed a retreating curtsy, but at the door she threw Joseph another glance.

"That was pointless," the viscount declared. "Whether one girl knows or does not know of one boy named Arthur proves nothing."

"Nor does it disprove anything," Geoffrey said. "I say, Uncle, that you and I accompany Mr. Tierney when next he meets this Arthur, and we settle the matter there."

"I will not have Arthur trapped, any more than I would Miss Hapgood," Joseph countered. "He has done nothing wrong, to be so ambushed by those who would likely frighten and overawe him. But we do intend to work tomorrow morning. If you should care to meet us at the copse that borders Pattergees and Bramleigh to the northeast corner—say, around seven o'clock, we will be prepared to lay this matter to rest." With a curt bow that bespoke his continued anger, he excused himself, leaving the family members to thrash out the situation to their satisfaction.

On his second visit to the Pattergees kitchen, Joseph found only William the gamekeeper's son, seated on an oak bench and staring gloomily into the fire. His gorgeous forest-colored livery coat was thrown off, and his collar loosened. One hand dragged through his tow hair.

"Excuse me, William."

The young man bounded to his feet, scrambling to tidy himself, his mouth thin with annoyance. "Sir."

"Please do not trouble yourself. I am looking for Tabitha. Do you know where I might find her?"

If possible, William's mouth tightened. "What do you be needing from her...sir? I'll be clearing the tea things, being as it's Mr. Girdles' night off."

"I wanted to ask her a few questions, William. It would not take a minute. You might be present, if you liked, if you would allow us the room's length, for privacy."

"Don't think she'll be too happy about. She's in a mood, all right. Fair like to bite a man's head off, that Tabitha."

On cue, hasty footsteps were heard in the passage, and the girl herself appeared, flushed and eyes glinting. "What was that you were saying about me, William? I'll thank you to keep your thoughts to yourself."

Scowling, the young man made no reply, and Joseph tactfully withdrew a few yards to inspect Mrs. Trapp's gleaming copper pans.

After a few moments of muttered conversation between the servants, he heard Tabitha's hesitant approach.

"Sir? You had some questions?" Her voice was low, but her eyes met his steadily.

"Ahem. Yes." Joseph rocked on his heels, wondering how best to come at the problem. "You see, when I was questioning you in the drawing room, it seemed to me there was more you might have said, if not for the others present."

She took a measured breath. "Yes, sir."

"Please—would you share what you know with me? Mr. Wynstanley labors under the misapprehension that there is no Arthur Baddely. That...I have been guilty of misconduct with Miss Hapgood when I pretended to work with Arthur. If we are to dispel this...notion...of his, there must be no mystery."

Tabitha nodded. Her bony hands clasped each other for comfort. "Mr. Tierney, I know no Arthur Baddely of Bramleigh."

"Yes." He fought that sinking sensation again. "You said as much. But you also described a similar boy you might know, in terms I had used before. I remember thinking, when I first asked about him in this very kitchen, that possibly you knew more of the lad than you would admit."

"I did," she replied, her voice dropping nearly to a whisper. William continued to watch them from the hearth, but Joseph drew closer to the girl, not to miss a word. "I do. It be not...certain, what I say, so if I be mistaken, I beg you not to hold it against me." Hardly daring to breathe, Joseph gave his assurances, and she went on. "My sister, you know, she works at Bramleigh. Has for years. Miss Alice there…it used to be that she wasn't all for being ladylike. She enjoyed the out-of-doors, you might say. Got in trouble with the squire who bad her give up the squirrels and fishes and keep to her embroidery. Well. My sister Dorcas says that, after the squire took after her, Miss Alice took to…disguising herself."

Joseph jerked backward, as if Tabitha had got him with the kitchen shovel. Across the room, William started up, but Joseph shook his head and the young man took his seat again. Tabitha watched the parade of emotion across Joseph's face: horror, doubt, horror again.

"…Disguising herself," he echoed after a minute. "What manner of disguise?"

"As…a boy, sir. In rough clothing. She puts 'er hair under a hat, and she's such a wee thing that you wouldn't know it right away, to see it. Wee and clever, Miss Alice is."

Wee and clever she might be, but could she be so deceitful? So *dastardly*? This was Miss Alice Hapgood they were talking about. The strange, shy girl who struggled to string three words together. The one who stared at her hands or her feet or a spot in the distance—anywhere but at one. The one who—Joseph suddenly felt the need to sit down. Magically, a bench scraped across the sanded floor and caught him, and Tabitha began to fan him, hissing away William's assistance.

Joseph's thoughts ran on, a mill race. Miss Alice Hapgood. The one who knew of Sir Joseph Banks' voyages in the South Pacific. The one who clapped spiders fearlessly between her bare hands and admitted to catching butterflies, and who, unlike Miss Edith, could well abide "dead things." The one with the injured ankle, an injury she claimed to sustain the same day Arthur tumbled into Joseph and lamed them both.

It could not be true.

His thoughts turned to Arthur. Arthur, with the Hapgood eyes. With the inconsistent grammar, the supposed gift for mimicking his betters, the hints of Latin and book-learning, and the terrible talent for spinning whoppers. Yes, Arthur's voice alternately squeaked and dropped, but, as the lad himself confessed, he had experienced that change of life only recently.

Joseph's brow clouded as he recalled how awkwardly Arthur received teasing and horse-play. Could he, Joseph, have been aiming teasing blows at a *young lady's* head? Clapping her by the shoulder? Shoving her up the bank by the bottom, blessed Lord? It could not be. It should not be. Perhaps Arthur's awkwardness was a product of his upbringing. As the orphaned parish ward, he likely had few friends his age and might have suffered some taunting and cuffs at the hands of village boys.

No.

No.

It was impossible that Arthur Baddely and Miss Alice Hapgood were one and the same person. If for no other reason than that it defied imagination. Or that he would do anything, if it only were not so.

No well-bred young lady would dream of such conduct! Such devious, compromising behavior—such trickery! Could the squire possibly be in on the game? In his eagerness to catch husbands for his many daughters? No, again. Impossible. What need had the squire of elaborate ruses, when Nature herself had given the eldest Miss Elfrida all the traps of beauty she could supply?

Nothing made any sense, and his head was beginning to ache.

It might not make sense, but that was not the catch. All that mattered was whether it was true.

And if it was? If Miss Alice Hapgood had indeed deceived him and posed as one Arthur Baddely, and he, Mr. Joseph Tierney, had spent hours and hours in her company, with no chaperones but the birds and bugs? That was all that mattered.

Because it meant Geoffrey Wynstanley would be right.

It meant he would have jeopardized his own reputation and stained hers. And the only remedy—

"Sir? Can William bring you some water?"

"No. No, thank you."

"Help you to bed, then?"

He didn't answer. Couldn't answer. But he felt his arm slung without ceremony over the shoulders of the strapping William, Tabitha snapping instructions and William muttering responses.

He found himself in his bedroom, with his man Chambers helping him to undress. He found himself in bed, staring blindly at the painted ceiling as the candle flickered.

He wondered what he would say to Arthur the next day. And to Lord Marlton and Mr. Wynstanley. And to Squire Hapgood.

He wondered what he would say to his mentor, Sir Edmund Chall.

And to his own father.

He wondered what would become of his life—of his hopes and ambitions—if this dreadful possibility hardened into truth.

If Mr. Arthur Baddely was none other than Miss Alice Hapgood, and he, Joseph Tierney, had compromised her.

CHAPTER TWELVE

Hence false tears, deceits, disguises.
—Alexander Pope, *Chorus of Youths & Virgins* (1718)

If Father Thomas of Bramleigh Downs wished from time to time for the services of a sexton to open and close the church building and to tend the churchyard, this was not one of those mornings. He had few parishioners abroad in the early mornings beyond those involved in farm work, and they would come to no harm until the day closed and the jug flowed. Nay, only one morning lark among his flock caused him concern, and his concern had grown as the weeks passed. When he saw Miss Alice Hapgood skipping past this morning, hand to her hat and a merry tune escaping her lips, Father Thomas emerged from the shelter of the steps to waylay her.

"Miss Alice."

She gave a little shriek that bubbled into laughter, and it made him sorrier still to see the bright look on her face that he would shortly drive away. "Why, Father—you gave me a fright."

"Another morning's work, Miss Alice, with the young naturalist?"

"Yes, indeed! We are cataloguing the birds. I never knew there were so many, and even some I had not seen before. To think, just yesterday we heard a nightingale and a song thrush singing together—"

"How beautiful that must have been," he said, repressing a sigh. "But Miss Alice, I have been turning this arrangement over in my mind, and I am afraid it cannot, in conscience, continue."

Instantly she was on her knees again in their rusty breeches, her eyes huge with pleading. "Don't say that—please! I know it's wrong to lie, but it will only be another fortnight or two at the outermost. I have harmed no one, except to make you keep a secret, and I would have avoided that, if I could."

"Dear girl." He pulled her reluctantly to her feet. "Who is to say the harm will not fall at any moment? If you are discovered, the damage cannot be repaired. I have been remiss as your shepherd, already, to let this continue so long, only I could not bring myself to disappoint you."

Two big tears brimmed and overflowed. "I know, I know. I never wanted to put you in that position. And now it has gone on, this long. What would you have me do, Father Thomas? To confess now to Mr. Tierney would do the very damage you envision."

"I recognize that." Taking her hands between his, he pressed them. "Listen. You must return home now and send word to Mr. Tierney that duty has called you elsewhere."

"You mean, I must say I cannot assist him today?"

"You must say you will no longer be able to assist him," the curate replied, "today or any day."

"But he will want to know why," Alice said, the tears flowing faster now.

"You must be as honest as you can and say that you cannot name the reason, but it must be so. And because you cannot confess what you have done to Mr. Tierney, Miss Alice, you must tell your father of it."

She dragged the coarse sleeve across her face and gave a woeful sniff. "Papa will lock me in a dungeon and throw away the key."

"He will threaten to," admitted Father Thomas, thinking of the squire's temper, "but that will pass. You are—how many years now—?"

"Seventeen. Nearly eighteen."

"Seventeen, nearly eighteen. And it is time to embrace what God has created you to be: a young woman. You have had this period of grace, and now you must do your duty. So go. We will talk again." He gave her a gentle push in the direction of Bramleigh, and she took several halting steps before turning back.

"But I don't want to spend my life sitting indoors, Father Thomas, doing fancywork and approving menus and practicing music and trimming bonnets! Those are things Elfrida loves. I am not Elfrida. I am Alice."

"Certainly, you are Alice," said the curate. "You know that, and I know that, and God knows that. And so we must wait and see how Alice will be Alice, and how she will come to say with the Psalmist that, 'The lines are fallen unto me in pleasant places; yea, I have a goodly heritage.' Go quickly, my girl, so you may send your message."

Joseph drew the watch from the pocket of his waistcoat and consulted it again. Arthur had never been late before. He paced the length of the small copse and retraced his steps, anxiety giving way to frustration. Today, of all days, this Arthur must come! Shortly the viscount and his nephew would join them, and Joseph intended to know the entire truth before that moment arrived.

A figure appeared atop the grassy slope, and Joseph's heart sped until he recognized the slouching gait did not belong to his erstwhile assistant. The figure caught sight of him and raised an arm, hallooing.

Joseph strode to meet him, quickening his pace when he saw the youth waving a note.

"Mr. Tierney, then?"

Nodding, Joseph snatched the missive. "Who gave this to you?"

"Err..." the rough lad dragged a barefooted toe in the dirt. "Came by way of Dorcas at Bramleigh, but don't think it's from 'er, if you ken my meaning. But she said there'd be no reply, so I'll be off now."

Joseph hardly waited for Hal to go before he tore the note open.

Mr. Tierney, sir.

Begging your pardon for this short notis, but I am un-able to assist you any longer in your work. I have other duties to attend to and cannot divide myself. I have very much enjoyed your teechings and compny and wish you God's blessing.

Arthur Baddeley

"Wait!" called Joseph after the servant. He dug in another pocket. "I will give you…sixpence, if you stay here and pass a message to Lord Marlton and his nephew Mr. Wynstanley."

The boy eagerly removed his cap and pocketed the coin. "What shall I tell 'em?"

"That I, Mr. Tierney, have gone to call at Bramleigh and will return to Pattergees thereafter."

"Gone to *call*?" echoed Hal. "It be not seven of the clock, sir. You won't be finding anyone but Miss Alice and the servants up so early. Mebbe the squire in another half-hour."

Joseph winced at the mention of Miss Alice's morning wakefulness, but he only said, "Then I will await the family's convenience there. Please pass my message."

With Hal abroad, not a soul at Bramleigh heard Joseph's knock except some chickens out pecking the graveled drive and one pig that glanced up before resuming its snorting in the shrubbery. Joseph stepped back to peer up at the windows on the floor above, but no telltale shifting of the draperies hinted at any human observers.

He would find somebody in the kitchen, he surmised, and he would do as well to wait there till the family was up. But as he made his way around the weathered-but-solid stone great house, he found a window to the drawing room open. There was someone within, seated with her back to him, her slim shoulders shaking with a burst of silent emotion. He recognized the line of the neck and the rich dark color of her hair.

Casting a glance in either direction and seeing no one, Joseph stepped in.

"Miss Hapgood."

For the second time that morning, Alice gave a shriek of surprise, and she tumbled from the settee as she spun to face him. "Mr.—Mr. Tierney!" she gasped, dashing at her eyes with the ends of her shawl.

"Forgive me for alarming you. No one answered at the door."

She reminded him of nothing so much as a cornered fawn, ready to dart away once she gathered her wits. "What—whatever can bring you here, so early?"

"I had hopes of meeting my assistant Arthur Baddely, but he sent word through your servant that he would no longer be able to help me in my work." His tone was light, but Alice had no such self-control. She blanched. Her eyes fluttered up to meet his searching gaze and then fell to the floor. She was certain he could hear her rapid breathing, if not her very heartbeat! And what was that expression he wore? So intent. So...bleak. It made his handsome face look older.

"That is too bad, sir. But why should you seek for Arthur Baddely here?"

He drew closer and Alice retreated, clutching the chair back behind her to steady herself. "You seem distressed, Miss Hapgood. May I call for a glass of wine?"

"No, thank you. I am very well."

"I am glad to hear it. Perhaps we might avail ourselves, then, of this opportunity for private conversation. Should you care to sit down? You tremble."

"I would prefer to stand," she said, her voice growing stronger. She did not understand what this unconventional call could be about, but as he was here, she must submit to it.

"Very well," rejoined Joseph, who also had been bracing himself inwardly. "Miss Hapgood—are you personally acquainted with Arthur Baddely?"

"I? With Arthur Baddely?" When he met her stalling question only with a silent nod, she was compelled to blather on. "Not—it is not a close acquaintance by any means. But I—I know of Arthur Baddely, to be sure."

"A most unusual youth, as I have told you. And it seems a shame that he should give up his work with me, when he shows such talent for it. I thought, perhaps, if it were a matter of money, I could speak to his guardian. But I do not know even the name of Arthur's guardian, and I cannot find Arthur to ask. But I know he is a ward of Bramleigh Downs, so I decided to inquire here, especially if he knew one of your servants well enough to pass messages through him. Arthur claims he is the illegitimate, unacknowledged son of somebody, with possible connections to your cook Mrs. Button and even to your family."

"I think I will sit down, after all, Mr. Tierney."

"Do you deny his claims, Miss Hapgood?"

"I...know nothing of his parentage," managed Alice, squeezing her hands in her lap. How unfortunate, that on the very day she chose to discontinue her deceits, she should be forced to add to them!

"You are right. It is ill-bred of me to put these questions to you. I should rather bring them to the squire."

"No! Don't ask him!" she cried. "I mean to say, I do know Arthur Baddely, and my father—we share a father. So disgraceful. I am the only one who knows. And my father does not suspect that I know. We none of us ever refer to it, and you must never, ever speak of it, if you have any courtesy." Alice buried her face in her hands and had no difficulty at all bursting into tears.

She heard his chair give a squeak as Mr. Tierney sprung from it to pace the length of the room. Toward the white-painted fireplace; away past the windows to the escritoire; back to his chair. Though mortified by her display, as well as her lies, she rallied, choking back her sobs and dabbing at her eyes once more with the soggy ends of her shawl. This could not continue. It must not.

Joseph had not expected to pity her. Indeed, he had come warmed by his anger at being so deceived and entrapped. But there was such earnestness in her distress that he could not help feeling a brute for harassing her. "Miss Hapgood. I'm sure you think me a monster, to come upon you unawares and throw these—accusations—at you—"

"Mr. Tierney." She raised one trembling hand to forestall him. Father Thomas told her that she could not confess her doings to Mr. Tierney, but surely if she did so in confidence—? She only knew she could no longer bear to deceive so kind and generous a man.

"Mr. Tierney," Alice repeated. "I beg you will not apologize. Indeed, I will have far more to beg your pardon for, than you of me. This sorrow of mine does not stem from any misconduct of my father's. I only add to my wrongs to let you believe so. You see, I have something to confess. You will be horrified. You will despise me, when I tell it to you. But I promise—no one knows of this, and if I share it with you I will tell no other soul. Not even my father or my sisters. And I meant no harm by my actions, though you will no doubt think my conduct unforgiveable."

So it was true.

Joseph felt the blood drain from him. He had hoped against hope in the dark hours of the night that Wynstanley's tale was but a wild notion born of jealousy, and Tabitha's corroborating evidence mere coincidence. It did not appear he would be so fortunate.

Sinking into the chair closest to her, he abandoned himself to his fate.

Out came Alice's confession, halting, low, broken by gulps and blushes and pauses. The whole time she kept her head bowed. She did not want to know his reaction. Did not want to read the anger and judgment there. Although she longed to make excuses, she forbade herself the relief. Likely Mr. Tierney would not find her unmaidenly desire to study the natural world a point in her favor, in any case. Alas. Button had warned her. Her father had warned her. But Alice had insisted on doing what she pleased and defying all, so who could she blame if the world crumbled to ash around her?

When he spoke at last, she would not have recognized his voice. Gone from it were all traces of cheer and humor. He did not upbraid her, but the despondency she heard lashed her more strongly than anger would have.

"How you must have laughed at me, Miss Alice, to find me so credulous."

"No," she breathed, wanting to weep again. "No. There was no possible reason for you to suspect."

"I blush to recall some of my own actions—" planting a hand on her backside came uncomfortably to mind "—as well as conversations we have had. Did your father suggest this scheme to you?"

"My father?" Startled eyes flew up to his. "Absolutely not! Suggest—? Did I not just say that I would confess to you and no other person? He knows nothing of it. Nor will he ever, by my tongue. Oh, Mr. Tierney, you must believe me that I regret my actions causing you pain. No sooner had I given Hal the note for you than I was overcome with not only sadness that we could no longer work together, but also remorse that I had deceived you. Please believe me that I have the highest, most thorough respect for you—I think you will be the greatest naturalist in all England—"

"I will be no such thing."

"You will. You *will*," Alice insisted. "I know it. How I envy you, Mr. Tierney. Your stuffed and pinned specimens, your researches, your monographs, your meetings of the Royal Society."

"Enough," Joseph broke in. He was pacing again, fists clenched. "I must speak with your father. When does he rise?"

Alice paled and leapt up to thrust herself in his path, her Paisley shawl slipping unheeded to the floor. With detachment, Joseph noticed she had a tea stain on her high-necked bodice, and the lace trimming one shoulder was coming loose. "I do not have the pleasure of understanding you, Mr. Tierney. I am repentant. No one but you has suffered from what I have done. If this matter goes no further, no one will be the wiser. Can you not see? If you tell my father, he will be angry. He will make a fuss. It might—endanger your future."

"I no longer have a future," said Joseph in that same grim tone, "of my own to speak for."

"What can you mean? Do you not hear me? The matter is finished. You may go your way, and I mine, and after a time you may forgive me. I give you my word that I will say nothing." In her earnestness she reached for his hand, and he recoiled as if a serpent had struck him.

"Forgive me for contradicting you, Miss Hapgood, but you cannot go your way and I mine. Had you not made your confession just now, I would have wrung it from you. Yes—you shake your head at me. I have my own admission to make—that I was so ignorant and blinded that I might never have realized, had not another informed me."

She clapped a hand to her mouth in horror. "Another? But *who*, pray—?" Names and faces ran through her mind, and she exclaimed, "It could not have been Father Thomas. He would never—was it Dorcas? Button? Hal?"

"I thought you had not told a soul, Miss Hapgood," he reminded her icily. "Now you name this host of possible informers?"

"No—no—not possible. That is what I am saying—" She was interrupted by the sound of footsteps and the grumbling and hacking of the squire's early-morning throat-clearings. "It is my father. You must go, sir." Darting a look over her shoulder as if she expected the squire to fling open the door at any moment, she gave Joseph a shove toward the open window. "Quickly."

Almost as if she were Arthur again, he elbowed her away, making himself an unmoveable rock. "I must speak with him. Our deeds are no longer our secret."

"Nonsense." Alice stamped an impatient foot. "Tell your...informant to be silent! Bribe him, if necessary. Threaten. Cajole. Tell him he must not endanger the reputation of a respectable gentlewoman." Putting her back into it, she shoved him again, and, just as resolved, he held his ground.

Alice recognized the distant sounds of bustle in the hall—Cook and Dorcas carrying the food to the breakfast room. Muffled thumping and oaths—her father descending the stairs. Mr. Tierney must have drawn the same conclusions because he took her by both shoulders and moved her bodily out of the way, calling, "Squire Hapgood? Squire, a word—"

"Hush!" squealed Alice, launching herself at him to clamp a hand over his mouth. His eyebrows shot up at this new proof of her complete want of propriety, and they struggled in silence some moments. When he managed to pin her arms behind her, her tea-stained bosom heaving against his waistcoat, he opened his mouth to call out once more, only to find her own mouth pressed to his in desperation.

Had he begun it, or had she? Or had their lips simply come together because their bodies had first?

Neither one could say. But resistance on his part, and panic on hers, gave way to something else. For one measureless moment, they yielded themselves to it. Her arms were somehow about his neck and his fingers in her hair, and all was softness and warmth.

"What in thunderation?" roared the squire, hurtling through the door just as Alice imagined he would, only he had a napkin tucked in the front of his waistcoat.

She felt Joseph's body harden to stone against her. Then his hands came up and set her firmly away. When she met his eyes, she realized the metaphor was wrong. He had not turned to stone but to ice. For the look he gave her was glacial. "My leg was already in the trap," he hissed, "you had no need of this."

Then he turned to the still-sputtering squire. "Sir, I was come in search of you. We must speak."

And to Alice's complete humiliation, her father dropped all pretense of outrage. He glanced from one to the other—rubbed his hands together! "Well, then. No need to stand on ceremony. I guess you could use some breakfast, eh?"

"No, thank you. This is business, and we had best deal with it as soon as we may."

"Whatever you like, Mr. Tierney, though I did think you might prefer my Elfie to this one, but so be it, so be it! Alice, child, you run along while the gentleman and I have a word. Clever girl. Good girl. What are you waiting for? Get you gone."

She did not need to be told again.

Alice fled.

Chapter Thirteen

**Since nothing else will do, I am engaged
by all the strength of Vows and Honour.
—Henry Fielding, *Love in Several Masques* (1728)**

"I say, Margaret—let me have a turn." Edith tugged on her sister's arm and was swatted away.

"Hush! My ears are better than yours, and this is too good to miss," Margaret whispered, pressing against the keyhole once more.

"Is she still crying?"

This time Margaret only put a finger to her lips and kicked at Edith. Edith pinched her in retaliation but hushed all the same. The keyhole was only necessary to catch Alice's replies—the Squire's resounding voice knew no barrier of walls.

After a quarter hour of this, the Squire gave his second-oldest daughter a final, bracing clap on the shoulders and made for the door, his two youngest scrambling to escape discovery behind an arras. They did not dare emerge until they heard Alice's swift footsteps and muffled sobs follow after. But where her father headed for the stables and his dogs, Alice escaped upstairs, seeking refuge in the bedroom she shared with Elfrida. There she could find solitude because Elfrida spent her days in the morning room or closeted with their mother.

"Poor Alice!" cried Edith. "Forced to marry a man she doesn't love!"

"She didn't say she didn't," pointed out Margaret.

"But she was crying so hard!"

"You don't understand anything," said her older sister maddeningly. "Come. Let's tell Elfie and Mother."

Mrs. Hapgood and her daughter were ensconced in Mrs. Hapgood's chamber, Elfrida sewing by the window while her mother lay in bed and tallied the day's symptoms and ailments. "—So much for my foot. And then the aching in my back that Mr. Lewis cannot make head nor tail of—why, goodness me, girls! Whatever can be the matter? I beg you not to make such a noise."

"Mama! Elfie—"

"Alice is going to be married!" declared Margaret, over the top of Edith. "To that Mr. Tierney!"

Utter silence met this announcement, but Mrs. Hapgood so forgot herself as to sit bolt upright, all thoughts of back pains and Mr. Lewis forgotten.

"Don't be silly, girls," Elfrida chided in her gentle voice, when she had recovered. "What can possibly have put that thought in your minds?"

"We heard it! We heard Papa saying so," cried Edith. "Just now in his study. It is too bad because she is not happy about it, and you were the one who was supposed to marry him, Elfie. You won't be angry with her, will you?"

"Of course I won't, if it be true, and Mr. Tierney prefers her," Elfrida assured her. "Though if I must marry someone, I would have liked him well enough. He is very kind and does not speak in that loud, bragging way some young men have. However, I do not see how Mr. Tierney should have spent enough time with either one of us to form an attachment."

Edith let out a happy sigh. "What a relief you will not die of a broken heart, Elfie! Although Alice might, she—"

"Shhh—let me tell it, Edie. I was the one who heard all." Margaret smoothed her skirts and straightened as if she were prepared to recite a lesson. "It seems Mr. Tierney called early this morning—"

"Called?" interrupted Mrs. Hapgood. "It cannot yet be ten of the clock."

"All the same, ma'am, he did so," Margaret insisted. "And found only Alice awake, naturally. Well, when Papa came down to breakfast and was tucking up, he heard someone call out his name. When he looked into the drawing room, he found Mr. Tierney and Alice *locked in an embrace.*"

"That's enough, Margaret." Elfrida frowned now. "You are inventing this from whole cloth."

"No, no—she isn't!" said Edith. "I heard Papa say as much, too."

"Begin at the beginning, Margaret," ordered Mrs. Hapgood, settling back against her pillows. She wagged a finger at her youngest. "And no more interruptions from you, Miss."

Casting her sister a superior glance, Margaret started over. "The first thing Papa said when he shut the study door was, 'Congratulations, my little Alice. You will be poorer, if possible, than we are now, but you have netted yourself a fine young man.' And Alice only cried and said that poor Mr. Tierney mustn't be made to marry her because it was not his fault. And Papa says, of course it was his fault, because if a young man thinks he can march into another man's house and kiss his daughter like the dickens and face no consequences, that man is sadly mistaken. And Alice leaves off crying for a minute and asks if that was the reason Mr. Tierney gave for offering for her—that Papa caught them embracing—and Papa says, 'Well, does a man have to give a reason, when he's discovered in such circumstances?' And Alice says, 'Then he doesn't have to marry me, Papa, because I threw myself at him.' And Papa says, 'You might have—you have your wits about you—but that doesn't explain what the young man is doing in my house at such an unholy hour—'"

"Margaret, for shame," interjected Elfrida, unable to stop herself from dimpling at her sister's perfect imitation of their father's voice and postures. "This information is all got from eavesdropping, and I think we had better wait until Papa or Alice chooses to share the news with us."

Mrs. Hapgood bit her lip, wanting very much to hear the story in its entirety but reminded of her obligations as a mother and model of conduct. She compromised. "Where is Alice? Fetch her, Edie."

Margaret flopped onto the bed, annoyed to be robbed of the moment's drama, but her mother's hand rumpling and petting her curls soon soothed her.

Edith's swift steps returned shortly, followed by the more dragging pace of her sister. Alice looked a fright. Her eyes were red and swollen, her complexion ashen, apart from her red nose, and her hair tumbled and tangled about her shoulders. "Yes, Mama?"

"My darling girl, what is this I hear about you and Mr. Tierney? That you are to be married?"

Alice looked in danger of brimming over again, but she fought it, only sinking down upon the coverlet beside Margaret and nodding.

"But how can this be, my dear? How came Mr. Tierney to be in our house this morning, and you two to have an understanding? Did this come about when he sat beside you at the assembly?"

Rolling the coverlet beneath her fingers, Alice attempted to speak—cleared her throat—tried again. "No, madam. He came this morning in search of his assistant Arthur, but—but—found me instead."

"And...?" pressed her mother, when Alice seemed in danger of saying no more.

Alice hardly knew how to answer. Her head was all in a muddle and aching now, from crying so much. She was longing to be by herself. To escape to the woods to sort everything out. Since she encountered Father Thomas by the church some few hours ago, she had experienced a year's worth of emotions. Nay, a decade's worth! Happiness to misery, fear to mortification, the shame of confession and its relief. And then to feel her lips pressed to Mr. Tierney's! To breathe his very breath and feel the thud of his heart against her. To find those capable fingers of his winding in her hair and her arms about his neck in a stranglehold. Alice felt her insides quicken just to recall it, but just as swiftly came the memory of him putting her aside with that cold voice. He did not care for her, as she had dared to hope in that moment. He thought her conniving, underhand. He would do his duty, and that was all.

"I...took advantage of the situation," Alice went on at last. She sounded like one talking in her sleep. "I threw myself at him. Papa found us. Mr. Tierney was forced to offer for me."

Margaret sat up again, scowling. "How ill you tell your tale, Alice! I would do a much better job. You must explain why you did such a thing."

"Whatever possessed you?" Even Elfrida sounded frustrated.

"And what did it feel like?" demanded Margaret, drawing the reprimands of her mother and eldest sister.

"Has not Papa counseled us, time out of mind, that we girls must marry? Marry, marry, marry?" Alice countered, answering none of their questions.

Edith crept to her side and took hold of her hand. "But Alice—we had thought Elfie must try and get Mr. Tierney. Papa said so. You were under no obligation. And see how unhappy it has made you."

But even this sympathy must be rebuffed, and Alice did it with a will. "Nonsense. I wasn't 'trying to get him.' He's handsome. I wanted to kiss him, so I did. I did not expect him to offer for me, for that. It was not necessary—for one kiss that no one but Papa saw."

"It does seem extreme," admitted her mother. "You are sure your father did not...force him to offer?" By which Mrs. Hapgood meant *threaten to set the hounds on him*.

Alice shook her head slowly. "No. Papa was triumphant when he discovered us, but I daresay Mr. Tierney could have persuaded him to calm down. No. It was Mr. Tierney himself who insisted that he must offer and be accepted."

"Because he's head over ears in love with you!" crowed Edith, clapping her hands.

"Because he liked kissing you?" Margaret suggested.

"I...do not know," said their sister. "When Papa came to me after Mr. Tierney was gone, I—I tried to apologize for my conduct. But Papa only praised and congratulated me and would hear no apologies. I then tried to ask—what reasons Mr. Tierney gave for offering for me, but Papa said, 'Reasons? He said he felt duty-bound to marry you, my girl. Isn't that enough?'"

"Well, you cannot expect him to make sonnets to Papa about you," said Edith, "but he must have meant he felt so strongly for you, that it was his duty to marry you."

"I never thought Papa would approve of any of us running at gentlemen and kissing them," Margaret said, "even if he would like to marry us off."

"I do not think he recommends it as a strategy." Mrs. Hapgood said.

"Nor does it always work," pointed out Edith. "Remember when Uncle Alwyn got into trouble for kissing that young woman, when he was supposed to be engaged to the heiress? Uncle Alwyn refused to marry the young woman, and the heiress thereafter refused to marry him."

"You are not supposed to know about that!" cried her mother, while Margaret rolled her eyes over her little sister's latest blunder.

"Passing over your conduct for the present, sister," spoke up Elfrida, "I believe it proves Mr. Tierney to be thoroughly the gentleman. A man with a fine sense of honor."

"One can't live on honor and bread crumbs," grumbled Mrs. Hapgood, perhaps resenting the slight to her dear Alwyn.

The resolute set to Alice's features melted away then, and she rolled over to bury her face in the bed coverings. "That is the worst of it, Mother—Papa asked Mr. Tierney how he intended to support a wife and family, and Mr. Tierney said he had no choice but to—withdraw from the Royal Society's project. That he must—must go and see his father about the family living and take orders as soon as possible."

"I would like to marry a clergyman," said Edith. "Only think how nice Father Thomas is."

"Hold your tongue, you ninny," retorted Margaret. "Can't you see how upset Alice is? She doesn't want to marry a clergyman and spend her life hearing sermons and bringing joints and soups to the poor."

But Alice whipped around to glare at Margaret with red eyes. "You don't understand anything. If Mr. Tierney should like to be a clergyman, I would listen happily to all his sermons and bring joints and soups *innumerable* to his flock. But he doesn't want to be a clergyman. He wants to be a naturalist. You see—I have ruined him. Ruined him and ruined his life. And he will never forgive me."

"This is serious indeed," murmured Elfrida. She had taken up her needle again and held her frame up to inspect it. "But besides being an honorable gentleman, Mr. Tierney appears to be a tall and strong one. Surely if he saw one kiss from you leading to the collapse of all his hopes in life, he might have fought you off. You need not blame yourself for everything."

Nine times out of ten this gentle raillery from Elfrida would have drawn a smile from her sister, but this time it only sunk Alice further into misery. Because it was certainly true that Mr. Tierney could have flung off her kisses, could have calmed down her father, could have gone about his business as a naturalist and fulfilled his life's ambitions—if only Alice had not made all these impossible by her own actions. She had not intended to, but she had trapped him and closed off every other option. And it tortured her that he would tell no one she had done so, that she might demonstrate her penitence. If Mr. Tierney would not have it known, how could she confess it? Elfrida thought him a gentleman of honor, but she little suspected how truly honorable he was.

If Alice had not already loved him, his silence on her wrongdoing would have won her heart. As it was, she almost hated him for it.

The Honorable Miss Agnes Birdlow would not deign to eavesdrop, but a parallel scene took place at Pattergees. Upon his return from Bramleigh, Mr. Tierney closeted himself with Lord Marlton and Mr. Wynstanley.

"Mr. Wynstanley, while I persist in objecting to the manner in which you made your findings known, I do beg your pardon for doubting your word," said Joseph, with an offer of his hand.

Having gained his point, Geoffrey was inclined to magnanimity. He did not need his uncle's pursed lips to encourage him to make peace. Shaking with Joseph, he said, "I am a brash man, when the impulses of honor drive."

"I can hardly believe yet, that there is any truth to the story," Lord Marlton sighed, "no matter if Geoffrey tell me, or you, Mr. Tierney. How can any young woman behave so? It beggars comprehension."

"Cunning little baggage," was Geoffrey's comment. "I would never have guessed it, when I sat beside her at the assembly and she said not a word. Busy plotting, I suppose."

Joseph drew himself up stiffly. "If it would please you to remember, my lord and Mr. Wynstanley, we speak of my future wife here. I will not have such things said of her."

"That's as may be, young man," rejoined the viscount, "but have you so swiftly reconciled yourself to how that young lady attained that position?"

"I must," said Joseph, no quiver of voice betraying the emotions warring within him. "I must, and I shall. And I pray you, out of kindness to me, make no mention of this matter outside these walls. It is enough that people be told Miss Hapgood and I are betrothed. We are each of us eligible enough—no further explanation is required for such an ordinary event."

Geoffrey threw back his head in scorn. "Have your wits gone begging, Tierney? You may well bid that fond hope of secrecy adieu. My cousin sits this very moment in the drawing room with her bosom friend Miss Porterworth come to call—"

"And who have we to blame for Agnes' acquaintance with the matter?" his uncle retorted. "Had you not raised it last night in so public a manner, Geoffrey, this might well have been hushed up. I have no quarrel with my neighbor Hapgood, no wish to triumph at his expense. No, I assure you, Mr. Tierney—insofar as it lies in my power, or that of my family, we will hold our tongues. And that includes you, nephew, lest you find yourself on the wrong side of me."

Geoffrey appeared on the verge of an imprudent reply, but he clapped his mouth shut again and crossed his arms over his chest.

"I thank you," said Joseph, quite cast down. While Lord Marlton showed greater courtesy than his nephew, Joseph suspected Geoffrey's words painted the likelier picture. He could not protect Miss Alice Hapgood or her family from the brush of scandal. The servant Tabitha might be reasoned with—she seemed a sensible, loyal girl—but if Miss Birdlow whispered of it to Constance Porterworth, the tale would spread from there like fire.

And why should he wish to protect Miss Hapgood? he asked himself as he strode to the window. If she had no care for her good name, why must he? Was it because he feared the taint of scandal himself? Was his fine honor only a pretext for his own fear of others' disapproval?

Joseph could not excuse himself from this last thought to his own satisfaction. Of course it would be mortifying to be spoken of as the man tricked into wedlock by a young girl's shameless intrigues. But there was not the rub, he suspected. Not entirely. A vision of Miss Hapgood's pleading eyes rose before him. He remembered the pity he felt for her. Had her offer to say nothing and to go her own way been genuine? And had such a course even been feasible, did she not negate her words the very next minute, by throwing herself at him?

Unless, of course, he had thrown himself at her. Had he?

"—Would not you say, Mr. Tierney?" finished the viscount.

Shaking his head, Joseph tore himself from his thoughts and looked back at them. "I'm sorry, sir. Can you repeat that?"

Lord Marlton and his nephew exchanged glances. "I said, Mr. Tierney, that however you found yourself in this situation, there is no hurry to act upon it. Let the nine days' wonder pass, and do what you can, by all fair means, to put off the day of reckoning."

Pressing the wood of the window frame until the blood left his fingertips, Joseph said softly, "Are you suggesting, sir, that I leave Miss Hapgood to bear the brunt of public scrutiny, that it might weaken her attachment to me?"

"Just so," agreed Geoffrey.

"I have given my word to her father that I will marry her."

"And you can keep your word," Geoffrey assured him. "But there is no guarantee she will play her part. It's plain she is the kind to take matters in her own hands. Promise her a long engagement. A *very* long engagement, in which you absent yourself. She may grow tired of waiting or find some new chap she likes better. She then jilts you, and all comes right in the end."

"If I am not mistaken, Mr. Tierney—and I hope you will forgive my impudence for mentioning it—" went on the viscount, "you haven't the means to support a wife at present. Let that be your excuse. You must work, and she must wait."

"I see your point," said Joseph. He inspected where the carved wood of the window frame had left grooves in his skin. "And I thank you for your counsel. Whether I have the means to support a wife at the present time depends entirely on my father's reception of this news."

"Will you write to him?" asked Geoffrey.

"I will see him. But before that, I must have words with my mentor Sir Edmund Chall. Whatever Miss Hapgood's part in it, I am nevertheless fully answerable for the situation in which I find myself. Lord Marlton"—he gave a quick bow— "if you will make my excuses to Lady Marlton and Mr. and Miss Birdlow, I fear I must be off to London by the afternoon stage. I stay only to have my man pack for me and to write a few notes of explanation."

"Naturally, naturally! You are wise to take our advice. Be gone as long as you possibly can, though my wife will be sorry you may miss our Midsummer Ball. We will do our part to smother the flames of gossip, and if I have news for you, I will send it by way of Somerset House."

They shook hands once again, and Joseph excused himself.

Once in his room, however, after Chambers had been dismissed, the pen mended, and a clean sheet of folded paper drawn before him, he found himself unable to write. The very walls of Pattergees seemed to press in upon him, with their expectations and rules, their observations and sentences.

He could scratch out the note to Sir Edmund at any rate, if he did not trouble himself with explanations: *Sir, I will be in London in three days' time and beg to meet with you at your earliest convenience. Leave word for me at the Dundridge. – Joseph Tierney.* Such a letter would perplex the man, but there was no help for it. Joseph blotted the sheet, folded it again, and sealed it, leaving it for Chambers to have franked.

Then he pushed back his chair and reached for his hat.

"Sir?" Chambers' inquiring head peeked around the dressing room door.

"Going for a walk. I'll return before we leave to catch the stage."

"Yes, sir. Very good, sir."

This drew a grimace from his master. Joseph might be at a loss for words, but those ones would hardly do the trick. The world was anything but very good.

Chapter Fourteen

Farewel, ye secret Woods, and shady Groves.
—John Dryden, *Works of Virgil* (1697)

Alice had not wandered the woodlands of Bramleigh without the comfort of trousers and loose shirt for years. But those days were gone, and she had wrapped Hal's clothing in a clean sheet and left the bundle for him in the kitchen. Instead, as she made her way among the ancient trunks of oak and ash, she found leaves and twigs and soil adhering to the hem of her gown and her shawl catching in the shrubbery.

"Blast," she hissed, when the trailing fringe snagged once again. She knew the word to be unladylike, but she was past caring. What more of her reputation could be lost? Stopping to detach the fringe, she found the silky threads had managed to wind themselves in myriad directions that were not easily untangled, and she was forced to remove the shawl from her shoulders altogether and kneel beside the bush. Her nimble fingers had worked most of it loose when she caught the approach of footsteps. They were slow and meditative, but she had walked beside those booted feet too many times not to recognize them.

Mr. Tierney.

Alice clutched at her throat, darting wild glances to each side. She knew how sounds carried in the quiet and was relieved to spot him at some distance, but before she could even release her bated breath, he abruptly altered course and headed straight for her.

"Blast! *Blast*!" Alice only mouthed it now, tugging at the fringe. The last threads hung on, and, in a panic, she abandoned the shawl, scrambling to her feet to flee—anywhere.

"Miss Hapgood. How fortunate to come upon you here."

Aware of her dishevelment, Alice only made her curtsy, resisting the urge to brush herself off. Her chin lifted in precisely the defiant manner Button advised against, but Alice could not help it. Mr. Tierney thought the worst of her—accused her of scheming to entrap him. He thought her guilty in both action and intention, and she had no recourse now but to hide how this wounded her. If he regarded her as a duty he must face, no matter the cost, she would not, by her conduct, give him more with which to upbraid her. By acting henceforth with dignity, she might one day recover his respect. There would be no more tears from her, no desperate kisses, no further attempts to explain.

Even as she made this silent vow, she nearly broke it because Mr. Tierney bent on one knee and patiently finished disentangling the shawl.

"Confounded nuisance, these fringes and fripperies," he said, holding the article out for her.

Alice snatched it ungraciously. To hide the constriction in her throat she said, "Perhaps you would prefer I wear Arthur's clothing again. So eminently practical."

The dimness of the sunlight filtering through the canopy did not prevent her seeing the shadow cross his face. "Miss Hapgood, I have never wished you to pretend to be other than who and what you are."

Silenced, Alice wound herself in the shawl to give herself a moment to recover. Dignified! She must be dignified. If only she were not at such a disadvantage. If only he would not be so kind. "You wanted to see me," she murmured presently.

"I did. I was going to send a note to Bramleigh, but then my thoughts were so...jumbled...that I had to take a walk."

Both his honesty and the remedy he sought caused another stab of sympathy to shoot through her, which she smothered with an effort. But she could not help saying, "I, too, needed the air and...escape."

"Shall we take a turn together, then? Or would you prefer to sit somewhere?"

"I suppose we should return to Bramleigh," Alice said with reluctance. "It would not do to be seen here by ourselves."

She thought she caught a gleam of humor in his eyes, but it was gone before she could be certain. "That horse has bolted, Miss

Hapgood," he answered. "Bolted. We need not worry now about shutting the stable door."

Of course. The worst had been done. If someone came upon them walking unchaperoned far from others, it made little difference.

Without answering, she began to walk, deeper into the woods, taking care to pull her shawl snug about her and to keep to the widest path. It was a quiet afternoon, the birds having given up their morning songs and activity, and the nocturnal animals having sought their hiding places. The day had grown warm, but the heat could not penetrate the cover of the longstanding trees, leaving the air chilly. If Alice pretended, it might just be another morning's work together.

Something of the same thought must have passed through Joseph's mind because, as they tramped through the light and shade, he began to whistle the familiar "Betsy Belle and Mary Grey," and Alice was surprised by an urge to sing along. She held it in check, however, and after a verse or two Joseph fell silent again.

After some minutes, the trees opened into a clearing, where a single whitebeam held place, surrounded by its fallen blossoms.

Joseph drew a sharp breath. "Why—that's no common whitebeam. It's—"

"*Sorbus devoniensus*," supplied Alice. "Devon whitebeam." She bent to scoop up the crushed and browning petals, tossing them in the air to flutter down.

"Were you ever going to show me this?"

"Eventually," she answered. "Maybe in the autumn, when the fruit ripened." Seeing his brow knit, she sighed. "I know. You think your work here would have been long finished by then. You hoped, rather. And I hoped not. And now it will never be finished."

His face darkened further, and Alice felt the tightening behind her forehead that threatened tears.

"Why do you say you hoped I would not have finished my work?" he asked.

Her troubled eyes met his and dropped again. "I enjoyed it," said Alice simply. "When you finished, you would have gone, and I would have...I don't know."

Shuffling aside the blossoms beneath her, she made her way to one of the tree stumps clustered beside the whitebeam and sat down.

Belatedly, Joseph dug his handkerchief from his pocket. "May I clean that off for you?"

"No! Stop!" she exclaimed, jumping back to her feet. "I mean—no, please, Mr. Tierney. Do stop treating me so courteously. When I know how angry you must be—how resentful. I know you feel you must play the gentleman, but I would rather—please—simply say what you wanted to say to me and let us be done with it."

Straightening with a sharp look, he turned and walked a few strides from her. She had provoked him, she knew, but she preferred his anger to his kindness. It simplified her own feelings. If he were angry, she could be angry in return, which hurt far less than thinking how lowly he regarded her. How unlikely he would ever be to care for her, as she did for him.

She watched him stare up into the branches of the whitebeam and wondered if he was remarking the leathery leaves, green on top and white on the bottom. Or if he was searching for the beginnings of the fruit, which would be hard and green the whole summer before ripening to an orangey-brown. One October, years ago, she had picked the berries and popped them in her mouth, but they did not appeal to her.

He folded his handkerchief meticulously and replaced it.

"Very well, Miss Hapgood." Both his voice and gaze were cool now. "I will spare you my courtesy, if you prefer, however much I might like to 'play the gentleman.' Though I do say, having gained your desired end, I would have expected rather more civility from you."

"My desired end!" Alice echoed, sitting down again with a bump, that she might not collapse. "You little credit me, but I tell you for the last time that I never meant to deceive you—or I did—deceive you, rather—but not to *that* end—" she broke off in confusion, too late remembering her resolution not to go on explaining and begging. Each time muddied the waters further. No—if he did not believe her, repeating herself and repeating herself would not make her case. There was such a thing as protesting too much. With an effort, she steadied herself, wrapping herself more firmly in her shawl. "Pardon me my clumsy speech, Mr. Tierney. I will try not to interrupt you again. Please speak your piece."

Her hard-won calm settled him as well. "Very well. I came to tell you that I leave Pattergees this afternoon. No—do not be alarmed. I will return and keep my word to your family. But I must—"

"You go to see Sir Edmund Chall and your father," she said, forgetting that she was not going to interrupt anymore. Taking the ends of her shawl, she began to knot them. "Papa told me. But I hoped you would defer that."

"Defer it. For what reason?"

"Oh, Mr. Tierney," said Alice, pulling the knots tighter, "this has all come about with dizzying rapidity. I wish you might take time and consider. If you reveal all to your mentor and your family, there will no longer be a possibility of change. You say I entrapped you, but—but I marvel at your determination to be trapped!" Meeting his gaze fully, she pressed on. "You never told Papa why you felt obligated to offer for me. You let him believe that it was because he—he stumbled upon us in a compromising situation—which need not have been compromising, had you only tried to reason with him."

"My dear Miss Hapgood," Joseph said, bemused. "Have you kissed so many gentlemen that I might have convinced your father it was all a matter of course?"

Though she went all over scarlet, her gaze did not waver. "*Why* did you say nothing, Mr. Tierney?"

He brushed this aside, reaching up to break a twig from the whitebeam and twirl it in his fingers. "Perhaps I was motivated by my desire to 'play the gentleman,' as you call it. I held some chivalric notion that the woman's honor, such as it is, must be guarded. It meant something to me, if not to you."

Alice wanted to say that it meant something to her—that it meant a great something to her, but she could not form the words.

"Whatever my motives were, Miss Hapgood," Joseph went on, "they little matter now. The second thing I have to tell you is that your secret is known. I warned you I had an informer. And before anyone could be bribed or cajoled, as you suggested some hours since, the seeds of scandal sprouted, as it were." Seeing the dismay and question in her eyes, he added, "I am afraid it was Mr. Geoffrey Wynstanley who raised the alarm, and he did so in the most inconvenient way possible." Briefly he described Mr. Wynstanley's method of discovery and drawing room theatrics, Tabitha's unwilling corroboration, and Miss Birdlow's bosom friend coming to call. "If I hesitate to leave Somerset now, you understand it would be because, however we came to be engaged, I would regret to see you weather scandal alone."

Little dots appeared in Alice's vision, and she experienced a curious sensation that her blood was ebbing from her head. Good heavens. She must not faint! Mr. Tierney would only see it as another feminine ploy. *Dignity, Alice Arbuthnot Hapgood!* Digging her palms into the stump until she feared it would break the skin, she let the pain recall her to herself.

"You regret to leave, and yet you will leave." It came out more accusingly than she intended.

"And return," he insisted. "It is my nature to settle things as rapidly as possible. I like to know my path, that I may embrace it. But I realize this tendency of mine, while making you more comfortable in the long run, might render the next fortnight more difficult."

"It would be no hardship for me to keep to Bramleigh," she replied, her voice seeming to come from far away, "let people talk as they may, but it grieves me that my entire family will be punished and made to suffer through no fault of their own."

"Hear me, Miss Hapgood." He tossed the twig away and came to lean against the tree. "There will be talk, of course. But only have your curate publish the banns this Sunday, and it will be dampened. By the second week it will cease altogether, and by the third, the only talk to oppress you will be your neighbors' congratulations."

"Publish the banns!" she gasped. "Do you think no one would raise objections, believing what they do about how we came to be engaged?"

"No objections that would be substantial, in a legal sense, considering your father and I give our consent."

Alice could not refrain kicking the stump with her boot. If a good fairy had whispered to her some weeks ago that Mr. Tierney would shortly speak such words—of consent and banns and marriage—she would have fallen on her knees in gratitude. But to have the man on such terms! To have him, as it were, not won by her beauty or even moved by their shared passion for nature, but come unwillingly—by duty, and cold honor, and resentment that would grow into loathing. No girl would care for a husband on those terms, be she ever so desperate to marry.

She stood up, impatient to move. "Well! You are right there. What objections could there possibly be, if the important parties are in agreement? Never mind what the prospective bride thinks! You and my father must do as you see fit, Mr. Tierney. Men always have the arrangement of the world."

His head reared back. "Unless they are manipulated by women into a course of action they would not otherwise pursue. You mystify me, Miss Hapgood. Your actions tell me you wish very much to be married—and be damned to the consequences—yet your words give your actions the lie. Which am I to take for truth?"

So much for Alice's vows of dignity. Her eyes flashed, and he thought for a moment she might run at him. When she mastered herself to speak, her voice hummed with anger. "I have wronged you by posing as Arthur Baddely, Mr. Tierney, and I have confessed my wrong and asked your forgiveness. But I persist in denying any and all attempts to manipulate you into marrying me. Can you not understand? Can you not see? I only wanted to have the freedom you desired for yourself: the freedom to make one's own choices and pursue the passion one loves, even in the face of disapproval. For that, and that alone, am I guilty!"

"My pursuits involved no deceit, madam," argued Joseph. "I made my choices, as you say, with the full knowledge and subsequent disapproval of my family. The consequences of my choices were therefore solely mine. I endangered no other."

"Yes, yes, you are right again, of course," Alice declared. "You made your decisions and abided by them like a gentleman. Like a man! But I tell you I could not do the same. A woman *cannot* do the same. I could not defy my father openly, as you did. I could not wander the countryside unaccompanied, as you could. If I wanted to study and learn and explore, I had no choice but to do it as you did it—as a Man!"

They were both of them breathing hard and looking daggers at each other. Alice half expected Mr. Tierney to wring her by the neck for her audacity, and her own hand itched to wipe the tight-lipped expression from his face. Her eyes dropped to those lips, pressed into a thin line. She remembered them otherwise. Responsive, seeking, urgent. And even as she watched them, they fell open slightly.

The world swayed.

She might have taken a step toward him in the next instant, had not the iron-hard ring of his voice frozen her. "You have ably defended yourself, Miss Hapgood. Your vehemence persuades me that, however your behavior might be subject to differing interpretations, *you* believed it justifiable. What more is there to say? Whatever our original motivations and subsequent actions, quarreling this way is bootless and ill becomes us. I...beg your pardon for railing at you in that manner. What is done is done, and we must make the best of it."

She shook her head slowly, as if she were awaking from a deep sleep. No—she was a fool! Had she not told herself that talking only made things worse, in this instance? She had bared her soul to him, and he had rejected it.

When his companion made no reply, Joseph said, "Let us part now, at any rate, with the appearance of civility. If you or your father have word to send me, I can be reached in care of Somerset House. Otherwise, I will return when my affairs are settled and we will be married."

Still she said nothing. Joseph looked one last time on her tense, white face. Then, retreating a step, he made his formal bow, turned on his heel, and strode away.

Alice felt her rage and confusion draining slowly as the minutes passed. She was aware of dim gratitude that she had not hurled herself at Mr. Tierney again and forever sunk in his estimation. Perhaps there was indeed something fundamentally wrong with her, if she could even think of kissing a man who deemed her such a deluded trollop.

"Not that wantonness could sink me much lower in his estimation," she said aloud to the whitebeam tree. Scooping up another handful of the petals, she let them fly. "I fear I did not forward my goal of gaining his respect. I did not overawe him with my dignity. And, my goodness—my tongue grows as sharp as Margaret's. I may not prove the designing harpy Mr. Tierney fears, but I certainly show signs of becoming a proper fishwife."

A breeze rustled the green-and-white leaves overhead and Alice pretended to listen.

"Yes, just so," she murmured, resting her chin on her gathered knees and clasping her arms about them. "It is a shame, indeed, the way things have come about.

"Because I fear I love him more than ever."

CHAPTER FIFTEEN

**Having thus submitted myself to
the Judgment of many Learned Men;
I saw that my journey must not here end.**
—Nehemiah Grew, *The Anatomy of Plants* (1682)

The coach rattled over the stones as it entered Glastonbury, throwing Joseph against the dyspeptic clergyman who had come on at Taunton. Joseph had been grateful for the fellow's discomfort, if only because his companion's sufferings kept him from conversing. Chambers at least knew his master's moods well enough to hold his tongue and had passed the jaunting, jarring hours staring fixedly out the window.

"All out," called the coachman, swinging open the door and lowering the steps. "'At's as far as we'll go, tonight. Nice enough inn, the Pilgrim. Better fleas than the usual."

Joseph hardly noticed the fleas. Or the hardness of the bed, the quality of the ale, the doings of his fellow travelers. As he tossed and turned and waited for the darkness to give way to dim daybreak, his mind worked only on what had passed, his thoughts occasionally drifting and twisting into dreams that gave him no more rest than wakefulness.

Onward the stage trundled.

Glastonbury to Wells. Wells to Bath. Bath to Chippenham. Another fitful night in a roadside inn. Marlborough. Hungerford. The miles grew smoother, but no less long, on the heavily traveled Bath Road. Newbury. Reading. At Reading he was joined by a talkative matron and her two daughters, whose presence forced his man Chambers to an outside seat, and all of whom eyed him with varying degrees of interest and flirtation. Humor flickered through him for the first time since the crisis, as he heard himself saying—in self-defense—that he was recently betrothed. The immediate relief from feminine ambition this afforded him was short-lived, and he was bombarded from Maidenhead onward by questions on his "fortunate lady" and their coming union.

Joseph might have pressed on to London in the long summer evening, but his companions proved too much for him in his present state, and he impulsively got down at the village of Slough, nodding and murmuring noncommittal responses as the ladies called out that he must certainly visit when he was in town—Portland Place, mind—and how they yearned to meet his bride as well!

"I will see about rooms, sir," said Chambers, when Joseph showed no sign of wanting to go inside the Crown. "And shall I order you dinner?"

"Thank you, no. I believe I will stretch my legs. I may be some time."

With the departure of the London coach, the High Street grew quiet again, and Joseph imagined he could make a circuit of all that was to be seen in town several times before he was prepared to retire. Perhaps he would walk so far as Windsor. It could not be above three miles. Turning southward, he came into a wide lane, where only one woman walked ahead of him, small and stooped and carrying a basket. With his quicker stride, he soon passed her, giving her a courteous nod and tip of his beaver hat, but in pausing along the road to regard a trim, ivy-covered house surrounded by outbuildings, she came up to him.

"Does my brother expect you?" the woman asked. She spoke with a barely discernible foreign accent. Graying hair peeped from her ruffled cap, and her face bore traces of long-healed smallpox scars. She reminded Joseph of an elderly pixy.

"Your brother?" he smiled. "Does he live here? No, I'm afraid. I am not acquainted with your brother."

She raised skeptical brows in answer. "Then you are the only one," she said. "For he is a very famous man. An astronomer and composer. The discoverer of what he called Georgium Sidus but others call Uranus. Not many come this way, but they are seeking him. Astronomers, royalty, men of science, foreigners, the curious—even the authors."

Staring, Joseph struggled to contain his surprise. "Do you mean your brother is Mr. William Herschel?"

"There." She nodded. "I knew it would be so. But if I had to tell you these things, you must not be invited to the supper, and so I beg your pardon." Hitching her basket higher up her arm, she made to pass on to the gate.

"Stay—please—if Mr. William Herschel lives here, and he is your brother, you must be Miss Caroline Herschel—the discoverer of comets. I have had the pleasure of seeing records of your observations at Somerset House."

A warm smile broke over her face and made her appear suddenly much younger. "Ah. I was entirely mistaken in my thinking. If you have been at Somerset House, you are a man of science."

"A naturalist, yes," cried Joseph eagerly. "What a signal honor to meet you like this, and what a quiet lane to hold such greatness." His gaze swept the house with renewed admiration. "My name is Joseph Tierney. I work under Sir Edmund Chall of the Royal Society and go tomorrow to London to meet with him."

"Sir Edmund...? Oh, but Mr. Tierney—you will find no Sir Edmund in London."

"Won't I? Then you are acquainted with Sir Edmund as well?"

"A little." She wagged her head at him. "Enough to know he is not in London. Because he is here, Mr. Tierney."

"Here?" echoed Joseph. "In Slough?" His excitement giving way to dismay, he remembered why he sought the company of his mentor.

"At the Grove." She gestured toward the house. "He accompanied Sir Joseph Banks, and they have stopped here for several days on their way to Bath. A meeting of the Philosophical Society has tempted them. And the waters. Sir Joseph will take the waters, you know. The gout."

To this Joseph said nothing, his mind working. Sir Edmund here! Should he send a message in? But how could he interrupt his mentor among these legends of science? How could he confess under the circumstances, that he must leave their ranks before he had even truly joined them?

Raising a hand to his hat again, Joseph withdrew a step. No—it was too bad. He would have to delay speaking with Sir Edmund. He would have to go first to his father, further into Buckinghamshire, and then treat with his mentor afterward.

Miss Herschel had been doing some thinking of her own. "Come. You did not know it, Mr. Tierney, but you are invited to share our supper."

"Impossible. I mean—I thank you sincerely, but I could not think of intruding."

"It will be no intrusion. I may no longer be the hostess here, but I can assure you your welcome. I am certain Sir Edmund will be delighted, and my brother and sister-in-law have long been used to unexpected guests." She gave Joseph a playful poke in the ribs. "And to judge from appearances, you will not eat very much. My dear nephew, who I think is only a few years younger than you, is the same: tall and thin, with the too-much brown hair."

He could think of no polite means of refusal, though he doubted such august men would welcome his unexpected company. Apart from Sir Edmund, whom Joseph had come to know well. A stray corner of his mind wondering if Miss Herschel meant his hair was too much in quantity or too brown in color, Joseph put his hesitations aside and followed her dazedly through the gate.

It was a dinner he would remember his whole life long, for more reasons than one. At the head of the table presided the most famous astronomer in the world, William Herschel, to whom all other leading lights in the field had been forced to give way. To his right was Miss Herschel, of her comets and *Star Catalogue*, the first woman in all Britain to earn a professional salary from the king for contributions to science. To his left was Sir Edmund, organizer of the largest, most ambitious natural history undertaking the country had seen. And across the board sat no less than the President of the Royal Society and onetime explorer with Captain Cook, Sir Joseph Banks himself, who surveyed the young man through keen eyes under heavy white brows. Dazzled as he was, Joseph nevertheless managed some polite talk with the plain and sensible Mrs. Mary Herschel and the Herschels' stripling son John, who would later become as famous as his father in astronomy and chemistry.

The conversation ranged from Herschel's researches into deep space and nebulae, to chemist Humphry Davy's recent illness after his marvelous lectures on electricity, to the ongoing war and its effects on the pursuit of knowledge. Only when the ladies left them to their port (somewhat reluctantly on Miss Herschel's part) and the son John excused himself to his another engagement, did Sir Edmund turn to his protégé. "Now, then, young Joseph. We have traversed the continent, the universe, and the mysteries of the mind of God, and now we have leisure to consider the minutia of the individual. What has brought you in search of me?"

Joseph immediately sat straighter in his chair. "Sir Edmund—yes—perhaps what brings me here would be better left for a private discussion."

"Dear me, dear me," returned Sir Edmund, tapping his glass to have it refilled. "Does Lord Marlton pose an obstacle to the advancement of science?"

"None at all, sir. He has been all that is hospitable and generous."

"You have grown tired of the work, then."

"Of course not. I love it better than ever, sir. Yet..."

"Yet he requires more in the way of stipend," suggested Sir Joseph Banks, his wheeled chair creaking beneath him as he shifted in it. "I have been applied to for monies too many times not to suspect a solicitation under every rock and around every corner."

"Begging your pardon, but you are mistaken in this case," Joseph replied, with some indignation, at which Banks only chuckled.

"No, no," put in Mr. Herschel, wagging his head. "He is a younger man than we. It is not money problems. It is love problems."

To this Joseph gave no answer in words, but the dark color that flooded his face spoke for him.

"Oh, dear," said Sir Edmund. "I see. Forgive these old codgers their banter, Joseph. It has been long since love stirred their blood."

"But not so long that we have forgotten the trouble it causes," protested Herschel. He gave a low whistle and nodded his head toward where the ladies had withdrawn. "Ten, twelve years, I think it took, before she forgave me."

"Surely not," said Banks.

"It is true. If not for their *rapprochement* over John's schooling, it might never have come about." Herschel gave Joseph a rueful smile. "You need not spill your secrets here, Mr. Tierney, but you see you are among old friends. Too old to be surprised or shocked by anything. I was referring just now to my own marriage and the difficulties it caused. For many, many years, my dear sister Caroline was my right hand. My colleague in astronomy, my housekeeper and companion. My manager, of sorts. But when I decided, some twenty years ago, to take a wife, it came as a terrible blow to Lina."

"Some of us did worry what effect your marriage might have on such fruitful collaboration as yours and Caroline's," said Sir Joseph. "We were so glad the work went on."

Herschel nodded slowly. "Ach, yes. The work went on. Such difficult times. And my Mary, always trying to make it right. But Lina decided she could not live at the Grove, if she could no longer be its mistress. Caroline has lodged in the village for some years, Mr. Tierney. A needless inconvenience, I say, when she still spends so great a portion of the day *and* night here, sweeping the heavens."

"You astronomers, male or female, prefer your independence and solitude," Banks teased.

"I am glad that Miss Herschel and Mrs. Herschel are better reconciled now," said Joseph politely.

"That's right," seconded Banks. "And thus you need not fear marriage, Mr. Tierney. Oftentimes a wife brings what can only be a blessing to man of science—that most coveted element: gold."

Banks and Herschel shared a laugh, but when Joseph only looked more ill at ease, Sir Edmund frowned. "Joseph, I say—*are* you planning on taking a wife?"

"Yes, sir."

"I assume, then, that what these cynics here propose bears on your situation—your intended bride will bring you financial independence?"

He took a deep breath and plunged. "I fear not. She is a gentlewoman, to be sure, but almost portionless."

His companions left off their mirth, and Sir Edmund's expression grew serious indeed. "Joseph, stay a moment. If you have gone so far as to engage yourself to this young lady—"

"I have."

"—Then at least resign yourself to a long engagement. Your stipend is, sadly, meager. You may have years of labor ahead of you, not only in the field, but also in securing further commissions and patronage, before you might be able to support a wife and family. You knew this. We had discussed as much."

"Sir Edmund, I remember our discussions clearly. But I am afraid I must—that Miss Hapgood and I—must be married sooner, rather than later."

"Dear God, you've gone and got her with child," declared Banks.

"No!" cried Joseph. "Not at all."

"Well, it wouldn't be such a crisis if you had," Banks resumed, "if you had the means to pension them off respectably."

"He could not behave so, with a gentleman's daughter," Sir Edmund reminded the President. He gave a heavy sigh. "Very well, Joseph. Somehow you have involved yourself with this young lady and you must marry quickly. I confess myself disappointed. You showed immense promise, and I had thought you considered yourself wed to science."

"I did, sir." It was on the tip of Joseph's tongue to reveal all, but if Miss Alice Hapgood was to be his wife, he would not bring further shame on her. That chivalry again, which she made so little of.

"How, then, do you intend to live, if you must give up our project?"

Joseph's heart sank. He had known, certainly, that he must abandon the project, and yet to hear Sir Edmund say so made it suddenly real. In a subdued voice, he answered, "I go from here to Aylesbury. I must inform my father of my change in careers. You know, sir, how he intended me for the church. Now I will gratify his wishes."

"At the cost of your own."

A silence fell, in which the men ranged about the table considered the young man's situation and their own follies of earlier days.

"The living your father has for you," began Sir Edmund again, "it is a good one?"

"I could have no complaint there. As my father has often pointed out, the income would easily allow me to hire a curate without feeling the loss in revenue. But—I am afraid my conscience would not permit me to leave all duties thus. I would feel obligated, as the rector of Stone Halt, to involve myself with my flock, such as it was. Too many parishes suffer neglect in these times, having only a fraction of an underpaid, overworked hireling to attend their needs and well-being."

"I say," spoke up Banks, "I admire your integrity, young man, but there is such a thing as taking it too far. If the living is indeed so bountiful, why not hire a curate, pay him decently, and share the duties? You might still be involved with your 'flock' as you say, while having a reduced, but existent, amount of leisure in your week to pursue your studies. Why, you could be the Gilbert White of Buckinghamshire! You must know his work on Selborne. Both a parson *and* a naturalist was White. Held a handful of livings and still identified some four hundred plant and animal species."

"No wife, however," Sir Edmund pointed out. "And therefore no children. Fewer claims on his time."

"And perhaps Mr. Tierney's intended bride might resent a further division of her husband's attentions," said Herschel. "We men of science, when allowed, would give all our time and thought to our work. Maybe this Miss Hapgood would prefer her husband keep his mind, when not on her, in the religious realm."

"Not a bit of it," Joseph blurted. "Miss Hapgood is as fanatic in her passion for the natural world as any naturalist could desire. She studies it herself—thoroughly and fearlessly. She was—in her fashion—a great help to me in my work."

In any other setting, such a declaration would have been met with doubt and a good share of dismay, but here at the Grove, the reaction was entirely the opposite.

"What? You say she shares your interest in the natural world? In your studies?" asked Herschel, leaning his elbows upon the table.

"'Shares my interest' is not putting it strongly enough, Mr. Herschel, to be plain. Miss Hapgood came to her passion on her own and without benefit of a formal education such as I received. Nevertheless, I would say I have learned as much from her as she from me."

"You take pride in this young lady," said Sir Edmund.

"I—I do," Joseph replied, startled. He had taken pride enough in his assistant when he thought him Arthur, and a boy. "I did not realize it myself until this moment. But, yes, Miss Hapgood—if given the opportunity—could bring as much credit to the field of natural history as—as Miss Herschel has to the study of astronomy."

"A bold claim," said Banks.

"Then why not give her the opportunity?" Herschel murmured. "You do as my friend Sir Joseph advises: you take the living, you hire a curate, you work sometimes for your parish and the rest of the time in your studies, assisted by this admirable wife." He rolled his eyes ceilingward, giving another shake of his shaggy head with its receded hairline. "You do not recognize perhaps a blessing has come to you, Mr. Tierney. How different my own life would have been, could I have found an assistant, a colleague, and a wife—all in the same person!"

Sir Joseph grinned. "Had such been the case with you, William, I imagine you would have discovered twenty more planets and solved all the riddles of the universe."

"Or nothing at all—I would have been so happy," answered his friend. His mood shifted before long, however, and he added regretfully, "Not to mention what Lina would have done."

"Yes," said Banks.

Herschel shook his glumness off. "All is not lost, young man! You do not need this long face. You must retire from Sir Edmund's project or take it up again in Buckinghamshire. Who have you placed in Buckinghamshire, Sir Edmund?"

"No one at present. I calculated we should begin with exploring the farthest reaches from London and work our way inward—"

"Indeed," interrupted Banks, "and a wise strategy, in these uncertain financial times. But here you have a *terra incognita* not two days' ride from London. I suggest you hasten to explore it, Chall. And who better to send than your young lieutenant Tierney, along with his faithful foot soldier of a bride? They will in short fashion map every inch of Bernwood Forest and the Chilterns, down to the number of bird nests in the trees and otters in the rivers."

"Hm." The great naturalist regarded his protégé thoughtfully. "I suppose it might be done. What say you, Joseph? Could you resolve yourself to hire a curate and let him share the burden of the parish? If it allowed you to continue with our undertaking?"

When the young man did not at once reply, Herschel pointed out, "You did not hesitate to share the burden of Sir Edmund's work with this Miss Hapgood. There was no crisis of conscience then. No man can set about great enterprises without the assistance of fellow believers, as it were."

Joseph could hardly argue that he would never have accepted Miss Hapgood's assistance, if he had not thought her a boy, but he understood the astronomer's reasoning. He felt the stirrings of hope, which he feared to indulge. Could he be both? *Do* both? Work with a curate to care for the parish, and work with—his wife—to further the world's knowledge of Nature? There could be no voyages to distant lands, to be sure, but with the war on those were a distant possibility, in any case. And in the meantime—he pictured wandering Bernwood Forest with Miss Hapgood beside him. They were holding hands, and she looked up at him with her wide brown eyes—

Blinking, he came to himself. The other men were talking again.

"—At least until his wife produces ten heirs," said Banks.

"There may only be one heir," Herschel sighed, thinking of his lone son.

"In Otahite, the natives were wont to dispose of infants they were not prepared to raise," Banks observed. "Shocking but practical."

"And, I may be permitted to observe, a custom not found in our own land," interrupted Sir Edmund. He rapped the table. "You need not decide at present, Joseph. As these gentlemen noted, no choice in life is without risk, but I am willing to transfer your work to Buckinghamshire if you are willing to continue with it."

"Sir Edmund. Gentlemen." Joseph's voice trembled, but he saw it brought smiles to the company. "My gratitude would know no bounds. I—that is, my wife *and* I, if we are not buried under ten heirs—would do our utmost to contribute to our country's advancement in the sciences."

"There now. It is settled," said Herschel. He signaled a footman, who rushed forward to have the steering of Banks' chair. "And we had better adjourn to the drawing room because Lina will be anxious to show Mr. Tierney the telescopes before she begins her sweeps."

"By all means," agreed Sir Edmund, grasping Joseph by the shoulder. "We would not deprive our soon-to-be reverend companion this marvelous view of the heavens. If you did not believe it before, Joseph, you soon will—we live in an age of wonders."

Chapter Sixteen

I say that these things will not keep him from
the charectar of a proddigal sun,
who hae spent his time idely abroad.
—Nicholas Owen, *Journal of a Slave-Dealer* (1757)

News of Miss Alice Hapgood's sudden and unconventional betrothal swept the county, but as the Hapgoods kept to Bramleigh, it was not until the Sunday that they reaped the consequences. There were glances and whispers among the parishioners when the Hapgoods entered their pew, and Alice was uncomfortably aware that the church was fuller than she could ever remember it being, but the voices of the newly-devout died away to a hum and ceased altogether when Father Thomas ascended the pulpit.

His sermon was pithy and heartfelt, if anyone had an ear for it, which Alice had not, in her distraction. It was only when Father

Thomas paused and began again that her attention, and that of all around her, returned from distant places: "I publish the banns of marriage between Mr. Joseph Tierney of Stone Halt, Buckinghamshire, and Miss Alice Hapgood of Bramleigh, Somerset. This is the first time of asking. If any of you know cause or just impediment why these two persons should not be joined together in Holy Matrimony, ye are to declare it."

The hum rose again and Alice caught snatches of "scandal" and "fine way to get a husband" and "run wild" and "take a strap to 'er." But as the congregation could not declare any obstacles in the legal sense, Father Thomas was suffered to continue in peace. Peace had departed the Hapgood pew, however. Alice noted a sudden rigidity in her father's posture. She heard Edith whisper to Margaret and be hushed. She perceived Elfrida's head inclining toward her, puzzled brows drawn together.

When the service concluded, the squire and his daughters were met with averted eyes and mumbled greetings from their tenantry. Old Mrs. Bramble favored Alice with a sucked-in lip and sailed past the squire, offering only a huff and a grunt to his "Good day, Mrs. Bramble." Father Thomas alone returned their pleasantries fully, and the squire was quick to take him by the button.

"What means this buzzing, Father Thomas? Why did none hasten to congratulate us?"

The curate glanced toward Alice, and she gave him a tiny nod. The truth had better be told and got over with. "Squire Hapgood, I fear there is word abroad about this match. Such things, swiftly done, will ever draw comment."

"What manner of comment?" pressed the squire, ominously.

"Papa—" Alice reached for his arm. "Mr. Tierney warned me before he left that there would be talk. May I please explain myself to you at home?"

Her father shook off both her hand and her request. "Comment? Talk? Nay—I will know it now! Who begrudges our family our good fortune? The jealous. The envious. Why do you not say a word to that from your pulpit, eh, Father Thomas?"

"Papa!" pleaded Alice. "Do not place Father Thomas in this position. I will tell you all at home."

"You shall tell me all *now*," declared the squire, stumping back to the pew and throwing himself down on it. "Girls, be seated! Elfrida! Margaret! E—E—"

"Edith," supplied Edith.

"Your sister has something to say."

Elfie squeezed Alice's hand in sympathy as she passed, and Edie was all eyes, but Margaret was hard put to hide her eagerness. "I knew there must be more to the story," she whispered.

Alice ignored her. "What Father Thomas would tell you, Papa," she said, "is that Mr. Tierney marries me out of obligation. For honor's sake."

"Yes, yes, we know as much. Can't be grabbing gentlemen's daughters and kissing and palavering without paying the piper."

"But Uncle Alywyn once—*ouch*!" Edith's interjection was nipped in the bud by a timely pinch from Margaret.

"It was not only that, Papa," Alice went on, determined not to be interrupted again, lest her courage fail. "In fact, it was hardly that at all. The truth is, I—I played a deception on Mr. Tierney. He was in want of an assistant in his observing and collecting, as you recall, and I took on that role. But, in order to do so, I—er—borrowed Hal's clothing—without his knowledge—and—and Idisguisedmyselfasaboy."

The very echoes of the church held their breath at this pronouncement. The squire's eyes started from their sockets. Elfrida gasped and covered her mouth with gloved hands. Even Margaret was stunned speechless and hardly felt Edith's tugs on her sleeve.

"I was discovered, it seems. Not by Mr. Tierney, who remained innocent throughout, but by Mr. Wynstanley—Lord Marlton's nephew. It seems he was about one morning, as Mr. Tierney and I counted the species of nesting birds, and somehow he recognized me. When he made his discovery known—before the entire Marlton family, I'm afraid—Mr. Tierney did not believe him. He then...confronted me, that morning you found us, Papa, and I confessed the whole thing. I had not meant any harm by it! Indeed, I wished it might all be forgotten. But Mr. Tierney assured me this was impossible—that if we were not married, my reputation would be ruined."

"Reputation?" roared the squire. "Re-pu-ta-tion?!" Taking his daughter by the ear as if she were five years old, he would have shaken her, had not Elfie thrown herself between them and prevented this fate. "Leave off, Elfie!" he barked. "Get out of the way!"

"Squire, I bid you," cried Father Thomas, "this is a house of God."

"Did you know of this?" bellowed the squire, rounding on the ancient curate. "Of this monstrous, unnatural, ungentlewomanlike, undaughterly behavior?"

"I did."

The squire let fly another roar and might have taken Father Thomas by the ear next, had not Alice untangled herself from Elfrida and flown to his rescue. "No, Papa! I made Father Thomas promise to say nothing! He did not want to keep silent—he did not feel right about it—but he did it because I begged him. It was Father Thomas who told me I must give it up at last and make confession to you, and I intended to, only Mr. Tierney came that very morning before you had risen."

"You will be locked up on bread and water for this, Miss. If that Mr. Tierney were not so complete a gentleman, what do you think might have become of you? Had you no thought to your sisters' reputations, if you cared nothing for your own?" She had braced herself for such a tirade and bore it with lowered head and no trace of defiance. After all, he only spoke truth. Alice had not considered the danger she put her family in by such an escapade—only her own desires. Finding her thus cowed, Squire Hapgood turned the attack to Father Thomas: "And you! Call yourself a man of the cloth! Hiding such a secret from me! Does not a daughter owe her duty to her father? 'Honor thy father and mother' and some such! You must get yourself a new situation—Bramleigh Church cannot afford such a cleric."

"No, Papa!" wailed the girls.

"I am afraid you must speak with the rector about that," replied Father Thomas.

"And I will! If you think you'll be in this pulpit even next week to publish the banns again, you are sadly mistaken. Come, girls. We must tell your mother of this disgrace."

Storming from the chapel and trailed by his four daughters, the squire found the rest of the congregation hastily dispersing outside. "What, hey! Not in a hurry to get to your luncheons today, I see," he called after them. "Get you hence. There will be no more fireworks today."

It required all of three days for the squire to calm down. The threatened imprisonment and starvation of his second daughter proved superfluous, as Alice immediately took to the bedroom she shared with Elfrida and could not be convinced by any arguments of her sisters or notes from her mother to emerge. Button sent up heaping trays of food at regular intervals, but Dorcas carried them back down hours later, hardly touched.

Elfrida sent for Mr. Lewis, who braved the squire's thunderings to examine the unwilling patient. When he descended the stairs a half-hour later, he found himself ambushed by his old friend.

"What means she, holing herself up in this fashion?" demanded the squire. "If she hopes to play something from her mother's bag of tricks, I'll not put up with it."

"Come, Richard," said the doctor, leading the way to the study where they might be out of servants' earshot. "This will never do. Your family was already the talk of the county without adding fuel to the fire. Next they will say you are behaving the veriest Bluebeard and locking your daughter up to starve."

"They should approve, then," retorted his friend. "If you had heard the chattering and whispers at church you would know I might tar and feather the girl and receive only my neighbors' applause."

"A life guided by avoiding the ill-judgment of neighbors would scarce be worth the effort," Mr. Lewis rejoined. "One day they call for Miss Alice's head, and the next they will require yours, especially if outrage turns to pity. For all their disapproval, the fact remains she will be honorably and respectably married. I would not be surprised if those same clucking hens were not gathered to toss wheat at their wedding and congratulate your family on such a prize won."

In answer to this common sense, the squire harrumphed and took up a post by the window, glaring out the murky panes at the lane, as if he might challenge any passerby who dared to glance his way. The doctor waited patiently, examining the few volumes on the shelves put there by one of the squire's more bookish forbears.

"I've not locked her in, whatever she may have told you, Lewis," grumbled the squire. "And if she be pale and half-starved, that is her own choice. Heaven knows enough food has been sent up to supply his majesty's army."

"Miss Alice does not keep to her room for fear of you, I grant you, but from unhappiness."

Another grunt. "And who has she to blame for her unhappiness?"

"She is all too aware that she has created the quandary in which she finds herself. In fact, she told me she could bear it all better, were she not ashamed of having involved both Mr. Tierney and her family in her misadventures."

If the diagnosis of Mr. Lewis was accurate enough, it was also incomplete. Alice did indeed feel dreadfully for what she had done to her family and to Mr. Tierney, but she neglected to mention that a good deal—if not the larger share—of her misery stemmed from a broken heart. She had won her prize of a husband in the worst way imaginable, in a way that made impossible the likelihood of ever winning what she wanted still more: his love. Now she only turned over and over in her mind how it might all be undone, without further harm and family disgrace.

Replacing *The History of the War of Cyprus* on its shelf, Mr. Lewis dusted off his hands. "If you ask me—"

"Didn't ask you. Elfie asked you."

"—If you ask me, Richard," the doctor persevered, "I think the cure for Miss Alice's ailment would be a long walk out of doors—"

"—That she might get into even more trouble out there, hey? I blame you for all. Were you not the one who prescribed such dangers in years past?"

"—and a little forgiveness on your part."

"Forgiveness!"

"Miss Alice has repented fully. She will never do something so willfully reprehensible again. Therefore, forgive her. Forgive her and ignore the gossip and get on with celebrating her wedding! One daughter launched into married life—is that not a marvelous thing, however it was brought about?"

"Mmph."

But the doctor had known his friend long enough to recognize his point had been made. "Come, Richard. Let us release Miss Alice to what will heal her most swiftly. And mind you greet the prodigal with open arms."

Alice was not the only scapegrace that day to be received once more into the bosom of her family. That very afternoon, as she made her way back to the house (having been duly forgiven and her spirits revived by a long, long, solitary walk), she was overtaken on the graveled drive by a man on horseback. Having no inclination for company, she darted into the hedgerow as soon as she heard the trotting hoofs, but she had already been observed.

"Alice! Allie! Ho there!" called the visitor, pulling up. He was a dashing man in his middle thirties, his fine figure tending slightly to paunch and his clothing a few years out of the fashion, but worn with such an air that nobody noticed.

Abandoning dignity yet again, Alice clambered from the bushes, yanking her skirts free of twigs and smiling up at him. "Dear Uncle Alwyn! We did not expect you."

"We Arbuthnots enjoy a good surprise," he beamed, leaning to extend an arm to her. "Hop up with me and we will give my sister a scare."

Alice thought of flashing her stockinged legs to whoever might be abroad in Bramleigh and decided she had offended propriety enough. "I will follow you on foot, Uncle."

"What? Oh! I say—quite the young lady now, are we? Very well. I suppose even little Edith will soon be grown too old to romp about with me. I will have to marry and settle myself, pop out my own progeny, if I am to have any amusement." With a tip of his hat he spurred his horse to a gallop. Alice knew he loved to arrive at Bramleigh with a spray of gravel and shouts up to her mother's window, but in this instance she did not shield her eyes to watch him do so. Her thoughts were occupied with his last remark.

Why, Uncle Alwyn was the very man to advise her! She would not think of approaching him if she sought good counsel, but as she found herself in a distasteful situation—coerced by social conventions into marriage with a man who neither loved nor respected her—Alwyn Arbuthnot's vast experience of scrapes and scandals, from which he emerged but little scathed, was exactly what she required.

Gathering her skirts halfway to her knees and forgetting all about possible onlookers, Alice hastened down the sloping drive.

"Uncle Alwyn, I need your advice."

The ne'er-do-well having been welcomed with varying degrees of enthusiasm by his Hapgood brethren, the invalid sister's quarters visited and the news shared, the luncheon eaten, and some of the squire's ready money transferred to his brother-in-law's capacious pockets, Alice took the first opportunity to draw her uncle aside.

"You see," she began, as they paced the drafty gallery, "—and I hope you will not take it amiss—I have no one else to ask with experience in these matters. You once were engaged, were you not, before the match ran into difficulties..."

"Hey, there. A young miss like you shouldn't know a thing about that."

"But I do, at any rate. And I believe the woman you were engaged to then broke that engagement?"

"The more fool her," Alwyn said, without rancor. He crossed his arms behind his back and stopped before a portrait of Obadiah Hapgood in his Elizabethan ruff. "Married a stooped old codger with a title. Nothing but her gold to hug to her, when all is said and done."

"Yes, too bad for her," agreed Alice to humor him. "But you see, I find myself in a similar situation. Needing to break an engagement, that is."

"That so? Your mother and father had nothing to say against the fellow, other than that he ain't got a fortune. Most of their complaining was about you, Allie." He nudged her and winked. "Taking after your uncles, eh? You'll find the first troubles the sharpest. After that, you may do what you please, and others pretty much make way for you."

"I hope not to make a career of it, Uncle, but this is certainly one scrape I must get out of. I find I cannot marry Mr. Tierney."

"Oh, ho! Too bad, too bad. You must have caught your young man in a flirtation with another chit. Probably harmless, I daresay."

"Oh...no. Nothing of that nature."

"Gambling debts, then? Creditors beating down the door and chasing him about town."

"No, indeed. Not that either."

"I suppose not. Your father wouldn't care for that one." Pretending to inspect the likeness of a plump Hapgood great-great-grandmama with the Squire's beetling brows, Alwyn's mind tiptoed around unpleasant reminiscences of presenting his brother-in-law with promissory notes. "Just so. Then it must be...the gentleman is too handsome for his own good?"

"Well, he is handsome, but nor does the problem lie there."

Having exhausted the objections usually raised against his own person, Alwyn appeared at a loss. "Then why not marry him, Allie? I've got it!"—with a snap of his fingers as he recalled another criticism—"He lacks ambition and direction in life!"

She laughed helplessly and patted her uncle's shoulder. "No, no. Precisely the opposite. I must break the engagement because Mr. Tierney *has* ambition and direction in life, and marriage to me would hinder both of those. He marries me only because he feels it his duty, and though he is a kind man, I would hate to see duty grow to resentment, and resentment to bitterness. So we cannot be married. People will talk—of course—but they are talking already, and thinking ill of me. It will pass. But you must instruct me how to go about it."

"How to go about *what* exactly?" demanded Alwyn, twisting the end of his blond mustache in puzzlement at this lofty talk.

"Why, uncle, I thought I made myself clear," Alice said. "You are the only one I can ask because you are the only one with knowledge of the matter."

Tugging on his arm, she coaxed him into motion again, that she would not have to meet his gaze directly. Her ancestors looked on—disapproving, no doubt—but Alice had enough to do with the living.

"You must instruct me how to jilt him."

Chapter Seventeen

Let brotherly love continue.
— Hebrews xiii.1, *The Authorized Version* (1611)

"Explain this to me once more. I am afraid I have not the pleasure of understanding you."

Joseph stood in his father's study, having chosen a position by the window which overlooked his mother's rose garden. He had seen her out there with the gardeners, ostensibly to trim and stake up the bushes, but he knew from her frequent glances his direction, that she meant to encourage him.

Laying a hand on the handsome globe beside him in its turned oak stand, he gave it an idle spin. How long ago had he stood in this precise spot, facing his father's ire, because he had painted onto the globe's surface the routes traveled by Captain Cook?

"Sir," Joseph began again. "I come to ask you if it be too late for me to take up the Stone Halt living."

"Yes, yes," his father Walter Tierney returned. He was his son's equal for height and build, but his hair was a silvery white at the temples and rather thinner at the crown. "That much I understood. What you have yet to make clear, Joseph, is what you want with it. And why, after such a summary rejection as you gave my career choices for you not six months ago, you should suddenly undergo this turnabout."

"I have decided that I might pursue my naturalist studies while serving as rector of Stone Halt."

"Well, of course you might! Did I not say as much a hundred times? Only get yourself some curate and you may have all the leisure and funds you require to study yourself to the moon and back."

Joseph lowered his eyes to the globe, where his fingers brushed over Labrador and the coast of Newfoundland. "You were right, father," he said slowly.

But the elder Tierney rose behind his mahogany desk, tenting his fingers on the green-leather inlay. "Has Sir Edmund Chall dismissed you from his service?"

"He has not," Joseph answered, as grimly as if the opposite were true. "Sir—let me be brief. I have decided to take a wife. In order to support her and—and any family that may follow after, I find I must increase my income." His father drew a sharp breath, but before he could interject, Joseph went on. "Sir Edmund offers to transfer me to Buckinghamshire, but the stipend, as you know, is modest. Therefore, if the living is still available to me, I will take orders and hire a curate as you suggest, and be both parson and naturalist. Although I do not intend to leave my curate all, or even the heavier portion, of the parish duties."

"Certainly Stone Halt is still yours, if you wish it," his father dismissed the parish with a flick of his fingers. "I will tell the solicitor Bradley to tear up the papers for the sale. And I care not a fig if the curate do all, or none, of the work. But a wife, Joseph? How came this to be? You swore, the last time we spoke, and to your mother's sorrow, that you did not know a time would ever come when you might marry. You disdained the living. You bid me invest all my hopes and expectations in your brother Frederick!"

"I know I did, sir. But you told me, if I may remind you, that a time might come when I would see things differently. And that time has come. Sooner, perhaps, than either you or my mother or I expected, but I hope you will not begrudge me my haste in coming about to your way of thinking."

Walter Tierney only blinked and sunk back into his seat. "I will not, certainly. I confess I was bitterly disappointed when you refused the living. You have always been—that is, your brother Frederick has sorely—Joseph, I hope you have not come to this because of our recent quarrel. I have thought much on it, as has your mother. At the time, I might have said things too harsh in nature—"

"I, too, sir." Striding across the room, Joseph laid a tentative hand on his father's shoulder, and Walter reached up to grasp it with his own.

"I will be glad to have you near again," his father murmured, "whatever the cause." When he turned to look up at his son, his eyes were moist. "But—please—sit. You must tell me of this revolution in your thinking. You must tell me of this young lady of yours."

"Young lady?" echoed a voice as the door flung open. In bounded the glorious Frederick Tierney in his wasp-waisted blue frock coat, cut away to reveal an embroidered ivory waistcoat and buff pantaloons. His boots gleamed; his golden, artfully-tousled hair gleamed; his teeth gleamed in a rich smile for his brother. Despite bearing no aristocratic title and being heir only to a modest fortune (if he did not burn through it while it was yet his father's), Frederick was a darling of the fashionable world. Deemed by many a Golden One, even among the charmed Five Hundred. "Did I hear our father say you have a young lady, Joe?"

"I say, Fred. Have you come from your own hanging?" Joseph indicated on his own throat where his brother's bore a reddish welt, but Frederick met this teasing with equanimity.

"If you knew a thing of the matter, Joe, you would know that the man of fashion must suffer some starch and chafing to maintain his cravat in a snowy cascade. Your own neckcloth is sadly limp. I should dismiss Chambers for such slovenly work, if he were my man."

"How fortunate, then, that Chambers is *my* man." Despite his quizzing of Frederick, Joseph was not well-pleased to see him. He often thought (as did most who knew the Tierneys) that two brothers could not be more unlike. Frederick loved cutting a dash in town, frequenting clubs and horse races and gaming hells and—so rumor said—taking up with the married Lady Wimpole. His parents were both proud of his handsomeness and air, and grieved by his resultant use of them. By contrast, Joseph had been the steadier son, well-enough-looking, studious, and reliable, until his refusal to take orders took his complacent parents by surprise. Frederick had shared their astonishment, having always believed he could never be as good as Joseph and therefore need not bother trying. He found his parents' estrangement from his younger brother as uncomfortable for himself as for the rest of the family. His father began to scrutinize his own activities and express greater dissatisfaction. His mother grew sadder and sadder, and Frederick hated to disappoint any woman. News of Joseph's return from self-imposed exile thus filled Frederick with delight, and he rushed back the thirty-five miles from London the very morning he heard, not listening at the library door beyond two minutes before he burst in.

Repressing a sigh, Joseph shook hands with his brother and turned back to his father. "The young lady's name is Miss Alice Hapgood. She is the second daughter of a respectable squire in Bramleigh, Somersetshire. They have been prominent in the county since before the Conquest, I believe."

"A Saxon shield-maiden!" crowed Frederick. He perched on the corner of his father's desk and threw his beautifully-tailored arms wide in a dramatic gesture. "A West Country warrioress!"

"You have altogether the wrong picture," Joseph said. "Miss Hapgood is somewhat small in stature." So small he mistook her for a pubescent boy, he needed not to add.

"Small, you say? 'Though she be but little, she is fierce,' eh?"

A sudden memory of Miss Hapgood, fists clenched and eyes blazing, confronting him by the whitebeam tree, flashed through Joseph's mind, and he almost smiled. "I thought her timid and shrinking, when first I met her, but I have since discovered she bears a mind quite her own and an admirable firmness in expressing it."

"On the subject of marriage, you must mean," said Frederick. "No discovery there. On that topic most women grow eloquent."

"That is not what I refer to at all," Joseph replied. "Marriage was not something we discussed until—until it was inevitable. I mean that she has a first-rate mind. She can speak with knowledge on anything from animacula to Zizypha, and what she does not know about the natural world, she is anxious to learn."

"Never say you contemplate getting wedlock-bound to this...this encyclopedia, Joe!" said Frederick, alarmed by his brother's seriousness.

"I do," he replied shortly. "If I mistake not, the banns have already been published this Sunday last."

"So soon, Joseph!" said his father.

Walter Tierney proving incapable of further speech for some moments, Frederick gave a low whistle and abandoned his seat on the desk, dropping into the chair beside his brother's. "Very sudden, indeed. Suspiciously so. There is something you are not telling us, Joe. And I believe, unless you intend to pass the remainder of your days solely in scientific conversation, the maiden must have more than a brain that attracts you. Else might you have been content with Sir Edmund and those tedious Royal Society rendezvous. Admit it, brother: this small maiden is also quite the Incomparable. She must be, to have cast the spell over you—the man who once spurned both marriage and career."

Joseph colored with annoyance. "I never spurned a career. I only thought I preferred another."

"A matter of semantics. Do not dodge me. Is this Miss Hapgood fair to look upon, or not?"

"She is—a pleasant-looking young woman."

"Such language! Such passion!" Frederick mocked on. "I see how you have been carried away. Your beloved must be a regular Circe."

"Enough, Frederick," interjected their sire, having recovered. "Joseph, have you her father's blessing on this match?"

Something passed over his son's countenance and as quickly disappeared. "Yes. Yes, we have."

"And—you will pardon me this question of prudence, Joseph—you have agreed on a reasonable marriage settlement?"

His son nodded again. That was to say, he and Squire Hapgood had agreed that Miss Alice was but eight hundred pounds away from being portionless, and that would have to do.

"What cares our Parson Joseph for pounds and shillings?" Frederick rallied him. "Her eyes and form are wealth sufficient, I am sure. Come, Joe. I insist on poetry, on this occasion, at least. Tell me of her yellow tresses—are they 'like a clue of golden thread, most excellently ravelled?'"

"Miss Hapgood has brown hair."

"Miss Hapgood has 'brown' hair, he says—and you call yourself a naturalist! Or you did. The world is well spared your 'brown.' How are we to know if her locks be chestnut or auburn? So brown as to be nearly black, or so little brown they are almost gold?"

"Say chestnut, then," Joseph threw at him.

"And so I shall. Miss Alice of the chestnut hair." Frederick sprang to his feet, pressing the back of his hand to his fair brow. "'But, O those eyes, Miss Alice!...Whence didst thou steal their burning orbs?'"

"Leave off, Frederick. You've been too often in Drury Lane."

"And her bosom!" his brother persevered. "Fain to deny that 'her bosom is love's paradise.'" Cocking an eyebrow at his sibling, Frederick added, "I hope, Parson Joseph, that this hasty match does not come of your romping too liberally in love's paradise."

"It does not," Joseph grated out. "As I said, Miss Alice Hapgood looks well enough, but she has other qualities that compel me to believe she will make a fitting wife."

"Ugh. That I might be spared such love," grimaced his brother. "You speak of the girl as if she were a new lens for your microscope. No, I pray you—do not suffer us to endure any more of your babblings of passion, brother. How Miss Hapgood possesses superior powers of magnification or how a union of two weaker lenses—read, *husband and wife*—minimizes spherical and chromatic aberrations."

Despite his unwillingness to subject his approaching union to scrutiny, Joseph could not help laughing at Frederick's antics. Only their father remained sober.

"Leave off, Frederick." Walter Tierney paced the room thoughtfully, hands clasped behind his back. Outside, his wife straightened up and relinquished the basket of roses to the undergardener. Her gaze met her husband's, and he smiled reassuringly, giving a nod before turning back to Joseph. "My dear son, your mother and I will welcome any bride you bring to Stone Halt. Welcome and love. We have faith in your judgment and your character. But I know your mother—that *we*—would not feel at ease, if we felt you married only from a sense of duty or…prudence. We would be glad enough of your return to these parts and taking orders. Finding a wife could well wait, especially if you felt no affection for this Miss Hapgood."

A silence fell in the study. Walter waited for his son's reply, and even Frederick held his tongue, sparing only an amused thought that he himself would never be offered such *carte blanche* in choosing a wife. Rather, his own liaisons were wont to provoke tear-stained letters from his dear mother and lectures from his father. Not that Frederick could blame them. The simpering debutantes in white muslin with their five thousand pounds apiece bored him silly. He much preferred women with some knowledge of the world and sympathy for men's foibles—alas, that such women tended to be married! Or perhaps it was all to the better, as Frederick was then not required to offer for them. Not like poor Joseph. Joseph might not own it, but Frederick had not been his older brother for twenty-four years without knowing when the young man was in a coil. Somehow this Miss Alice Hapgood had him in her power, Frederick was certain.

Joseph gave his head a shake, but his thoughts remained snarled as undergrowth. Did he have affection for Miss Alice Hapgood? Who, indeed, *was* Alice Hapgood? Joseph's memories of her—in the Bramleigh drawing room, at the assembly, by the whitebeam tree—were inextricably tangled with his memories of Arthur Baddely. He might boast of her fine mind and firmness of expression to his family, but was he describing Miss Hapgood or Arthur, or both? Or neither? Was the real Miss Alice Hapgood shy and awkward, or was she clever and resourceful and full of fun? Had she laughed behind her hand at deceiving him, or had she admired him? Was she scheming, as the world would have it, or was she, as she claimed, sadly trapped by the limitations placed on her sex? Had her kiss—their kiss—been the product of design, or of innocence?

For just an instant he allowed himself to relive that kiss. (He blamed Frederick for drawing his thoughts down that avenue, though they went swiftly enough, like horses too long held in check.) He thought of the softness of her mouth and warmth of her breath. The stranglehold around his neck which yet did not bring her close enough. The silky feel of her hair—her chestnut hair—as he buried his fingers in it.

Mrs. Tierney's high, clear voice carried to them, and Joseph looked over to see her near the window. "Make it three vases on the sideboard in the dining room, Falkes, and two by the entrance."

They must wind up their discussion speedily, or his mother would come in, and Joseph would have it all to do over. If he could make his father comfortable, however, Walter could win over his wife with ease.

"You and Mother need not worry," said Joseph at last, "about my feelings for Miss Hapgood." Drawing in a steadying breath, he prepared himself to lie to his father and brother, and a half-smile curled his lips as he recalled how ill his betrothed had gone about it when dressed as Arthur. She panicked. She over-reached. She told lies that required more lies because they gave rise to questions. Joseph would not make those mistakes.

"I may not be able, as Frederick is, to rhapsodize and spout poetry," he said, "but I can assure you of this: I love Miss Hapgood and expect, with time, to love her still more."

From the immediate softening of his father's features and the surprise apparent in Frederick's, Joseph realized he had succeeded. Why, lying was not so hard to do, after all! Were it not that he wished he might hereafter have only truth from his intended's lips, Joseph would be tempted to offer her some instruction in the practice.

The trick, he would say, was to meet your interlocutor's gaze without fear, to breathe evenly, and finally, in telling the lie, to adhere as nearly as possible to the absolute truth.

CHAPTER EIGHTEEN

...No more of this, God may you bless;
Your tale's a nuisance, you annoy us by
Such talk, it isn't worth a butterfly.
—Chaucer, *Prologue to* The Nun's Priest's Tale (1386)

Another week passed, and nearly another, and Joseph had yet to leave Buckinghamshire. First there was the testimonial from the master at Emmanuel to be obtained, after Joseph wrote with explanations of his change in plans. Then there was the appointment with the bishop, that Joseph might be given his ordination exam. He feared the prelate would quiz him on arcane church history and theological fine points, but the jolly man merely regaled him with tales from his own days at Jesus and congratulated Joseph on his good fortune in securing so comfortable a living.

"Not an easy thing, in these days," Bishop Arnot sighed. "Most men have to scramble for enough curacies to keep life and limb together. You'll keep a curate, naturally? If your father has no one in mind for the post, I know of several gentlemen who would welcome the opportunity to put themselves forward..."

Then there was the parsonage to inspect and workers to be hired before it could be occupied again. Though modest in size and haphazardly designed, the house was comfortable, with the windows of the study facing south and east, and plenty of shelves and cabinetry to store years' worth of specimens. As Joseph walked the grounds with his father and Stone Halt's overseer, nodding and asking occasional questions as they surveyed the gardens, the orchard, the small dairy, and the condition of the surrounding wall, he found himself wondering about his intended bride. About *Alice*. He should call her that now, should he not, as they would be married shortly? He should call her Alice, and she should call him Joseph. Somehow he had forgotten to ask her if he might address her by her Christian name. Would...Alice...like it here? Would she like leaving the woods and wetlands and streams of her corner of Somerset, which she knew so well, for the rolling landscape of Aylesbury?

He found himself impatient to show his home country to advantage and planned which of his favorite childhood haunts he would share first. He knew every inch of Stone Halt and the beginnings of the neighboring Chilterns as she did Bramleigh, and he would have treasures as hidden as her Devon whitebeam to reveal. So much for nature. How Alice would like her share in the duties of the parish, however, he knew no better than how he would like them himself, but he judged from her close relationship to this "Father Thomas" that she would have no objections on religious grounds. Then there would be the housekeeping. If, as Joseph suspected, she had no great passion for it, at least "so comfortable a living" as Stone Halt would afford them as many, if not more servants than the Hapgoods enjoyed at Bramleigh. And Bramleigh was clean and vittled enough. It did not compare with the luxuries of Pattergees, to be certain, but Joseph hazarded that Alice would be as indifferent as he to opulence.

As the days went by, he thought more than once of writing to her. Only the pain and confusion of their last encounter prevented him. He could describe how he had been occupying his time easily enough, but how would he begin the thing? "I realize, madam, that we parted on bitter terms..." or, "Although, madam, I accused you of entrapping me, and you accused me of merely 'playing the gentleman' rather than actually being the gentleman, I hope you are well and write to inform you..."

No.

It could not be done.

When he was finished here, he would return to Somerset, and they would begin again. Joseph had determined on it. If they were to be married, however their union had come about, they must make the best of it, for their own sake and for the sake of the parish. He did not doubt that they had enough in common to make a life together, even if the timing of that life had not been left to him.

In a shorter space than he would have believed possible, Joseph found his anger and dismay over the situation not only faded, but entirely gone, to be replaced by a curious contentment. Even eagerness.

His time at Slough accounted for much of this change of heart. If the great William Herschel could work side by side with his sister, year after year, unraveling the mysteries of the universe, could not Joseph and Alice do the same, in their smaller, more earthbound manner?

But the encouragement of those he revered was not all, he admitted.

There was the easy rapport they shared when working alongside each other. Well—the rapport Joseph and *Arthur* shared. But surely that could be recaptured, even if it was Alice beside him? Surely they could learn to abandon the ceremony and rules of propriety that hindered men and women, and jest and interrupt and correct and collaborate, as they once had. That hope accounted for much of Joseph's change of heart.

Much of it.

As for the rest—what portion, he asked himself, was due to Miss Hapgood's personal appeal? That she was indeed appealing to him, he could not deny. Once he allowed himself, the number of times his mind returned, unbidden, to the soft curve of her neck and the shape of her lips, the richness of her hair, was proof enough of that. Joseph realized he was fast finding it difficult to recall why, precisely, he objected to losing Arthur's assistance, after the shock of Arthur's transformation into Alice was got over. And, for her part, Alice must not find him physically repulsive, if she was so determined to marry him. Lasting unions had been built on less.

It would have to serve.

Still, he did not write.

But on his final morning at Stone Halt, he found that Miss Hapgood had been doing some thinking of her own, coming to rather different conclusions, and she had not waited to share them.

"Post for you, sir."

"Thank you, Wright." The missive from Sir Edmund Chall had come directly to Walter Tierney's home, but the other letter and parcel were sent first to Somerset House and forwarded from there to Stone Halt. Joseph did not recognize the handwriting on the brown paper of the flat parcel, but when he saw the address he hastily excused himself from the breakfast room for the relative privacy of the east drawing room.

Throwing the letters aside, Joseph untied the string on the parcel. He found rolled inside an illustration of three butterflies: a Grizzled Skipper, a Marsh Fritillary, and a Green Hairstreak. They were meticulously and accurately rendered in black ink, and then most delicately brought to life with watercolors. He noted that Miss Hapgood—that *Alice*—not only drew the butterflies as they appeared in the case he brought her many days past, but she added small details from where they might habitually be found. There was dried grass beneath the Skipper. A violet Devil's Bit flower beside the Fritillary. Thorny brambles around the Hairstreak. She must indeed have worked with her sister because the initials "A.H." and "Ed. H." appeared in the lower right corner of the sheet.

Joseph admired the work some minutes, even thinking how he might have it framed and hung in the parsonage to welcome Alice there, before he shook out the brown paper that had enclosed it and discovered a second, folded sheet. A note. In the same neat, simple, and small writing from the parcel, he read:

My dear Mr. Tierney,

I pray you forgive the forwardness of my writing to you. You did not say precisely how long you might be absent, and I find myself too anxious to wait longer. When you read what I have to say, you will certainly agree that it is better you know these things beforehand.

I thank you again for your offer of marriage. I realize that, for your honor's sake, you felt you had no alternative, and yet you overcame much and sacrificed much to engage yourself to me. If I have appeared disdainful or ungrateful for this in the past, I once again beg your pardon.

As you predicted, the wave of scandal has washed over us and begins to recede. The banns have been published, and everyone only awaits your return for us to be united.

But, Mr. Tierney, despite everything—I find I cannot bring myself to marry you. It is impossible, after such a

beginning of deception, mistrust, and reproach. I there-
fore release you from your obligation.

I will naturally say nothing of this to any beside your-
self until you have reappeared in Somerset, lest you be
accused of abandonment or breach of promise. Then
you may declare that I have jilted you. You may say
that you were content to marry me, but I chose disgrace.
After we have taken this step, I need only weather a few
more weeks of gossip, and you will be free to go about
your life as you had planned, before I interfered.

Please send word to Bramleigh when we may expect
you. Do not fear another unpleasant interview with me.
When I know your call to be imminent, I will prepare
my father, and you need only speak with him.
As I have said before, I greatly admire your work and
wish you all future success. May God bless you.

I am, sir, very sincerely your most humble servant,
Alice Hapgood

It required several readings before Joseph's brain could compre-
hend this extraordinary message. If she had schemed to entrap him,
why would she relinquish the prize at the eleventh hour? Did she

doubt he would keep his word? Did she think it thus necessary to lure him back, with promises of freedom?

He read the missive again, a creeping unease filling him. Her words could be subject to an entirely different interpretation. Far from being another subterfuge, they could be the bare truth. But if she wrote the bare truth now—here his unease mushroomed into outright apprehension—would it not be likely that she had spoken truth all along? That she had been innocent of all deceit, save posing as Arthur, in order to pursue her love of nature? If it were so, he had wronged her gravely. If it were so—

He dashed into the hallway, calling for his man.

"I say, Joe—what do you mean by this confounded hallooing, so early in the morning?" grumbled Frederick as he descended the staircase. Although he was glorious, spotless from his golden hair and bottle-green coat to his gleaming boots, he considered eleven o'clock a deucedly provincial hour to be about and only rose by then at Stone Halt to oblige his father.

"I must be gone. On the instant."

"Gone where?" demanded Frederick, catching his arm. "Has our uncle popped off at last?"

"Uncle? What? No—I must catch the morning stage and return to Somerset at all speed. There you are, Chambers. Please have my trunk and valise packed immediately. If you cannot make the stage, I will take the valise, and you may follow as soon as possible."

"Brother, I thought you a man of sense," drawled Frederick as he watched Chambers scurry back up the stairs. "How can you talk of speed and taking the stage in the same sentence? If you wish to be in

Somerset this sennight, you had better let me drive you in my gig. I wager I could have you to Taunton by tomorrow eve."

His features clearing, Joseph clapped Frederick by the arms and narrowly avoided embracing him. "Say you'll take me all the way to Patterton, and I'll buy you the finest supper the Wheel and Crown affords."

"Supper? Nonsense. Rather, say you will introduce me to the finest heiress the county affords and I will consider myself recompensed. But you must explain yourself, Joe. Whence this haste? Has the girl bolted, your peerless betrothed?"

"Had she merely bolted, I might pursue her," replied Joseph, already turning to go in search of his father. "She's done worse." His hand on the door of the breakfast room, he paused and looked back. "She's decided to be noble."

Only two people besides its recipient knew of Alice's letter. Her uncle Alwyn, who shook his head over it (—"Too long by half. I would not be surprised if he threw it in the fire after the second paragraph"—) and her sister Elfrida.

"Alice, dear," said the latter, upon laying it down and crawling into the bed beside her, "my eyesight must be as dim as you all claim it to be. I think I read that you mean to end your engagement."

"I do." Alice leaned to blow out the candle, but Elfie stopped her and drew very near, her limpid blue eyes searching her sister's.

"You have not been confidential with me for some weeks. I know it has been a dreadful time for you. A trying time. But how I wish you would trust me with your heart, as you were used to do."

"Oh, Elfie," Alice gulped. How much might have been avoided if she only had, as Elfie fondly declared, been truthful! The tears which threatened constantly of late welled up, but Alice dashed at them with the end of her braid. "Breaking my engagement will bring further scandal on the family, I fear, but I hope it will be brief in duration."

Elfie snapped her fingers at this. "What care I for further scandal, as you call it? Another unpleasant Sunday in church and whispers behind our backs until something new claims our neighbors' interest. Besides—*refusing* to marry Mr. Tierney cannot compare to the outrage of how your betrothal came about. You will only add to our disgrace by increments."

"Why, that's just what Uncle Alwyn said—that the first scandal was always the worst."

"And he would know better than anyone, except perhaps Uncle Alec," Elfrida agreed dryly. She squeezed her sister's arm. "I mean, Alice, I wish you would tell me why you must jilt Mr. Tierney. Do you not feel you like him already and could learn to love him?"

Alice rolled away from that steady gaze and plumped the pillow beneath her cheek. "Yes."

"There! He seems a kind, educated, steady young man. And certainly handsome. How winning his eyes are when he smiles! I very much enjoyed the supper dance with him at the assembly some weeks ago."

The tart reply of "Then you had better marry him yourself!" nearly escaped Alice's lips, but she succeeded in smothering it by screwing her mouth up and pushing it into the pillow. Practical Elfie only meant to be comforting.

"If only *you* could have cared for him, Elfie, instead of me!"

"I might have," her sister replied in her matter-of-fact way. "If circumstances had thrown Mr. Tierney and me together more often. But I suspect I could never share his interests as you do, Alice. To be sure, I asked questions and recalled little bits from being around you over the years, but feigning any deeper interest in larks and larvae would have grown tiresome."

To this, Alice said nothing.

"And think how pleasant to be a clergyman's wife," Elfrida went on, "if one is not too poor. To keep a snug parsonage and call upon the members of your flock and perhaps teach a school."

More silence.

Elfie prodded her. "I know from your avowal earlier that you do not object to Mr. Tierney's vocation. Or do you, on second thoughts?"

"I do *not* object to his vocation," insisted Alice, rolling back to face her. "That is exactly it. Don't you see, Elfie? Mr. Tierney's true calling is not the Church—it is the study of the natural world—the larks and larvae! If he were not in this embarrassment now—if I had not landed him in this embarrassment—he would be free to pursue his true vocation."

Elfrida huffed out an impatient breath. "Mr. Tierney is a man grown, Alice. You speak of him as if he had no choice in the matter."

"He hadn't."

"And I say he had!" Elfrida sat up and gathered her knees to her. "Why, if I were Mr. Tierney, and I felt everyone expected me to marry some girl I didn't want to marry, I would drag it out as long as I could. I would go away for a while, and see if those expectations didn't die a natural death on their own. And if they didn't when I came back, I would engage myself, but say it would be ever so long before the marriage could take place because I was a naturalist and couldn't support a family, see? Then, I would sign on with some long expedition to the Antipodes and hope, in the three years I was gone, that the odious girl would meet someone she liked better."

She succeeded in rousing Alice from her dejection enough that Alice swung a pillow at her. "Elfie, you are as bad as our uncles, if you would behave so dishonorably!"

"Who said anything about behaving dishonorably?" Elfrida countered. "Nothing I suggested would be dishonorable. Can I help it if Mr. Tierney, beside being handsome, educated, and steady, is also something of a gudgeon?"

Now Alice was on her knees, eyes firing indignantly. "He's not a gudgeon! You take that back or I will tie your braid to the bedpost." The two sisters wrestled, half in earnest, half giggling, until the bedclothes tumbled to the floor and Elfrida was sitting on the smaller Alice.

"Admit it, Alice—you have other reasons to jilt Mr. Tierney than the noble ones. If you do not confess, I will put it about that you were ashamed of how easily you gulled him and could not bear to tie yourself to such a simpleton."

"You wouldn't dare!" Alice wriggled to no avail, kicking her feet on the bolster, and then gave in when Elfrida threatened to drip candle wax on her. "Very well, you brute. I have another reason."

Her sister released her instantly, reaching for the tangled linens and sitting back demurely against the headboard.

"Sham," grumbled Alice. "The entire world thinks you so mild and proper, but you are ruthless as Tamburlaine."

"Tamburlaine and I would call it being practical," replied Elfrida, unperturbed. "Only come closer when you confess—I should like to see if you lie."

As she obeyed, Alice muttered another imprecation, this time related to Elfrida's weak eyesight, which the latter just as serenely ignored. She waited, and Alice spoke at last. "You see, I cannot bear for Mr. Tierney to marry me from duty or pity or honor. To save my reputation or his reputation."

"And why can you not? Duty and honor are no poor foundations. They speak much of his character."

"Because I want him to love me!"

"Who says he will not?" said Elfrida, with a shrug. "In time."

"He thinks me a schemer—a liar!" cried Alice.

"If he said so, in so many words, you might make allowances for the suddenness of it all. And you did lie to him. To all of us."

At this her sister scowled. Elfie and her practicality! She was indeed as merciless and inexorable as Tamburlaine. "Yes. All right. The lying bit was true, in the main," Alice conceded. "And I've apologized all 'round for it. But to accuse me of scheming! He is as bad as Edgar Mandlebert with Camilla! You cannot expect me to love him for thinking so, and you cannot expect he will grow to love me, if he thinks me capable of such intrigues."

"Camilla loved Edgar, despite his constant suspicions."

"Camilla," pronounced Alice, "was a chuckle-head."

Elfrida smoothed the tendrils which had escaped her sister's braid. "Sweet Alice—why do you not admit it? What is most wounded by Mr. Tierney's offer is your pride. You would have him think well of you—love you—and you cannot bear it that he does not. Therefore you cast him off."

Burying herself in her sister's shoulder, Alice sniffed. "It sounds wretched when you put it so baldly, Elfie, but I suppose that is the crux of it. You would not understand—you are so beautiful that everyone loves you at once. I saw how Mr. Wynstanley stared! And even Mr. Tierney would not have kicked up such a fuss, I imagine, if he discovered Arthur Baddely to be *you*."

"Perhaps you overrate the power of beauty, my love. Mr. Wynstanley's attentions passed as swiftly as they came, and for all Mr. Tierney's admiring looks, they never struck me as more than that. He admired me as he admired the butterflies he gave you—as pleasing examples of Nature's variety."

To this Alice only made a face, which Elfrida intuited, even if she did not see it. She gave her sister a shake. "Come now. If you love Mr. Tierney and wish him to love you, I advise you to tell him, when he comes, that you have changed your mind about jilting him. If he thinks you inconstant, he can just add that to the list of your flaws."

"No! It cannot be done, Elfie. Just let it be."

Elfrida squeezed her sister. "All right! I give up. If you insist on making yourself miserable, do so. I daresay you will recover eventually. We all will. Whatever your reasons, if you want to be rid of Mr. Tierney, be rid of him. I will back you against Papa, and the whole matter will be forgotten in six months. Twelve at the utmost. In the meantime, you must put on a happy face and be seen in the neighborhood and remind all those gossips what a good girl you are. I will help you trim your yellow silk for Pattergees' Midsummer Ball."

"No ball! I cannot be seen at a ball!" protested Alice.

"Yes, ball. If you have been accepting Uncle Alwyn's advice, I insist you temper it with my own. We Hapgoods have been skulking too much at home of late. Your recent conduct apart, we are a respectable family of long-standing, and people would do well to remember it."

Alice saw a most Tamburlaine-like line of jaw appear through Elfrida's soft cheek and abandoned further argument. She sighed. While she dreaded the remarks and cutting looks that might be directed at her if she attended the ball, she could not condemn her family to social exile. Soon enough, she and Uncle Alwyn would execute the second part of their plan, and Alice would be too far out of sight and mind to inflict any more damage on the beleaguered Hapgoods.

"Very well," she said. "The yellow silk and the Midsummer Ball. Thank you, Elfrida."

CHAPTER NINETEEN

Why this is verie Midsommer madnesse.
—Shakespeare, *Twelfth Night* (1623)

The village of Patterton was nearly deserted in the long twilight of Midsummer Night when Frederick and Joseph Tierney drew up in the inn-yard. They soon discovered that whoever was not gone in attendance at the Pattergees Midsummer Ball was gone to wait on those in attendance.

"You may get me a room, to be sure," Frederick answered the sour bar-keeper compelled to double as ostler and host, "but I will not retire there anytime soon. Let us see this ball, Joe! If these Marlton folk be as grand as you say, one guest more or less will make no difference."

"With our road dust, we are hardly presentable," answered his brother doubtfully. "And given the circumstances under which I left, I hesitate to make so public a reappearance."

"Pshaw!" Frederick dismissed this. "Utter nonsense. Weeks have slipped away, and with them the uproar—did not your delinquent beloved say so much?" Mischievously he began to whistle Handel's "See, the Conquering Hero Comes" as he followed the bar-keeper up the narrow staircase. "Come—we'll use my room here to rig ourselves out. I daresay I can tie your cravat better than that man of yours. And I have won our bet; therefore you must present me to the reigning heiress."

The great house at Pattergees glowed with the light of hundreds of candles. Stringed music drifted through the open windows to the wide, arcing drive where carriages drew up to deposit their passengers. Lord and Lady Marlton, the Honorable Mr. and Mrs. Birdlow, and the Honorable Miss Birdlow, rustling and glinting in their finery and jewels, anchored the base of the sweeping staircase to greet each guest with courtesy, though Miss Birdlow was obligated to abandon her post after an hour, that she might open the ball.

The Hapgoods drew up in their creaking barouche, with the squire driving and Hal scrubbed up and wigged to serve as footman. Mrs. Hapgood had, of course, pleaded her health and declined the invitation, and Lady Marlton omitted Miss Margaret and

Miss Edith after some discussion with Miss Birdlow, who declared them "too young by half, and certainly not out." Elfrida and Alice were glad to sit facing forward with their gowns uncrushed, and the novelty of viewing the balmy, dusky world from such a perch almost made Alice forget her dread of going once more into society. To the squire's annoyance, Alwyn Arbuthnot lounged across the rear-facing seat, regaling his nieces with tales of balls and London crushes past, assemblies glittering with the wealthy and renowned.

"Lady Molyneux favored me particularly, when I was last at Almack's," drawled Alwyn. "Said I had an air—and she would know, being married to Lord 'Dashalong' himself."

"Air, my foot," grumbled the squire, audibly enough. "Only air he knows of is which way the wind blows." The sight of his brother-in-law tricked up in his best finery (finery Bramleigh rents conferred upon him) provoked the squire, and he told himself for the thousandth time that Alec and Alwyn must be made to stand upon their own feet now, howsoever their sister might weep for them.

If Lord and Lady Marlton were surprised to see the Hapgoods ascend their front steps and join the line of those paying their respects, they were too well-bred to show it. Others, glancing between the two parties, took their cue from their hosts and nodded deliberately at the squire's party, their eyes just flitting to the blushing Miss Alice Hapgood and skittering away, to be hidden behind fans. What comments followed, made in low whispers, Alice could not catch—nor did she wish to.

"Dear Squire," said the viscount, extending a gracious hand while his wife curtsied, "what a pleasure to welcome you under my roof again. It has been too long. And two of your lovely daughters—Miss Hapgood, Miss Alice Hapgood. We congratulate you on your recent betrothal, Miss Alice. Mr. Tierney is a fine young man."

"We wish you very happy," added Lady Marlton, unable to equal her husband's warmth. Her nose tipped higher as she acknowledged Alwyn Arbuthnot's exaggerated bow. There was a time when his boasted "air" made her own heart beat faster, but that was long ago, and all present, not excepting Alwyn himself, would declare she had made the wiser choice.

After their father did his duty in greetings and marching a matron or two about the floor, he escaped to the card room. Alice was relieved to see Elfrida did not lack for partners. Whatever damage Alice had done the family reputation, the hospitality of Pattergees was sufficient to counteract, although offers to partner Alice herself were in short supply. The portly Mr. Birdlow claimed her for a set and conversed perseveringly on dog breeds. Norman DeWitt who danced two sets with Elfie and returned her to Alice's side found himself unable to avoid asking the sister as well, as Elfie was abruptly whirled off by the next gallant. But after these two episodes, Alice passed a half-hour in silence beside deaf Mrs. Trumbull, the grateful recipient of summer apricots and autumn haunches of pork from Bramleigh. Mrs. Trumbull, who would make no quibbles about being seen with the squire's wayward girl. Alice listened to the woman's chatter penitently, but she was young enough to find the decline in her own popularity humiliating. She even wished Mr. Tierney were there because he would be obliged to dance with her until she officially jilted him. *But I will never have the opportunity to dance with Mr. Tierney now*, thought Alice, twisting her gloved fingers.

The fog of depression which had enveloped her in recent weeks descended again. She heard Mrs. Trumbull's talk of elderberry wine no more; her eyes stared blindly at the couples prancing and twirling to the intricate patterns.

"What's this? Such a long face at a ball?" teased her uncle, appearing before her. "Good evening, Mrs. Trumbull. I hope you can bear to part with your companion because I mean her to stand up with me for the cotillion."

Mrs. Trumbull, not hearing a thing, nodded and waved at the dashing man as he gave Alice a bracing shake of the shoulder and led her to the floor.

"Can't have this, Allie," said Alwyn, as they took their place with the other couples in the square. "No moping, your first time out. Little smile and glow. There."

Rousing herself, Alice favored her uncle with a smile that nearly reached her eyes. He was right after all—she found it better to be dancing, concentrating on the chassé and balance and rigadoon. While she suspected Uncle Alwyn asked her in order that he might clasp hands with Miss Porterworth, to whom he had not been introduced, she saw he also meant to cheer her and remind her of his advice. They had neither time nor privacy for discussion during the dance, but when he saw Alice's efforts, her cheeks growing pink and her smiles almost genuine, he took her hands in the cross and said, "Well done, girly! That's the way." And when they stood together again before the final figure, she whispered, "Thank you, Uncle! May I speak to you after the next set?"

"Only let me secure Miss P for the supper dance, and you may speak to me till my ears fall off," was his low reply. "And don't call me 'uncle' here—it ages me."

A country dance followed. Uncle Alwyn—*Alywn*—and Miss Porterworth met in both-hands-round, and he squeezed the lady's hands so hard she squeaked, feigning indignation before letting loose a cascade of giggles. Clearly Alwyn Arbuthnot saw fair to boast another conquest. Mrs. Lade nearly toppled her feathered headdress when she marched with her partner beneath the archway of the other couples' arms. Then Mr. Harbo stumbled during the gallop and trod upon Roscoe DeWitt's shining buckled shoes, and the latter was forced to transform the oath that escaped him into a more proper "Odd rabbit it!" By this point Alice was giggling and clapping with the rest, her notoriety and proposed future scandal forgotten in the fun of the moment. Her uncle took her hands when it was their turn to lead the reel, and off they went, circling and interlacing with the others, laughing when they came together.

Mr. Joseph Tierney paused at the foot of the room, starting when he saw that glowing face upturned to her partner. It had been re-markably easy to single out Miss Alice Hapgood in her butter-yellow silk, matching slippers flying, hair curled and dressed and wreathed with flowers. Though when she arrested him, he could hardly say how he recognized her. Could that radiant young woman truly be Miss Alice Hapgood? Joseph had only seen, to this point, the unapproachable aspects to her character: shyness, diffidence, mortification, resentment, anger. Perhaps as Arthur Baddely she had looked this eager on occasion—the time she found a baby badger eating grubs came to mind—but he could not even picture this young lady in Arthur Baddely's floppy disguise at present. And who—managing to tear his eyes from his soon-to-be-erstwhile fiancée—was the man so happy to coax this sunbeam into appearing? Joseph failed to identify him from his previous time in Somerset. Whoever he was—some big, bluff fellow with dandyish aspirations and an overly familiar manner—Joseph detested him. Look how he put a hand to Alice's waist and leaned down to murmur something! And how she plucked at his sleeve, as they made their way to the French doors that opened on the gardens.

"Whew. Looks like she's found metal more attractive," said Frederick at his elbow, his gaze having followed his brother's. "His tailor's done his level best, but the man still smacks of brewer from Bristol. Which doesn't say much for the lady's taste. And you called her noble!"

The hot words bubbling to Joseph's lips had to be swallowed because the viscount descended upon them, his face lighting. "Mr. Tierney! You are welcome here again. How glad I am you could grace our ball."

"Lord Marlton. Forgive me for not writing to inform you of my return. I arrived here sooner than I expected because my brother was so good to drive me." Masking his impatience, Joseph performed the necessary introductions, barely attending his lordship's comments on how little the brothers resembled each other, how Mr. Frederick

Tierney was also welcome to stay at Pattergees however long he might be visiting his brother, and did he enjoy shooting, fishing, dancing, etc. etc.

"You will excuse me," Joseph said abruptly, interrupting the pleasantries. "There are matters I must tend to at once."

"But you have only arrived! Lady Marlton will wish to greet you," protested the viscount, watching Joseph's back disappear through the guests crowded along the edges of the ballroom.

"We are wont to joke in my family, of Joseph's narrowness of focus," said Frederick, his light manner soothing Lord Marlton's ruffled feathers.

"He will dance, surely? After he has tended to whatever could not be put off?"

Frederick just glimpsed his brother's brown hair and quick stride stepping through the French doors after Miss Alice and her partner, and he turned with a heartier smile to his companion. "Certainly, certainly," he assured his lordship, directing his attention back to the dancers. "But in the meantime I will do the courtesies for both of us, if I may. Many will vouch that I far outshine my brother in treading a measure."

Lord Marlton shook his head free of wondering about Mr. Tierney's vagaries and considered the young man before him. Tall, golden, handsome. Certainly possessed of an easier charm than his scientific brother. Mr. Frederick Tierney would be an addition to any ball, and though the glories of his embroidered waistcoat were not to the viscount's taste, he would not be surprised if the ladies praised it up and down. As for this Mr. Tierney being an oldest brother—well, anyone of sense would prefer the heir to the spare. Particularly to a spare who was already betrothed and embarking on a humble career in the Church.

"Mr. Frederick Tierney, the young ladies of our county would be delighted to partner you, I am certain. If you will come with me, I will perform the introductions."

The French doors opened on the Pattergees gardens, laid out in neat, old-fashioned geometries of parterres and topiaries. Despite the urgings of his daughter, Lord Marlton had not seen fit to tear up the design, that something more picturesque might be constructed. Here there were no clashing cataracts to be contemplated, no ruined temples, no folly. The viscount's guests this midsummer evening must content themselves with walks among the orderly paths or forays into the surrounding hedges.

Joseph scanned the lantern-lit scene as he paced the terrace, seeing no flash of yellow silk, no burly figure looming over a small one. But as he reached the corner and leaned over the railing to glance down upon a darkened pocket in the greenery, his well-trained ear caught the notes of the voice he sought over the lively strains of the musicians within.

"What I mean to say, Un—"

"*Alwyn*, my dear."

"But—Alwyn—what I mean to say is, I think it would be better if I accompanied you to London with my father's consent."

A bark of laughter. "He would sooner part with his precious hounds than trust you to my company! If you require your father's approval, Allie, you will end your days in Somerset, mark my words."

"But they have been so kind to forgive me. I hate to anger them again, if I could avoid it," Alice sighed. "Elfie asked me only the other day to open my heart to her. And how guilty I felt to keep this back."

"Where is your pluck, my love? Everyone will forgive and forget, in time. They always do. Your father may kick at you living with Alec and me, but after he has railed about and made his usual threats, he will be made to see reason again. He is not a man to cut family out of his heart."

"No," agreed Alice, though in so downhearted a tone that her uncle put an arm around her shoulders and dropped a resounding kiss on her head.

"What's this, Allie? Drooping again? What do you say we take another turn about the floor?"

"We cannot dance together *three* times," she answered dully. "It would not do."

"Ha! Soon you will soon run away and make your home with me—and you hesitate to stand up with me more than the biddies would approve? Come now." He poked a finger into her side as he used to do when she was younger. Alice pulled away with a squeak, and Alwyn gave a triumphant whoop and tickled her in earnest.

"Stop! Oh! Un—Alwyn—stop!"

"What will it be? Me and London, or that milksop clergyman you're betrothed to?"

"Eek! Do stop!"

Alwyn Arbuthnot did cease then to tickle her, but not from any impulse of mercy. He had to leave off because something had fallen on him from above. Or leaped. A great something, large and heavy enough to send him tumbling into the hedge.

"Is it a wolf?" cried Alice as the shrubberies shook and muffled oaths and grunts and blasphemies issued forth. "Un—Alwyn! Shall I go for help?"

"It is—no—wolf!" gasped her uncle, dodging blows from what he now realized was a mysterious assailant. "Oof! Varlet! Ruffian!" He was bigger than his opponent, but the man had the advantage of sitting on his chest and fighting like a fiend.

"Oh! Oh!" Alice dashed in a confused circle, trying to scrape her wits together—at first thinking she would run for the nearest footman, and then deciding her uncle would be run through by his attacker before she could return. "Oh, help!"

Throwing herself upon them, she climbed the shoulders of the upper man and attempted to pry him off her uncle. Her additional weight overbalanced them and flipped them all top-to-bottom, like a turtle knocked onto its back. Twigs and leaves stabbed Alice, tearing her gown and plucking off her flowered garland, and Alwyn Arbuthnot managed several clumsy but heavy blows to the brigand's face before he worked out that Alice's shrieks no longer came from beside the hedge but rather underneath.

"Allie! Allie! I got him!" called Alwyn, when his attacker fell still. "But where are you?"

"Down here," came her stifled reply, from below the man he had just succeeded in knocking out.

"Ods bodkins, girl—however did you come to be there?" Grabbing the unconscious man by the boots, Alwyn dragged him off his niece and out of the hedge. "Don't know what sort of ball this is—highwaymen and villains falling from the sky, not ten steps from his lordship's very presence. Marlton'll thank me for handling this one. Suppose he had made a sally at Lady Marlton! He's not an enormous fellow, but if he had landed straight upon the woman's neck, I couldn't answer for her diamonds staying clasped."

By this point Alice had straggled out, attempting to put her gown in order, only to let the torn petticoat trim drop when her eyes took in the fallen desperado. No direct moonlight shone on this section of the garden (hence her choosing of it for their conference), but there was something disturbingly familiar in the lines of the body. "Alwyn—Uncle—please—fetch a lantern."

"Hadn't I much better fetch his lordship?"

"No! No—we had better first be certain we are in a condition to be seen."

"But supposing the miscreant should recover his senses before I return?"

"Only *hurry*!" insisted his niece, her voice rising in a wail. "And pray do not draw attention to yourself."

Never able to bear women's tears, Alwyn Arbuthnot hastened away. Alice sank to the paving stones. *Dear Lord—let it not be—it cannot be—*

The man beside her gave a groan and raised tentative fingers to his brow. Groaned again.

Her stomach turned over. She scooted further away into the shadows, wrapping her arms about her middle.

"Damn," uttered the man thickly. "Damn and *blast*."

"Oh, dear," whispered Alice.

The man groped and fumbled in the half-light until he pulled a handkerchief from his pocket and applied it to his face. Music from the ballroom swelled above them into another country dance. One hundred conversations hummed on, and a burst of laughter broke from some open window, but the two of them were silent.

For what seemed an eternity to Alice, Mr. Tierney did not move. Had he died? Had Uncle Alwyn struck him so hard that he would never rise again? But no—he breathed yet. She made a soft gasping sound of her own. Steeling herself, she crept closer. Had his voice not given him away, Alice would have recognized his hands, even in the semi-darkness. Those long-fingered, capable hands. How many times had she seen them at work? The knuckles were swollen and the skin broken in places, but she knew them.

Oh, Lord.

Ever since she had seen him, she had loved him. And ever since she had loved him, she had only brought disaster into his life. Scandal, horror, an unwanted marriage, an unwanted career. Shame. And when she tried to release him—tried in all good faith—before she could do more than put her plan in motion, she visited more calamity upon him!

Not daring to sniffle, Alice dabbed at her nose and eyes with the edge of her chemise. But why had he thrown himself upon Uncle Alwyn? Had he overheard their conversation? And if he had, why

should he object to his former betrothed making plans to visit her
uncle? Perhaps he had only heard her squeals and protests when
Uncle Alwyn tickled her, and he thought her a damsel in distress.
Yes! That must be it. He had not known it was Alice, and Mr.
Tierney in his native gallantry would attempt to aid any woman. If
Alice could escape now without being seen he would merely wonder
whom he had saved—

She backed up one step, and then another. The stairs to the terrace
were behind her. If she fled up them, she could intercept her uncle
before he returned and gave them up.

The heel of her slipper scraped on gravel and she halted, but Mr.
Tierney didn't move. Rising to her tiptoes, Alice gained the third
step before he spoke.

His words came musingly, as if they were at work one morning
in the wood or beside a stream. As if Alice herself had just asked a
question.

"You can never call yourself a naturalist, Miss Alice," said Joseph,
"if you do not know that wolves have not been seen in England these
five hundred years."

CHAPTER TWENTY

See, the conqu'ring hero comes!
Sound the trumpets, beat the drums.
—George Friedrich Handel, *Judas Maccabaeus* (1747)

Whirling about she said, "Then you do know it is I!"

"My dear Miss Hapgood." He labored up on one elbow to regard her. "Would I interfere with any other woman's elopement plans?"

"Elopement plans!" echoed Alice. "How dare you! Who is eloping? You cannot be referring to me."

Mr. Tierney's desire to sit up increased, never mind the blood running from his nose and the fact that one eye was swelling shut. With another groan and a heave, he managed to prop himself up, resting his back against a marble bench.

"Do not, I beg you, Miss Hapgood, take me for a flat. I have been deceived by you in the past, but I will not be again. There was no mistaking what I overheard."

Alice found her heartbreak and trepidation giving place to indignation. Or perhaps the indignation protected her from further misery. "Indeed, sir, there would be no mistaking what you overheard, had there been anyone else to do the overhearing! Not that there would be—few people of manners and gentle behavior would stoop so low as to eavesdrop."

"We'll leave aside the right and wrong of my actions for the present," he replied curtly. "I heard you say you would accompany that mutton-fisted oaf to London, and he answered that you would run away and live with him! What is this, if not elopement?"

Even in the dim light he could see her eyes fire up and her white-gloved arms akimbo. "How, may I ask, could I elope with my own—no—wait—if you believe such of me—you have ever believed the worst of me! I need make no excuses to you. Indeed, I make none. Believe what you will, you—you *Edgar Mandlebert!*—" here her voice broke, and she hoped he would believe only anger choked her "—I owe you no more explanations. Did you not receive my letter? All connection between us is at an end."

If she would not come down to his level, then he must rise to hers. Bracing himself on the corners of the bench, Joseph got to his feet. Much better. Now she had to tilt back that delicate head of hers, with her lustrous hair fallen down on one side, if she wanted to look him in the eye, and the defiance of her pose shrank in proportion.

"I am not acquainted with this Edgar Mandlebert," said Joseph, "but to answer your question—you wrote, madam, that you found it impossible to marry me 'after such a beginning of deception, mistrust and reproach.' I believe these obstacles might have been overcome, however, if you could only bring yourself to give them up!" Her bosom swelled, but before she could speak, he went on. "Your letter nearly convinced me that I was mistaken in thinking—" here his own voice grew unsteady. He swallowed and took a moment to gather himself. "Why not simply tell the truth, Miss Hapgood? That you found—that you preferred another and wished to be set at liberty?"

"Whom do I prefer?" Alice all but shrilled. "Whom do I prefer, you great gape-mouthed clod-pate?" Gentleman most likely did not prefer wasp-tongued young women with vulgar vocabularies, but what was that to her now?

Joseph drew back, as if her vehemence had physical force. "Lady, you astonish me. I refer, of course, to that hulking ass-head of a booby who forced himself upon you not five minutes ago."

An Alice in her right mind would have giggled over this description of her uncle, who so prided himself on his appearance. But she was not in her right mind. "And I suppose you think you rescued me, sirrah!"

Joseph was too provoked for caution. "Base ingratitude! That was exactly what I supposed! Next time I will not interfere. Small blame to me, if I could not distinguish between unwanted advances and the coy, feigned reluctance of the female species!"

The sound of Alice's slap rang louder in her imagination than in reality. For one thing, Joseph's face was already too slick with blood and swelling to provide a satisfactory surface. For another, she wore gloves. For a third, the horror and irretrievability of her action raced through her brain—even as that brain directed her arm to strike—softening the blow considerably. Nevertheless, Alice reeled away, staggering to the bench and collapsing upon it, her hands flying to cover her face.

It was this scene that Alwyn Arbuthnot disclosed when he reappeared on the terrace with the lantern. He had not, in his rumpled, harassed state, managed to avoid notice, and he was flanked by several liveried footmen and Lord Marlton.

"There he is, the knave!" bellowed Alwyn, pointing down dramatically. "Alice—you have blood upon you! Has he harmed you, my love?"

Joseph glared up at his accuser with his good eye, clenching his fists. "Call Miss Hapgood that one more time, and I will fall upon you again."

"Oh, will you?" taunted Alwyn, much emboldened by the numbers at his side. "You are hardly in a position to make threats. I am far more likely to fall upon *you* from up here, with my fists and the full weight of the law."

"Can that be you, Tierney? What is the meaning of this?" demanded the viscount.

"I am uninjured," replied Alice wearily. "Uncle—do stop."

"You know that rogue, my lord?" Alwyn gasped.

"Did you say your *uncle*?" blurted Joseph.

A babble of tongues broke out, ensuring nothing could be heard or understood beyond repeated notes of astonishment and dismay. Lord Marlton held up his hands for order. "Let us seek greater privacy for this discussion. Arbuthnot, come with me. William, bring that lantern. Kester, meet us inside and unlock my library window. Joram, fetch some dressings for Mr. Tierney and bring them there. Make certain no one disturbs us."

Like a pied piper of the bloody and disgruntled, Lord Marlton led his train of stupefied guests through a garden gate and along a walkway beside the house until they reached his library. Momentarily, Kester appeared inside and unlatched one of the long windows for them to step through. He then lit the lamps and withdrew to guard the door, likely by pressing his ear to it.

Alice found herself surrounded by all manner of wonders. On every surface of the room lay cases and drawings, notes and reference books, instruments and specimens. The very bookshelves were cluttered with jars and bottles and boxes, and many of the books had been pulled from the shelves and upended in stacks, no doubt enlisted to press flowers. Upon a table by another window stood a microscope of shining brass! Without thinking, she began to explore. She wandered from table to shelf to desk, peeling off her blood-stained gloves that she might run bare fingers over things. She poked; she lifted; she pried. She leaned closer to inspect. She looked through the eyepiece of the microscope, though it was too dark to see anything. She nodded, remembering.

She smiled.

"Why, it's marvelous!" Alice breathed.

"I don't see a marvelous thing about it," her uncle grumbled. "And this is hardly the time for you to be inventorying his lordship's household effects. We are in a pretty pickle, my girl."

"Oh, yes, of course." With an effort, Alice tore her eyes from several jars of water bugs, each neatly labeled. "Forgive me," she said. Just as she spoke the words, her gaze crossed Joseph's.

He had been watching her, uncomfortably aware of a melting sensation in his middle. For he saw, in Alice's delight and curiosity, shades of his sometime assistant Arthur Baddely. Faithful, enthusiastic, clever Arthur. Every item in the room held a memory for them. Those selfsame water bugs—Joseph remembered how their first attempt to capture the pond skater and the water scorpion had been thwarted by slippery slopes and twisted ankles. How he had confided in Arthur his career misgivings and grief at disappointing his family, and how Arthur—how *Alice*, rather—had spun some tale about living with a farmer. That was not the only tale she spun. She lied that day—lied desperately—about her health, her sex—about everything, really.

Joseph's mouth twisted. He ought to rejoice that she wished to be rid of him. That he had destroyed all hope of persuading her otherwise by leaping on and pummeling her uncle, of all people, and then accusing her of wanting to elope with the man! Good Lord, what a mess.

But he felt no rejoicing. No—he made full confession to himself at last—it had been some weeks since he considered his impending marriage to Miss Alice Hapgood as anything but a full and unmitigated blessing.

Alas.

For her part, Alice felt that familiar tightening in her chest, as if Dorcas were pulling her stays too tight. How horribly wrong things could go. If this would be the last time she ever met Mr. Tierney—how could she waste her time with anger or argument? Should she not, rather, leave him with one pleasant, one true memory of her?

Gathering the rags of her dignity at the same time that she adjusted the neckline of her gown and tried to straighten her petticoat, Alice forced a smile. "Forgive me," she said again to all. "I have never seen the results of all Mr. Tierney's work. They quite rob one of speech."

"All *our* work," he said softly. "I would not have accomplished the half of it without Arthur Baddely's help. Without *your* help, Miss Hapgood."

She flushed almost painfully and her trembling fingers smoothed out her gloves before wadding them up again. "Thank you." Clearing her throat, she turned to Lord Marlton. "Your lordship—I am afraid what has passed was all the result of a misunderstanding. You know Mr. Tierney and I were—have been—engaged. He happened this evening to overhear a conversation in which I discussed visiting my Arbuthnot uncles Alwyn and Alec in London—a plan I have not yet shared with my father, I am ashamed to admit—and Mr. Tierney...misunderstood. Having never met or heard of my uncle Alwyn, he assumed I spoke of...running away with a strange gentleman. Of eloping. He thus saw the need to stop such an enterprise.

I can see—upon reflection—how he might have interpreted our conversation thus.”

“It was foolish of me,” Joseph broke in. “Completely unwarranted. I must certainly have known such conduct to be impossible for one of Miss Hapgood’s character.”

The raised eyebrows and sucked-in breath of Alwyn Arbuthnot and Lord Marlton indicated they thought jilting and elopement entirely within the realm of capability for a girl like Miss Alice Hapgood, but both men were too wise to put this sentiment into words. Alice herself noticed nothing of their auditors’ skepticism—she was too conscious of the wave of incredulous joy rushing through her.

“If you believed so,” she murmured, “why then did you attack my uncle?”

“Good point!” cried Alwyn. “I should like an answer to that myself.”

“As should I,” added the viscount. “Such unaccountable violence under my roof, in the presence of ladies.”

Joseph chewed the inside of his cheek for a moment, his unswollen eye blinking. “I’m afraid my only excuse for it all—for everything—is that I was...insanely jealous.”

“Lady Molyneux—Almack’s patroness, don’t you know—did say I have an ‘air,’” Alwyn informed Lord Marlton, who paid him not the smallest heed.

Alice had ceased to breathe. Without knowing how she got there, she found herself next to Mr. Tierney, her hand stretching out to him before she realized what she was about and dropped it to her side again. “Mr. Tierney...”

"Joseph," he corrected her. "If we are to part, I should like, just once, to hear you give me my name."

Checked, some small flame of hope in her breast died. She nodded. "Part?"

"Part?" echoed Lord Marlton.

"She intends to jilt him," explained Alwyn helpfully. "That's why she was planning a visit to town with me. Until everyone got over the fuss, you know. Possibly longer. My brother Alec and I could use a woman's touch in the house. And we do get about in society. Could probably find the girl a more suitable husband."

"You might find a more suitable husband," Joseph said, never taking his eyes off of her, though the one was throbbing painfully, "but I should never find a more suitable wife."

Her flame of hope rekindled, and this time she did reach for him and find his damaged hands taking her own in a grip that would have pained her, had she the attention to give it. "Do you—do you mean that...Joseph?"

"Yes. I do." His voice was rough, but it grew stronger as he went on. "For some weeks, I have been conscious of a very great revolution in my feelings toward our marriage, and I only knew how much they had altered when I received your letter. You see how I rushed back, only to jump to another foolish conclusion?"

"Your conclusions are never foolish, Joseph," Alice contradicted, abandoning with feminine ease what she had, till this hour, most strenuously insisted on. "I have, all along, given you every cause to mistrust me. But had you only known my heart, you could never have doubted me."

"I hope to know your heart," said Joseph.

"Then know this: it is all, entirely, yours."

"Shhh...when will you grasp, my girl, that you are *not* a boy? You mustn't say such things until you are certain of me." This teasing reproach he delivered with another, playful, squeeze to her hands. Then, with a faint grimace, he managed to sink to one knee. "My dear Miss Hapgood. You have, from the first moment of our acquaintance, impressed me with your knowledge, your thorough study of and passion for the natural world, your cleverness, and your fundamental desire for truth—nay, Alice, let me speak—I say, your fundamental desire for truth, even when you felt bound by circumstances to stray from it. Will you forgive me my accusations? My insults to your character and essential honesty?"

She could not find words. If not for the wringing grasp he had on her hands, she might think herself asleep and dreaming. But she nodded in her dream. Vigorously.

"I tell you I understand now," Joseph continued. "What you were trying to express to me. You see, I met a female astronomer after I left here—you may know the name of Miss Caroline Herschel—"

"He got off on the right foot, but I don't know where he is headed now, with this talk of women astronomers," muttered Alwyn to the viscount. "If you want to win a girl's heart, you don't mention other females."

"Hush," answered Lord Marlton.

"Yes! Yes, I have read of her," Alice replied. "You met her?"

"And learned how well she and her brother William Herschel complemented each other in their work. How each went further, accomplished more, because they worked together. The only sad thing was that Mr. Herschel married, and his sister felt the need to draw away. And I thought, how fortunate am I, that nothing can come between me and my very best partner? We will work side by side. Live, side by side. Love."

For a minute Alice could not speak, for fear she would cry. But a greater fear, that her uncle or the viscount would interrupt this all-important discussion again, if she did not speak, impelled her to her master her emotions. "Do you love me, sir?"

In answer he could only drop his head and press his lips to her hands.

"You do not feel obligated to marry me because I have trapped you," Alice persisted, "or that we have found ourselves, once more, in a compromising situation?"

"Most lovely of all Alices—I welcome my obligation." A mischievous grin flashed over his distorted face, cracking the crust of dried blood. "I would assault one hundred uncles of yours, if you would consent to live with me instead of them."

"But—but—we cannot be naturalists together like you say because, if you marry me, you must be a clergyman!"

"*Must* be?" The grin returned. "My love—that is the other confession I must make. I already am. If you will have me, then you must have the Reverend Joseph Tierney. And if you say you will work by my side, we will have both the natural world and the spiritual to contend with."

"I—I—"

"Beloved, most lovesome Alice!"

"But you did not wish to be a clergyman, Joseph!" she wailed.

"Do you think I will do it ill?" he asked. "I have a sermon for you: 'Two are better than one, because they have a good reward for their toil. For if they fall, one will lift up his fellow. But woe to him who is alone when he falls and has not another to lift him up! Again, if two lie together, they keep warm, but how can one keep warm alone?'"

"Oh, Joseph."

"Tell me quickly, dear. I might never be able to rise from this position, as I feel my head growing light. Will you make me the happiest of men? Will you marry me?"

Sinking to her own knees, heedless of her torn petticoat and fallen hair, the presence of witnesses, and her beloved's own beaten and disheveled appearance, Alice lifted his hands to lay them against her cheek.

"My dearest and yet more dear Joseph," she whispered.

"I will."

Epilogue

The banns having been duly published the previous three Sundays, Reverend Joseph Tierney of Stone Halt, Buckinghamshire, wed Miss Alice Hapgood, lately of Bramleigh, Somerset, in Bramleigh Downs church three days past Midsummer on the Nativity of Saint John the Baptist. The bride's mother made a most rare appearance for the occasion, consenting to be wheeled in a chair and lifted up the steps and over the threshold by the squire, as if she were newly wed herself. The bride's sisters attended her, everyone agreeing that the eldest Miss Hapgood far outshone her sister, both in beauty and in proper feminine conduct, and that little Miss Edith was a trim and quiet girl, but that sharp-tongued Miss Margaret would be trouble enough in future days, mark their words.

Poor Margaret had been guilty of nothing worse than saying, "Do look at Mr. Tierney's brother, Edie. What a popinjay he is! Lace at his cuffs and fleur-de-lys embroidered on his waistcoat. You would imagine him dressed for his own wedding, and to a princess of the blood, no less!"

Mr. Frederick Tierney was indeed resplendent. Margaret's were not the only eyes fixed on him that morning, and many forgot the bride's latest scrape in contemplation of her brother-in-law's glory. Nephew and heir to a baronet, possessed of a modest fortune, and so very, very handsome! If Miss Alice Hapgood had known on which side her bread was buttered, she would have practiced her unladylike stratagems on the elder. Oh, well. The girl looked happy enough.

And she was. Alice cared not a whit for what anyone thought. She saw only her bridegroom. His lacerations and bloody nose were cleaned and healing, he was very well turned out by his man Chambers, and he had covered his black eye with a patch. In Alice's estimation, her dandyish new brother could not hold a candle to the Reverend Joseph.

"Elfie!" hissed Margaret, pinching her sister after the last handful of wheat had been tossed. "Do not turn your head directly, but I assure you that that Mr. Frederick Tierney has looked your way a dozen times, if he has once."

"How interesting," said Elfrida with maddening calm, not turn- ing her head one degree. She tucked her mother's shawl more firmly about her in the chair, and Mrs. Hapgood just as quickly untucked it because of the warmth of the day.

"You did not say—" Margaret paused. "Were you introduced to him at the Midsummer Ball?"

"Not precisely."

"I suppose he is our brother of sorts now," spoke up Edith, regarding that over-tailored Adonis with her artist's eye. "Does one still require an introduction in that situation, Mama?"

"Tell your papa to bring it about, dears, I'm sure. I do hope the squire gives over talking to Father Thomas soon, or I will faint in this heat."

"Never mind any introductions," Elfrida said. "And we needn't hurry Papa. I will push your chair home, Mama."

"Oh, heavens," protested her mother. "If you do you will make yourself all red and blowsy, Elfrida."

"It is not very warm yet," Elfrida insisted. "And if it were, I should bear the heat better than Papa. Besides, there is no one but family to see me."

"But I should so like to meet Mr. Frederick Tierney before we go!" Margaret cried, following reluctantly after her sister. "Only see how everyone gathers 'round him."

"I should like to meet him, too," Edith agreed as she skipped backwards in front of the wheeled chair. "I would ask him if he would sit for me. What a fine Apollo he would make! And he could not refuse, could he, Mama? Not when we are related by marriage. May we send word and invite him to dinner? He will probably leave Somerset shortly."

"Such a lot of bother about a young man!" sighed Mrs. Hapgood. "After the bustle and fuffle of Alice's very sudden match, I should be pleased if we were spared young men for the present. Not that I do not wish Alice and her gentleman very well."

"Do not you think Mr. Frederick Tierney handsome, Mama?" asked Edith.

"Handsome enough. I think my brother Alec has the advantage in height."

"But the disadvantage in hair," pointed out Margaret, "for Uncle Alec must sweep his from the sides upward to cover his bald patch." Twirling to see her skirt bell out, she glanced back once more at the party in the churchyard. "If you don't find him handsome, Elfrida, it can only be because your eyesight is so poor. Perhaps you did not see him clearly by candlelight at the ball."

"Mr. Frederick Tierney? I saw him as clearly as anyone present, I daresay." Her low, sweet voice carried more than she knew in the still summer air. "And I confess, I deemed him then and still do, a very plain young man."

"*Centaurea cyanis,*" Alice murmured, after Cox set in motion the gig decked with blue cornflowers and ribbons and her husband had left off kissing her breathless. "If they are a sign of my love, Joseph, they will never fade. I hope you will prove as faithful."

"Always. Did you not see the forget-me-nots on the whip, my sweet naturalist wife?" Plucking the bouquet, he gave it to her and kissed her again.

"Your sweet naturalist wife," she repeated. "I like the sound of that. Almost as much as I do 'clergyman's wife.'"

His hand stole around her waist and drew her against him. "Shall I preach you another sermon?"

Giving a tiny shiver, she whispered, "Yes—please."

"I have the very one in mind." He bent down the brim of her hat, that no one might see, and pressed his lips to the hollow of her neck, trailing kisses upward to her ear. "It begins, 'Thou hast ravished my heart, my sister, my bride...'"

"Oh," said Alice, shutting her eyes. "I do so like that one."

The adventures of the Hapgood family continue with Elfrida's story in *A Very Plain Young Man.*

THE HAPGOODS OF BRAMLEIGH

The Naturalist
A Very Plain Young Man
School for Love
Matchless Margaret
The Purloined Portrait
A Fickle Fortune

THE ELLSWORTH ASSORTMENT

Tempted by Folly
The Belle of Winchester
Minta in Spite of Herself
A Scholarly Pursuit
Miranda at Heart
A Capital Arrangement

PRIDE AND PRESTON LIN

www.christinadudley.com